Certainly Sensible

by

Pamela Woods-Jackson

Certainly Sensible

COPYRIGHT © 2015 by Pamela Woods-Jackson

Cover Art by *Debbie Taylor*

The Wild Rose Press, Inc.
PO Box 708
Adams Basin, NY 14410-0708
Visit us at www.thewildrosepress.com

Publishing History
First Sweetheart Rose Edition, 2015
Print ISBN 978-1-5092-0450-2
Digital ISBN 978-1-5092-0451-9

Published in the United States of America

Caroline felt terrible for her sister,
but Allie had been so secretive about what had actually happened with her and Mark, and now she wanted answers. "All this started July third. You have to tell me what happened."

Allie grabbed a tissue and blew her nose. "He told me he thought I was getting too serious."

"That doesn't sound unreasonable."

Allie put the chilled water bottle to her throbbing temples. "I told him I was falling in love with him."

Caroline groaned, her worst fear realized. "Love? You barely knew him, Allie."

"But we'd spent practically every waking minute together since we met. He told me...or he let me believe..." Allie broke off with a sigh. "He said he was too worried about his dad's money problems to get involved in a relationship." Allie laughed a humorless laugh. "Can you believe that? Money problems? We live in a tiny house, no money, no school..."

Caroline gave that some thought. "It sounds like a lame excuse, like he wasn't really that into you."

"Starving artist—that's what he called me," Allie said with tears streaming down her face.

"Oh." Caroline was finally seeing the big picture, and she didn't like the view.

"I just thought he needed more time," Allie said with a sniffle, "but I guess what he really needed was someone to bankroll his family's debt."

"And when he heard the name Benedict, he thought that was you. Then he found out you didn't have a trust fund, so he moved on to a richer woman—Misty Peterson."

Dedication

To Robert, Faith, Tom,
and my real-life Caroline,
who graciously allowed me to borrow her name.

Chapter One

Caroline Benedict had just walked into her boss's office late in the day when her phone pinged with yet another text message. She pulled her phone out of the pocket of her blue blazer and quickly glanced at it.

Mom's message this time merely read —*Call me ASAP!*— Her sister Megan's was more detailed. —*Mom's in a funk so be prepared when you get home from work. And no way Mom's cooking tonight, so bring home a pizza.*—

"Do you need to take that?" Richard asked as he looked up from his laptop.

Caroline slipped the phone back into her pocket, smoothed out her black dress slacks, and checked to make sure her hair was still neatly tied in place. Even though it was late afternoon, she wanted to look her best for the boss she admired so much. She smiled at Richard and shook her head. "Stuff going on at home, but I think I know what it's about. So you wanted to talk about…?"

Richard leaned across his desk and smiled at her a bit too long. "Oh, yes, sorry, about this week's Hamilton Hardware ad…"

Caroline sat down in the chair opposite Richard's desk and gave him her full attention. Whatever was going on at home could wait.

****

Her eldest daughter still wasn't answering. Susan tossed her cell phone on the step as she sank onto the bottom stair of the mansion's entry hall and buried her head in her hands with a moan.

"Hi Mom!" Megan, her youngest, slammed the front door and walked across the large entryway to where her mother was sitting. She carelessly tossed her unzipped book bag on the floor with a thud, its contents partially spilling out onto the marble tile. "Mom, hello?" She waved her hand in front of Susan's face. "And why was Dad here?"

Susan was reeling from the shock, dizzy and disoriented. She heard her daughter speaking, but it was as if she herself was in a tunnel and nothing but muffled sounds were coming through. Susan slowly lifted her head to see Megan staring at her, hands on her hips, waiting for an answer. She tried to clear her head. "What?"

Megan untucked the blouse of her school uniform and kicked off her loafers. "Dad. Just now. He was backing out of the drive as my bus dropped me off. What did he want? And why are you just sitting here on the stairs?" Susan didn't move, didn't respond. "Mom? Are you even listening to me?"

Susan looked dully at her daughter's *Willowby Preparatory School* day planner on top of an art tablet that had tumbled out of the overburdened schoolbag. It took all her strength just to fight back the tears.

"Your father just got remarried," she said at last. "He and Sharlene eloped to Las Vegas last weekend."

"Huh. Well, that's lame." Megan shrugged. "Did you call Caroline yet? I'll bet she already knows." Megan nonchalantly pulled the ponytail holder off her wrist and tied back her long blonde hair.

Susan nodded and swallowed hard. "I sent her a text. She's probably in the middle of something at work."

Megan rolled her eyes. "That's not work; that's Caroline pining for Richard." She picked up Susan's phone off the bottom step and checked for messages. "Nope, nothing." Megan handed it back to Susan. "But seriously, Mom, you and Dad have been divorced for three years. What's the big deal?"

Susan rubbed her throbbing temples as she tried to focus on what Megan was saying and bit her tongue to keep from screaming something profane about her ex. She didn't want to ruin what little relationship Megan still had with Daniel by telling her about their conversation. She first wanted to discuss it with Caroline, certainly the most sensible of her three daughters.

Megan had spent so little time with her father after the divorce anyway. Caroline and Allison were young adults, but Megan was still a teenager and craved his attention. Yet Daniel always managed to find an excuse to avoid spending time with her. "I have a dinner meeting tonight," he frequently told her, or "I'm sorry, Megs, but Sharlene and I are going out of town this weekend." Eventually Megan quit asking him if she could visit.

Susan couldn't bring herself to go into detail about the conversation she'd just had with Daniel—if she could call his one-sided announcement a conversation—and she needed time alone to process it. "There's a little more to it than just his marriage, Megs, but right now I'm going to take a hot bath and try to let this all sink in." She gripped the handrail tightly for support and started up the winding staircase.

"Let all *what* sink in?"

Susan took a deep breath, turned to face Megan, and tried to sound cheerful. "How was school?"

Megan glared at her mother. "It was *school*. And quit changing the subject. What did Dad want?"

"Any homework?"

Megan narrowed her eyes. "Yes, Mom, I have homework. Stop stalling. Why are you so upset?"

Susan paused, wondering if she should just tell Megan what her father had said. She thought better of it, at least for the moment. "You'd better get busy on that homework, since your grades have been falling this semester."

"I've got a new art project!" Megan exclaimed.

"Megan, art class aside, you know you're on probation there, and your dad said…" Susan shook her head. "Well, I guess you could go to Belford High School."

"What are you talking about? I have to stay at Willowby because of the art program, Mom. Remember?"

Susan just nodded as she walked upstairs to her room. Life would never be the same, not that anything had been normal since Daniel left. She quietly shut the door and collapsed onto her bed in tears of frustration.

****

Sharlene waited in the car while Daniel had his "discussion" with Susan. She happily imagined the changes she would make to the house once she took possession of it: replace the carpet with wood flooring, of course, and fresh paint in every room, just for starters. Then she would order new furniture and throw out everything Susan and Daniel's daughters didn't take with them.

Draperies! Tear down those hideous curtains Susan picked out years ago and replace them with something light and airy.

Sharlene began imagining the first dinner party she would hostess for Daniel's friends and business associates, all from Belford society's A-list, once all the redecorating was done. Then there was that piano, right in the middle of her formal living room. What to do with that?

Daniel opened the driver's side door and, without looking at her, got in and started the engine. He checked his rearview mirror, shifted into reverse, and backed his late model Lexus out of the driveway, narrowly avoiding a collision with the surprised school bus driver. Sharlene gripped the seatbelt as Daniel put the car in drive and sped down the street, but she didn't have time to fasten it as the car lurched ahead.

"Daniel, darling, slow down." She reached for the door handle as the Lexus careened around a sharp curve, tossing her against the door and nearly banging her head on the passenger-side window. "Daniel? Did you hear me?"

He muttered a few expletives under his breath and slammed on the brakes, this time nearly catapulting his wife into the dashboard. "I heard you, Sharlene, but this isn't right! My family..."

Sharlene smoothed the skirt of her expensive, green, polished cotton suit and hastily fastened her seatbelt. "Darling, don't forget—*I'm* your family, now."

He turned on his hazard blinkers. "This isn't easy, you know."

"But Daniel, it's been three years! And you've been more than generous, darling. Private school tuitions and thirty-six very large mortgage payments, all while your ex-wife and daughters lived for free!" Sharlene looked over at Daniel to gauge his reaction.

Daniel sighed. "That was in the divorce settlement." He turned on his signal, put the car in drive again, and drove more slowly down the wide residential street. It was lined with stately oak trees in front of executive-style mansions, all with perfectly manicured lawns, similar to the one his ex-wife and daughters would soon move out of.

Sharlene didn't have time to admire her soon-to-be new neighborhood, though. She smiled sweetly and adjusted her tone. "You really only agreed to pay the cost of public college, Daniel, but it was generous of you to let them stay in the house a while longer, and to pay for private schools for your daughters."

Daniel shrugged as he waited his turn to enter the roundabout. "You know I can afford it, so why does it matter where the girls go to school?"

It mattered to Sharlene, because when she married a wealthy man, she wanted access to all his money. "But Daniel, darling, Megan hasn't been doing well at that expensive prep school you pay for, so you're wasting your money there. And Allison—why she's only a sophomore at that music school, barely getting started at, uh, at—"

"Bryce Anthony Music Conservatory."

"Yes, Bryce, so it wouldn't be hard for her to transfer to a public college nearby, and you'd still be in compliance." Sharlene loosened the seatbelt and shifted herself so that she was looking directly at her husband. "We've talked about this, remember?"

Daniel kept his eyes on the road. "I suppose so."

"And then there's Caroline. With that degree in marketing from Indiana University, it's time she got out in the real business world."

Daniel snorted as he pulled into the roundabout, cutting off a sedan that had the right of way. "I thought Meadows Advertising Agency *was* the real business world."

Sharlene winced. "Well, of course, it's a real business, but Caroline is a grown woman! You're not doing her any favors by coddling her with that allowance. As it is, she has no incentive to look elsewhere, and she'll eventually regret putting her career on hold."

Daniel tightened his jaw but didn't respond. Instead, he loosened his tie and growled at the sedan's driver as she honked loudly.

Sharlene checked her seatbelt, making sure it was securely fastened as Daniel spun the car out of the roundabout. "I think you've done enough for those girls, and you have no reason to feel guilty about getting on with your own life."

Daniel shook his head. "Susan doesn't even have a full-time job, never has had one. Even if she did, teachers don't make much money, and part-time substitute teachers make even less."

Sharlene dug in her heels. "So she'll just have to exert herself! It's time Susan stood on her own two feet and quit depending on you. I—we've waited three long years to get married, only to have your ex-wife continue to live in *our* estate. Honestly, Daniel, our future as a couple and our place in Belford society is at stake if Susan and your daughters don't move…uh, get on with their lives."

"Maybe we should give them more time," Daniel suggested as he hit the gas pedal and speeded up to just over the limit, "to adjust."

"They've had plenty of time, darling. I don't think the judge meant for you to support your daughters into old age. For heaven's sake, Daniel, they won't be destitute! Four women should be able to live comfortably on much less than you've provided up till now."

Daniel drove in silence for a while. "I suppose it's time we all moved on."

Sharlene turned her head so Daniel wouldn't see her gleeful smile when she realized Daniel had finally agreed with her. Instead she pouted in mock sympathy. "Look how much you've had to sacrifice, darling, living by yourself in that apartment, instead of in your own home."

Daniel threw his head back and laughed, and then winked at her. "I live in a three-thousand square foot penthouse, Sharlene. And I've hardly been alone all this time."

Sharlene fought to control her temper. "You know what I mean. You've been a martyr long enough. We had to run off to Vegas to get married on the sly so you wouldn't upset the girls."

"You're in the middle of planning your brother's wedding," Daniel retorted, "and you said you didn't have time for anything else. I thought I was doing you a favor by taking you to Las Vegas."

"Well, then, the least you owe me is a decent standard of living." Daniel raised an eyebrow but looked straight ahead at the road. Sharlene folded her arms. She didn't want to keep having this same argument with him. "It's *your* house, Daniel, and you're entitled to live in it!"

"I told Susan what you wanted, so that's the end of it." Daniel turned his attention to the traffic in front of him as he waited to make a left turn onto Meridian Street.

Sharlene smiled smugly and let Daniel drive the rest of the way home in silence.

****

Susan finally pulled herself off the bed and went into the master bathroom. *I told Megan I was going to soak in the tub, and that's what I intend to do.* She turned on the warm water, reached across the tub for the bubbling bath salts, turned on the Jacuzzi jets, and stepped into the oversized tub. Susan's whole body felt like one big, twisted nerve. Her neck was tight, her back ached, and she found it difficult to even step into the tub. Once in, she relaxed into the bubbles and leaned her head back on a folded plush towel, hoping to alleviate the pounding migraine.

This is what I get for marrying such an ambitious man when I was only twenty-two. Daniel always knew exactly what he wanted to do—Human Resources Management—and immediately after college graduation set about seeking just the right job with growth potential. He found it, not in their home state of Oklahoma but in Belford, Indiana, at the headquarters of a large health maintenance organization. They moved away from friends and family, and his career launched into high gear before Susan could catch her breath.

Career! Susan snapped out of her reverie as her heart raced. *How am I going to support my daughters? I need a job! But how will I ever convince a school in Indiana to hire a middle-aged woman with no real teaching experience?*

She sank back into her tub in despair. A moment later she pulled herself back up and fumbled around on the floor next to the bathtub, searching for her phone. She found it, dried her hand off, and pushed a button on speed dial.

"You've reached Emily Martin with Kinley Real Estate. I'm either on the phone or with a client, but if you'll leave a message, I'll call you back as soon as possible."

Susan groaned in frustration. "Emily, it's Susan, and this is an extreme emergency! You've got to call me back immediately!" She hung up the phone and hoped she didn't sound too desperate, when in fact she was very desperate. She sank back into the tub and tried to relax in the bubbles.

After three daughters and twenty-one years of being Daniel's supportive wife—managing charity events, doing volunteer work, and then finding private schools for the girls with their various talents—what did she have to show for it? A divorce, a large house she was about to be evicted from, no career, no direction in her life, and now she had to deliver the bad news to her girls. Daniel had dumped that on her, too. Caroline would be home from work soon, but Allie was still at school up in Chicago, finishing her final music exams.

The piano! What are we going to do about the piano? They'd be forced to downsize, so wherever they moved, there would be no room to put such a large instrument. The thought that Allison would have to give up her beloved grand piano gave Susan a sick feeling in the pit of her stomach. Allie's whole life was her music, ever since she was a little girl and got one of those toy pianos for Christmas. Susan and Daniel had laughed at their little Schroeder, like in the *Peanuts* cartoon, but it turned out their middle daughter actually had talent. A few years later, Susan arranged for private piano lessons, and Allie showed signs of being a musical prodigy. *And now what will happen to my daughter's career ambitions?*

Susan fought back tears. She wished Emily would hurry and call her back. Her friend might be able to help solve the housing problem at least.

Where are we going to live? Can I even afford a house? Will we have to move to an apartment?

She shuddered at that thought, and as if in response to the chill, ran more hot water into the bath. The immediate future looked bleak, and Susan needed the help and advice that her best friend would certainly give her.

If I find a house, will all four of us be able to fit? And where will Megan and Allie attend school? Why didn't I listen to my attorney when she tried to warn me?

Susan collapsed back into the bubbles, but just as she was about to relax, her phone buzzed. She sat up and grabbed for it.

"Susan, for heaven's sake, what's the big emergency?"

"Oh, Emily, thank God. I'm in a panic!"

"So I gathered," Emily said. "Do you mind telling me why?"

Susan took a deep breath. "Daniel was here."

"That doesn't sound good."

"It's the worst, Em. He and Sharlene got married."

There was a pause on Emily's end. "And *that's* what you're upset about? He's been carrying on with her for years."

"No, it's not about that. Well, a little, but it gets worse."

"With Sharlene involved, I can only imagine."

****

Caroline threw her handbag and car keys on the breakfast table, set the pizza on the kitchen cabinet, and ran up the stairs to Megan's room. She didn't even bother knocking, but Megan didn't notice anyway because she had her eyes closed, listening to music on her iPad.

"Megan!" Caroline pulled the ear-buds out of her sister's ears.

Megan sat up. "Hey! Why'd you do that? And where's the pizza?"

Caroline took her jacket off and tossed it on her sister's bed. "Megan, please. What's wrong with Mom?"

Megan shrugged. "I don't know, but Dad was here earlier, and Mom was crying when I got home from school."

Caroline took a deep breath to ease the queasiness in her stomach. Despite her dread, she piloted Megan down the hall to their mother's bedroom and gently knocked on the door. "Mom?" Poking her head in the door, she saw her mom lying in the middle of the king-sized bed, down comforter askew, wearing old jeans and a t-shirt, her hair still wet and uncombed from the bath. The TV was on and blaring. Susan lay on her back pretending to watch, but she was really just staring at the ceiling. Caroline grabbed the remote and turned the set off.

"Mom," she tried again, "what did Dad say to get you so upset?" No answer. "Was it because he got married?"

Susan sat up and looked at Caroline, eyes wide with surprise.

"Yes, I know about it. Dad texted me." Silence. "Mom, really, Sharlene's a social-climbing snob, but she's not worth all this drama."

Susan grabbed a pillow and hugged it to her chest. "I couldn't care less about Sharlene. I care about you girls."

Caroline sat down on the edge of the bed and patted her mother's arm. "We know that, Mom. But what exactly did Dad say that's got you so upset?"

Susan slowly stood to face her daughters and sighed, her shoulders slumped, "Your dad wants this house back."

"Well, I guess that's no surprise," Caroline muttered.

Susan shook her head. "In one month."

Caroline sucked in her breath, and Megan's mouth dropped open. "One month?" Caroline's head was swimming. "How is that even possible?"

"There's more."

"More?" Caroline looked over at Megan and winced.

Susan took a deep breath before blurting out the rest of it. "Your dad will no longer pay Megan's private school tuition or Allie's. And Caroline, your dad says it's time you were on your own financially, so he's cutting off your allowance."

Megan gasped. "What? Where am I supposed to go to school?" Caroline tried to put an arm around her sister, but Megan brushed her off.

"You can finish out the school year at Willowby, but then you'll have to go to public school next year," Susan told her. "You and I already talked about Belford High School…"

"Mom! Public school? *You* talked about it, but I didn't think you were serious. Anyway, I can't! Belford High's art department sucks!"

"Be honest, Megan," Susan said. "You haven't been doing very well at Willowby for the last couple of years. Except for the art classes."

"I haven't been in any fights for months, and my grades are…"

"Mostly Cs and Ds," Caroline finished for her.

Megan glared at her sister before turning back to her mother. "Willowby is the only school I've ever gone to!"

"Yes, I know, but your dad stipulated in the divorce settlement that he would only pay the tuition if your grades and behavior improved."

"And you're just now remembering that?" Megan cried.

Caroline tried to stay calm despite her rising panic. "Dad can't be serious. How does he expect us to manage a move so quickly? One month? That's not nearly enough time to find a house, to—"

"I called Emily."

Caroline nodded. "But even Emily can't work miracles."

"Why now?" Megan demanded. "After all this time?"

Caroline glanced at Megan, met her mother's eyes, and knew the answer. "Sharlene?"

Susan nodded.

Megan glowered at both her mother and sister and stormed out of the room, slamming the door behind her. Caroline and Susan stood there in silence. Caroline tried to let their situation sink in, to absorb the reality of their predicament, but she noticed the tears in her mother's eyes.

"Mom, are you okay?"

"Don't worry about me, I'll be fine, but Megan?"

Then Caroline slapped her forehead. "And Allie! Mom, we've got to call her."

"Absolutely not. If she fails her performance final because she's too distracted…" Susan shook her head. "No, this bad news can wait till she comes home from school." At that, Susan collapsed back down onto her bed, scattering pillows everywhere, turned the TV back on, and resumed staring at the ceiling.

Caroline, confused about how to help her mother and sisters, recognized the familiar churning in her stomach. "I need an antacid." She headed down the hall to her bedroom.

Chapter Two

A week later, Susan had had a chance to regain her perspective and dignity, and had formulated a plan. She checked her look in the master bathroom's full-length mirror, snatched up her comb for one last swipe at her short brown bob, and then did a complete turn for a final assessment. Dressed in a navy blue suit that fit snuggly on her tall, slim body, she outwardly looked like a professional woman. But inside she was a mass of insecurities.

I'm a forty-six-year-old divorcee, interviewing for my first real job. She took a deep breath, adjusted her jacket, picked up her newly-acquired briefcase off the foot of the bed, and headed downstairs to the kitchen. Megan was sitting at the breakfast table eating a bowl of cereal and reading a story in her English textbook. "What's that, Megan? Homework?"

Megan looked up from her breakfast. "Where are you going all dressed up like that?"

"I've got a job interview in Indianapolis, so if you hurry I can drop you at school on my way. Unless you'd rather ride the bus?"

Megan gave her mother that *yeah-right* look and went back to eating her cereal. "Hey, Caroline, can you drive me to school?"

Susan turned around to see her oldest daughter taking some yogurt out of the refrigerator. Caroline was dressed in crisply starched jeans, an off-white linen blazer, and low-heeled sandals, her strawberry-blonde hair pulled back in a ponytail. "Caroline! I didn't hear you come in."

"You look nice, Mom." Caroline stuffed the yogurt into her bag. "Where are you headed?"

"I have a job interview," Susan said, nervously smoothing out her jacket.

Megan continued chewing, not even looking up from her book. "What kind of job?"

Susan cleared her throat. "Well, I got a call from the English Department at Rosslyn High School in response to my application, and they have an opening for next school year, teaching ninth grade English."

Caroline beamed as she gave her mom a quick hug. "Good luck and let me know how it goes." She unlocked the door leading from the kitchen into the garage and hit the automatic garage opener button.

"Caroline!" Megan called. "I asked you…"

"Not this morning, Megs, I'm running late!"

"Yeah, late to a *non*-job!"

Megan dropped the spoon in her bowl with a clink. "Mom, why didn't you just apply for a job at Belford High School? They've got a huge English Department."

Susan blew out a puff of air. "I did apply there, Megan, along with about fifty other candidates, most of them fresh out of college."

Megan got up off the barstool and set her bowl and spoon in the sink. "Mom, I know you're exaggerating about Belford High, but aren't there any other schools up here in Hamilton County where you can teach? Indianapolis is like thirty minutes away. That's a long commute."

Susan picked up her daughter's dirty breakfast dishes and loaded them into the dishwasher. "Since I've had no response to my applications from any of the other districts up here, I guess an inner-city school in Indianapolis is my best shot." She grabbed her briefcase and headed to the garage. "Are you ready?"

Megan picked up her book bag from the floor next to the breakfast table, stuffed the literature book inside, and zipped it up. "But, Mom, you aren't even giving them a chance to call you back." She followed her mother out into the garage with the door still open from Caroline's hasty departure.

"Sweetie, I can't wait for them to call. I have to have an actual paying job, and soon. Just wish me luck, okay?"

Megan shrugged and tossed her book bag into the backseat. "Let's go. It's almost eight, and I'll be marked tardy again."

****

Caroline pulled into the drive-thru at Peterson's Coffee Emporium on her way to Meadows Advertising and placed her order for a caffeinated latte, skim milk, no sweetener. At the payment window, she dug into her bag for the cash and realized she was quickly running out of money. Not just coffee money. MONEY. "I'll have to make coffee at home from now on," she mumbled as she handed the attendant a five dollar bill. She glanced at the dashboard clock. If she didn't hurry, she'd hit rush-hour traffic, so she decided not to think about her financial situation for the moment. Besides, the year she had negotiated with Richard was almost up.

"Working nine to five..." blasted through the

radio. Caroline cranked up the volume as she made her turn onto Meridian Street, hoping to drown out her conflicted thoughts.

****

Susan sat nervously in a hard, wooden chair just inside the English Department office. It was designed as a waiting area for students, with several closed office doors belonging to various administrators and their assistants encircling the reception area. A row of chairs lined the wall, but she was the only one there at the moment, and she felt conspicuous because two of the office staff kept sneaking glances at her and whispering. Susan tucked her hair behind her ears and then pushed it back again, crossed and uncrossed her legs, opened her briefcase to check again for copies of her résumé, and looked anxiously around the room for signs that she hadn't been forgotten.

"Ms. Benedict?" A distinguished-looking older woman emerged from an office.

"Yes," Susan said, rising to meet her.

"I'm Catherine Renfrow." Susan shook the woman's extended hand and then followed her through the open office doorway.

"Please have a seat." Mrs. Renfrow indicated a wooden chair opposite her oversized desk, and then settled herself into a comfortable swivel chair, its back turned to a large picture window. The view was breathtaking in late spring: lush green lawn, large stately trees, and a well-manicured flower bed surrounding the cement marquee that read *ROSSLYN HIGH SCHOOL, Established 1925*. Susan fumbled in her briefcase for a copy of her résumé.

"Oh, that's okay, Ms. Benedict—or may I call you

Susan?—I have the résumé you emailed with your application." Mrs. Renfrow smiled at Susan as she donned her reading glasses and looked over the résumé on her computer screen. She was a matronly woman in her late fifties, wearing a navy skirt and loose-fitting cardigan sweater over her ample frame.

"Susan would be just fine."

"Well, Susan, I see you've never had an actual teaching position before."

Susan squirmed, sure the interview was over before it had even begun. "Yes, that's true. But it's not because I didn't want to teach or that I don't love children. It's just that, what with my husband's career—ex-husband now—and raising children, who are mostly grown except for Megan—she's still in high school—substituting was all I had time for." Susan realized she was rambling and stopped. Not a good beginning.

Mrs. Renfrow nodded. "I understand, and in my opinion, raising children to be productive adults is an admirable occupation." She adjusted her glasses and went back to reading. "From your résumé, I see you've done quite a bit of volunteer work, though. Organizational skills can come in handy here."

Susan jumped at the chance to talk about something she was so proud of. "Oh, yes, I've been involved with a number of different charities. I also spend time volunteering at the public library as a storyteller, and for years I taught Sunday school when my children were younger." She stopped and swallowed. "Am I talking too much?"

"Not at all," Mrs. Renfrow said with a polite head nod.

Susan took that to mean she should continue. "Well, then, I also read a great deal on my own, both fiction and nonfiction. I know what books are included in the ninth-grade curriculum, and I've read them all. I've kept up with all the latest research on how children learn, and I'm up-to-date on the new state standards."

"Wonderful!" Mrs. Renfrow said as the corners of her mouth tilted up in amusement. "And I'd like to offer you the job."

Susan nearly fainted. "What?"

"I know you lack experience as a classroom teacher, but I'm impressed with your community involvement and obvious love of children. I've interviewed several newly-graduated teachers, but frankly none of them seemed mature enough to take on the challenge of our urban students."

Susan felt like clapping her hands together with joy, but managed to maintain her dignity. "Thank you for this opportunity, and I'm looking forward to the challenge. Oh, and I'm not planning to use this job as a springboard to someplace less demanding."

"Well, you'd be surprised at how many teachers do that very thing."

Mrs. Renfrow shuffled through some forms on her desk and handed them to Susan. "Of course you realize you won't start until August."

Susan nodded. "I appreciate you taking a chance on me."

Mrs. Renfrow stood up and shook Susan's hand. "Welcome to Rosslyn High School's English Department. You'll need to fill out these forms and turn them in to HR." Susan placed the forms in her briefcase. "I'll take you down and show you where your classroom will be." She walked around her desk, opened the office door for Susan, led her through the outer reception area and out into the school's main lobby. Susan felt like she was floating on air as she followed Mrs. Renfrow on the tour.

****

Caroline glanced at the clock as her car inched along in rush hour traffic along southbound Meridian Street. It looked like she was going to be late to work again. She loved working for Richard at Meadows Advertising Agency, even without a title or much of a salary, and she wasn't ready to face the inevitable.

"You always seem to know exactly what I need even before I know it myself. And you have the ability to see the smallest typographical error," Richard had told her during her first summer as an intern.

Caroline had blushed. "It's a knack I have."

During her internship year, Caroline gradually took over most of the copy editing duties as well as functioning as Richard's assistant, taking his messages, scheduling his appointments, and fielding any unwanted phone calls. Now here she was a year out of college, voluntarily working full time with little pay, and all because Richard said he couldn't do without her. If she was being honest, Caroline couldn't tear herself away from Richard, either. Salary hadn't really mattered until a week ago, because Dad was providing her with a generous allowance and she was living rent-free in their family home in Belford.

Now I need a job, probably one that puts some distance between me and Richard and—

Caroline slammed on her brakes as traffic came to a standstill. She glanced at the clock again. "*Move!*" she shouted as she pounded her hand on the steering wheel in frustration. She honked at the car in front of her, whose driver didn't notice the light turn green. *I'm good at what I do, I know I could earn more money, so why can't I force myself to leave Meadows Advertising?* She knew the answer: She could never refuse Richard anything, and in fact felt guilty telling anyone no. *Life was so much easier in college. Have I learned anything since then?*

In school she was always being asked to proofread other students' college essays, for no pay of course. Despite the drain on her time, she'd managed to keep up with her own assignments and excelled in her classes. Junior year, Caroline's academic advisor had suggested she sign up for a summer internship. Caroline had immediately called her father.

"Dad, do you know any ad agencies or marketing firms where I can get on as a summer intern?"

He said he'd give it some thought. The next day he called her back. "You know my friend Sharlene?"

"Yes, Dad," Caroline had said as agreeably as she could.

"Well, she and her brother are willing to take you on as an intern in the family business." Caroline cringed, just imagining what it would be like working for Sharlene. *Friend indeed.*

Her dad had met Sharlene—what? four years ago?—and Caroline didn't think for a minute that Sharlene had made the internship offer out of the goodness of her heart. Sharlene never did anything without an agenda. Naturally her gesture had impressed Daniel. At least Sharlene had been useful in getting Caroline the opportunity, but work for her? Just as

Caroline was about to politely turn down the offer, she'd met Richard.

Caroline rolled into the parking lot at eight-forty-five. She pulled the ponytail holder out and shook her hair loose, picked up her handbag with the now-warm yogurt, balanced her Peterson's coffee and went into Suite 100. Meadows Advertising Agency was a small company consisting of Richard, the CEO, receptionist Lucy Rosen, a part-time sales associate who was rarely in the office, and Jack Anderson, Richard's best friend from college and now his accountant.

"Good morning, Lucy," Caroline said.

During Richard's senior year at IU, his father's sudden illness had forced Richard to commute back and forth from Bloomington, Indiana, to Indianapolis, finishing his last semester of school mostly online while keeping his father's business running. His sister and business partner Sharlene was no help at all, since she'd all but abdicated her responsibilities when she met Daniel Benedict. Caroline couldn't imagine how Richard had managed to juggle both school and work and still cope with his father's death, but Meadows Advertising was thriving under his leadership four years later.

Caroline knew what a difficult position Richard was in a year ago, what with the tight economy and Sharlene controlling the purse strings from home, but never bothering to step foot in the office. Caroline had thought she had a possible solution. "Richard, I know you need to hire an assistant, but the finances aren't there right now, so what if I work for half-time salary the first year after I graduate? I live at home with Mom, and Dad pays most of my expenses anyway. It's a win-

win."

Richard had looked dubious. "That's not fair, Caroline. You're worth more than that."

"Just for a year, until the economy improves. Then we can renegotiate."

Richard had given that some thought. "Well, I guess Sharlene couldn't object to that. She'd have to pay that much for a part-timer anyway."

Caroline had felt elated about getting to stay on with Richard. Sharlene had gleefully agreed to the low-ball salary, and then of course bragged to Daniel about how she'd helped launch his daughter's professional career.

"Morning, Caroline!" said a cheerful Lucy.

Caroline snapped out of her head just in time to save her coffee from spilling onto the floor. "Hi, Lucy. What's new?"

"Not much, but the day is young," Lucy said with a wink. "I'm ordering Chinese for lunch today. You in?"

"Absolutely!"

"The usual?"

Caroline nodded.

"I'll meet you in the break room at twelve-thirty then," Lucy said as she put her earphones back on and turned her attention to the caller on the line. "Meadows Advertising. May I help you?"

The small break room down the hall was shared with the other office suites on the first floor of the Koffman Building. Suite 102 housed a law firm, Suites 104-120 were a branch office of Kinley Real Estate Company, and Suite 122 was vacant at the moment. It was rumored that the "investment" company that had been renting the office had fled overnight amid financial improprieties that were being investigated by the state Attorney General's office. Lucy had gotten a lot of mileage out of that piece of gossip. In fact, Lucy seemed to know everyone's business and was always happy to spread the news.

Caroline headed to her desk in the far back corner of the suite, down a hallway and wedged between the file cabinets, adjacent to Sharlene's former office. Sharlene had slowly removed most of her personal belongings, but there were still some photographs on the wall—Sharlene posing with the mayor, Sharlene posing with the runner-up of the Indy 500, Sharlene posing with Daniel in front of Truitt Wellness Corporation—all monuments to Sharlene's social agenda. Caroline wanted the photos gone, as well as the dead plant in the window. She could make good use of that space, but it remained firmly "Sharlene's Office." Richard's tastefully decorated office was right next to his sister's nearly empty one. Above the mahogany desk, his father's golfing mementoes hung on the wall along with Richard's framed diploma and snapshots of him with family and friends. Four wingback leather chairs ringed the desk in a semi-circle, making the office both businesslike and inviting. *Richard Meadows III—CEO* read the sign on his open door.

Caroline set her coffee carefully on her desk and then logged on to her email. She pulled the tab on her yogurt, found a plastic spoon in the desk drawer, and sat down to concentrate on her messages. First and foremost, she wanted to complete whatever task Richard had for her, so she opened his message right away. Just opening an email from him made her tingle. *Good morning, Caroline.*

I have several appointments today and will be in and out of the office. I know you will handle any phone calls in your usual professional manner until I get back. Would you proof that Hamilton ad before sending it to the printer? It needs to be ready as an insert for this Sunday's newspaper.

Thanks! R

Caroline smiled to herself as she replied to his email.

Will do. Have a nice day. Hamilton ad will be a challenge—Mr. Hamilton can't spell or punctuate!

Caroline steeled herself before reviewing the proof. Hamilton Hardware was one of Meadows Advertising's big accounts. Mr. Hamilton had several stores in the Indianapolis area, plus one in Belford and one in Muncie. The man had built his business from the ground up, so Mr. Hamilton was very hands-on. He even wrote his own print ads, emailing them to Richard weekly, and those ads were always in need of correction. The current one had a picture of a bathroom sink, with the following copy:

If your in need of plumbing supplys, stop by Hamilton Hardware We have the best for lest!

Caroline smiled to herself, knowing it was an easy fix, and went back to her emails. She went through them quickly but decided she could handle them later, since that Hamilton ad needed to be at the printer by noon, and Richard had asked her to get it done. Then one more message popped up, from Sharlene. She sighed as she opened it.

Hi Caroline!

I changed my email address to reflect my new status as your dad's wife.

Love, Sharlene
P.S. If thirty-five is too young to be your stepmother, you can think of me as Mrs. Meadows-Benedict LOL!

Caroline cringed and deleted that one. "A thirty-five-year-old stepmother," she mumbled to herself.

Sharlene was youthful looking, medium-height with a Barbie-doll figure, and always wore the latest fashions bought at high-end stores. She was also a highly successful saleswoman and had been an asset to Meadows Advertising till she met Daniel Benedict, who was no match for her charms.

Medical insurance companies had attracted some bad press in the deepening recession. CEOs like Daniel were earning huge salaries while their employees worked for low wages and their clients' premiums skyrocketed. Sharlene had arrived in Daniel's office four years ago to sell him on the idea of a positive publicity campaign for his mega-corporation, a bold move for so small a company as Meadows Advertising. She had flirted with Daniel, flattered him, and generally inflated his ego to the point that he could not resist her or her advertising proposal.

Officially they were business associates, but when Dad divorced Mom a year later, no one was surprised. Sharlene had proclaimed her love for Daniel and her intention to marry him to anyone who would listen, and to some who didn't care to listen, like Caroline.

Richard was as unlike his sister as two people could be and still share DNA. Both were very attractive people, even resembling each other somewhat. Both had dark brown hair and deep blue eyes, and since Richard was just under six feet tall and Sharlene always wore very high heels, they often appeared to be the same height. However, Richard was definitely overshadowed by his domineering older sister.

Despite losing Sharlene's capable sales acumen to her social ambitions, Richard pulled in clients of his own, including the large contract with Hamilton Hardware. Sharlene no longer wanted to work, and she didn't need to anyway, having the use of Daniel's credit cards, the run of his penthouse, and soon, the Benedict family home.

Caroline laughed to herself, remembering what her mother had said. "Sharlene will fit in nicely with the suburban housewives in Belford."

****

Caroline rushed back into the air-conditioned office a few minutes late for her Chinese lunch with Lucy. The late May temperature was hotter than normal, and she was already overheated, but she hurried down the hall to her office nook to deposit her handbag and the mail from the post office. She stopped to dig through her desk, looking for that half-drunk bottle of water she'd stashed in there yesterday, but after opening and closing every drawer, she came to the conclusion she'd either accidentally thrown it out or the custodian had gotten it off her desk for the trash bin. She sighed and dug two dollars' worth of loose change out of the bottom of her handbag to buy a fresh bottle, and then headed down the hall to the break room to join Lucy. As she walked by Jack's office she heard Richard's voice, and they probably should have closed the door, judging by the conversation they were having. Caroline paused in the hall just out of view. She knew she shouldn't eavesdrop, but she couldn't make her feet move.

"…and anyway I have a date with that hot new attorney down the hall, the one with the long brown hair," Jack said.

"Yeah, women always go for tall, blond, blue-eyed charmers like you." Richard chuckled.

"You don't have to settle for Misty, you know. There's a certain petite redhead…"

Caroline saw Richard blush. "Caroline Benedict is my assistant. My intelligent, efficient, creative assistant."

"Not to mention attractive," Jack said with a wink.

"I like her business sense," Richard shot back.

"Business sense. Yeah, right."

Richard narrowed his eyes at Jack. "So did you figure out yet if we can afford to take her on full time or not?"

"Not with your assets alone. You'll have to talk to your sister again, since you're required to get her okay on company financial matters."

Caroline thought she'd already heard too much, so she cleared her throat. Richard turned to face her and blushed.

"I just wanted to let you know I'm back from the printer and I'm going to lunch," she told them, trying to sound breezy. But she didn't fool anyone, least of all herself, because none of them wanted to discuss the elephant in the room—her lack of salary and status with the company.

Lucy was already in the break room, unpacking the just-delivered Chinese food in white cartons. Caroline shoved the change into the vending machine and pulled the bottle of water out of the tray when it landed with a thud.

"It's getting hot outside," Caroline said, fanning herself with a copy of the menu lying on the table and taking a swig of water. "And I'm starved. Where's that *moo goo gai pan?*" She tossed aside the menu and began rummaging through the sack. "How much do I owe you?"

Lucy smiled. "Never mind, you buy lunch next week."

Lucy Rosen had been working at Meadows Advertising for about five years. She and her husband Jonathan had a two-year-old son and another baby on the way. Even when not pregnant, Lucy was short and round, but despite her penchant for gossip, to Caroline, Lucy was a voice of sanity who could advise her about her insane family situation.

They sat down at a table under an air conditioning vent. Caroline tore open her chopsticks and began eating out of the carton.

Lucy handed Caroline some napkins. "How are things in Bel-ville?"

Caroline snickered and nearly choked on her food. "What?"

"Well, I'd have to be blind, deaf and dumb not to know that Sharlene is moving into your—I mean, Daniel's house." Lucy bit into her egg roll. "So how's everyone handling it?"

Caroline put her chopsticks down and frowned. "Mom's got a job interview today, Megan's in denial mode, and Allie doesn't even know yet. As you'd imagine, I'm crazed. And broke."

Lucy pointed a chopstick at her. "You, dear crazy girl, need a career path. Like I've been telling you for a while now."

"I need to do something fast," Caroline admitted. "The last of my allowance from Dad is almost gone, and I can't stay at Meadows indefinitely, at least not without a pay raise. And I really don't know if I can stick around after the wedding. Talk about painful..." She pushed her food aside, her appetite suddenly gone.

"So what's the plan? Tell Aunt Lucy all about it."

Caroline laughed in spite of herself but shook her head. "I don't have a plan."

****

Susan walked in the back door dressed in her workout clothes: black calf-length capris, sleeveless t-shirt, and worn athletic shoes, her hair pushed back from her face with a headband.

"Megan? I'm back!" she called out. "Fresh from the gym!" She laughed at herself. *Well, okay, not so fresh.*

After the tension she'd built up this morning before her interview, a workout had been just what she needed. Susan never felt like she fit in with those suburban moms at the gym, but she should have. She had everything they had: good looks, a wealthy and influential husband, a large home in the right neighborhood, gifted children. When she and Daniel had first moved to Belford, she'd tried to make friends with the other moms, but Susan just couldn't stand the incessant chattering about clothes, money, the country club, the latest parties, and the vicious innuendoes about each other. So she began spending more and more time with her old friend Emily Martin, who was then living in Indianapolis.

Megan was sprawled on the living room sofa, watching TV and munching popcorn. She was long out of her school uniform, lounging in shorts with her bare feet propped on the coffee table.

Susan walked over and tousled her daughter's hair. "Hey, Megs. I have some news." She waited for a response, which didn't come. "I don't suppose I had any phone calls?"

"*Mom!* You're in the way!" Megan never took her eyes off the television but shifted her position to regain a clear view of the program, some rerun of a reality dating show. "No one ever calls you anyway, except Caroline or Emily."

"Gee thanks." Disappointed at not getting the important conversation started about her job, Susan went back into the kitchen to wait till her oldest and most mature daughter got home. *Caroline will care.*

****

Caroline pulled her year-old Kia, a birthday gift from her dad, into the garage right next to Susan's five-year-old Jeep Cherokee, hit the garage door closer, and walked in the back door. She dropped her handbag on the kitchen counter, tossed her jacket on a chair, and went to the refrigerator for a bottled water.

"How did the job interview go, Mom?" Caroline twisted open the bottle and took a swallow.

Susan looked up from the stir fry on the stove and smiled. "Well, I was nervous at first, but Mrs. Renfrow put me at ease. I really liked her, and I also felt very comfortable inside the school itself. You know, it has a fabulous history." Susan paused and a sly grin spread across her face. "Anyway, it turns out being a substitute teacher was pretty good experience after all—that and all my volunteer work…"

"So?"

"So—*I got the job!*"

"That's great!" Caroline gave her mom a big hug and then called out, "Hey, Megan, did you hear that? Mom got that teaching job!"

Megan slowly got up off the sofa and ambled over to the kitchen island, popcorn bowl in hand. "What kinds of kids are you going to be teaching there anyway?" she asked. "Aren't all inner-city kids, like, losers?"

Susan shot her daughter a withering look. Megan shrugged her shoulders and went back to the sofa.

Susan frowned but turned back to Caroline. "I report to work sometime in the middle of August, and school starts about a week later. Your mom has officially joined the working world! Well, almost."

"Congratulations, Mom." Caroline reached into the fridge for another bottle of water, opened it, and handed it to her mother. The two of them clinked the plastic bottles together in a toast.

Susan motioned for Caroline to follow her into the living room. "There's one more thing." Susan approached Megan on the living room sofa. "I drove around Rosslyn Village after the interview and wrote down some addresses of houses for sale near the school. Emily's coming down from Chicago tomorrow, and we have an appointment with a realtor."

No one said a word.

Finally Megan spoke up. "Rosslyn Village? What are you talking about? We can't squeeze into one of those tiny houses down there!"

"We have to move somewhere," Susan said, "and we have to do it soon. A small house of our own is better than an apartment. From now on, we only have my salary as a teacher and your child support to live on, which means we'll be on a tight budget."

Megan groaned. "Mom! All the way down in Rosslyn Village?"

"Some of those cottages are cute," Susan replied.

"Cute? What does that mean? Small?"

Caroline saw the fear and emotion in her mother's face and jumped to her defense. "Megan, stop it. Mom's doing the best she can."

Susan exhaled. "That's why I called Emily. This is all so overwhelming. I need her moral support, as well as her real estate expertise."

Caroline was dubious. "Emily and Sara have been living in Chicago for two years. Isn't she kind of out of touch with the Indianapolis real estate market?"

"That's what the Internet is for. And she told me she's always available to help her best friend."

"So you're going house-hunting in Rosslyn Village," Caroline restated.

Susan looked down at her shoes, noticed an untied lace, and propped her foot on the coffee table to retie it. "Emily knows people in Indianapolis real estate. That's how she made a name for herself here. I'm sure between the two of us we'll find something affordable."

"Did you even bother looking up here in Belford?" Megan demanded.

"Even the small houses here are too expensive, Megan," Susan sighed.

"Mooommm…" Megan whined.

Susan planted both feet firmly on the floor. "We're running out of time, girls, because your dad and Sharlene are still planning to move in here June first."

Megan sank listlessly down into the sofa cushions.

She turned up the volume on the TV and pretended to be engrossed in the program.

Caroline grabbed the remote and muted the volume. She turned to Susan, determined to bring up the subject none of them had mentioned. "Mom, you still haven't talked to Allie, have you?"

"No, not yet, although I'm sure she's already had an email from the new Mrs. Benedict." Susan shook her head. "That's a sentence I never thought I'd say."

"Okay, she probably does know that Dad got remarried, but you can't keep the rest of this from her," Caroline insisted.

"I think it would be best to wait until she finishes final exams." Susan returned to the kitchen. She turned off the burner under the stir fry pan and slid it to the back of the stove. Then she went to the fridge and started pulling out vegetables for a salad.

Caroline got between her mother and the open fridge door. "You know Allie doesn't handle change well, Mom, and she doesn't like to be blind-sided either."

Susan nodded. "All I'm trying to avoid is telling her bad news while she should be concentrating on her exams."

"Maybe you're not giving her enough credit," Caroline said.

"I'm just going by past experience. Do you remember when she was in high school and she lost that statewide piano competition? She thought she played brilliantly, but she was upset because the boyfriend *du jour* had dumped her, and she lost."

Caroline shuddered at the memory. A small private college in Indianapolis, Bradley University, was hosting the finals in their Central Hall. Allie played well despite her distraction, but unfortunately, her main competitor played better, and the judges awarded first prize to the other girl.

"Second place? *Second*?" Allie had screamed. "No way! I was better than that no-talent fraud!"

Obviously Allie hadn't played her best, but she refused to accept that. She yelled and cried so much it brought on a migraine, and she went to bed for three days. It was the longest three days of everyone's lives.

Caroline nodded. "Oh, I remember. All too well. But she's not in high school anymore, Mom."

"Allie may be older, but she still reacts in the same dramatic way, and I'd never forgive myself if telling her this news caused her to flunk." Susan reached around Caroline for the bag of lettuce and went to the sink to start rinsing its contents.

"I should call her," Caroline said, drumming her fingers on the laminate countertops. "She'll be furious if we don't tell her."

"Not until after her exams," Susan insisted. "She doesn't know it, but this is her last semester at Bryce, so let her have a few more days to enjoy it. Please, Caroline, promise me."

This secrecy didn't feel right to Caroline, but for her mother's peace of mind—and her sister's—she finally nodded assent. "But what if—"

At that moment Megan yelled into the kitchen. "Hey, Mom, if Allie's leaving Bryce and I don't go back to Willowby, where am I supposed to go to school next year?"

Susan turned her back to both daughters while tossing lettuce into the salad bowl. "If we're going to live in Rosslyn Village, probably Rosslyn High School."

Megan jumped up off the sofa, looking both stunned and angry. She shrieked, "No! Transferring to Belford High would be bad enough. But Rosslyn? Are you crazy?"

"You'd have to live here with Dad and Sharlene if you want to go to Belford..." Caroline didn't finish her sentence because Susan quietly shook her head and made a slash mark under her chin. Caroline understood what her mom meant. Sharlene would never allow that.

Susan tried to hug Megan, who pulled away. "I'm sorry, Megs, but circumstances being what they are, things have to change."

Tears spilled out of Megan's eyes as she ran up the stairs two at a time and slammed her bedroom door. Caroline and Susan both stared after her, helpless and frustrated.

"Mom, don't worry. Megan will adjust."

Susan nodded. "I hope Allie will, too..." Susan's voice trailed off as she went back into the kitchen.

Caroline stood there bewildered. And despite her mother's insistence that Allie be kept in the dark, Caroline made up her mind to at least give her sister a hint of what she was coming home to.

Chapter Three

The next morning Caroline sat on her bed, phone in hand, alternately punching in Allie's number and hanging up before it rang. Her mother's objections kept replaying in her head, but Allie needed to be told. So she gathered her courage one last time and hit her sister's speed dial number. It rang several times and Caroline was about to give up, thinking it was going to voice mail, when her sister answered.

"Hi, Allie, I…"

"Caroline, hang on," Allie said. "I've got Nathan on the other line."

Caroline sighed and tapped her foot nervously while she waited on hold.

Allie clicked back in. "Sorry. Nathan's on my case. I haven't even started packing up my dorm room, and he's ready to leave and head back to Belford. I told him to give me a couple of hours."

Caroline remembered when Allie and Nathan had been in orchestra together at Willowby Prep and agreed to commute back and forth to Bryce. Since Nathan didn't have a car but didn't mind driving in Chicago, and Allie hated it, and Dad had given Allie a Toyota hatchback to transport her belongings to and from school, she and Nathan always carpooled.

"Are your exams over?" Caroline asked. "If Nathan wants to go ahead and leave, I could drive up

39

there to get you. There's something…"

"Well, if I let you do that," Allie interrupted, "then what about my car? And how will Nathan get home? Your car isn't big enough for all three of us." Her voice trailed off, and Caroline could hear her kicking boxes around the room. "Are you still there, Car? Nathan's mad at me because I went over to the music hall for one last practice session and lost track of time."

That made Caroline cringe, because it was her sister's last practice session there ever. Now she needed to spit the words out, let Allie know they were being forced out of their childhood home. "Well, yeah, but, Allie, we need to talk about…"

"Thanks anyway, Caroline, but I'll just see you when I get home. I gotta go. I've got empty boxes and suitcases everywhere and nothing packed."

"But…" Too late. Allie had already disconnected. Caroline chided herself for not speaking up. Now she had no idea how she was going to break the news to her sister about their impending move.

Getting accepted to Bryce Anthony Music Conservatory had been Allie's dream, something she'd worked for all through high school. Allie had blossomed musically and academically at Bryce for two years, and now…

Caroline shook her head and slipped her phone in her handbag. *Mom was right. This bad news would be better delivered in person.*

****

Caroline's phone pinged with a text from Allie late that afternoon, just as Caroline was preparing to leave work and fight the rush hour traffic home.

—*Toyota's packed, Nathan cooled down, and*

we're trying to get out of Chicago. Bumper-to-bumper traffic. Nathan stored his stuff on campus. Mine's in the car. Stopping for dinner in Lafayette. Tell Mom I'll be home late.—

Caroline typed in a reply.

—I'll wait up. We need to talk.—

She grabbed her bag, slipped her phone in the pocket of her slacks, and headed for the front door, intending to stop and commiserate with Lucy at the front reception desk. However, Lucy was gone, the lamp next to her chair turned off, and the phones set to night messaging. "I sure could use a friend right now," she said to herself.

"If you need a sounding board, I'm here."

Caroline spun around to see Richard standing behind her, his briefcase in hand. "Oh, Richard," she said, her heart fluttering, "you startled me."

Richard smiled at Caroline, and she momentarily forgot all about the problems with Allie. "Walk you to your car?" he asked.

Caroline nodded as Richard held the door for her, then locked it, and set the alarm. Her Kia was parked at the other end of the office building's open air parking lot from where Richard's BMW was sitting under a shade tree, so the two of them walked leisurely toward her car. She beeped it open and tossed her bag on the passenger seat.

"So what did you need to talk to Lucy about?" Richard asked. "Not business, I imagine."

Caroline looked up into Richard's blue eyes and again almost lost her train of thought. Suddenly she felt over-heated and regretted that she was still wearing her denim jacket, even though she'd needed it inside the chilly air-conditioned office. She slipped it off and tossed it on top of her purse. "I was going to ask Lucy's advice about Allie. Mom didn't want her to blow her finals, so she still doesn't know we're moving."

Richard leaned against Caroline's car door, folded his arms in front of his chest, and frowned. "I feel like I should apologize for my sister's behavior, but then again, no one's ever been able to control Sharlene, not even Grandmother." He glanced over at Caroline. "I guess Allie's going to be surprised."

"Shocked is more like it."

Richard stood up straight and faced her. "I don't know what Lucy would have told you, but my advice is to pull the bandage off and just get it all out there."

Caroline realized he was probably right. "I'll give it a try, but you know Allie's kind of a drama queen."

"Let me know how it goes," Richard said. He opened the driver's side door for her and shut it again once she was inside and settled.

Caroline rolled down her window. "Thanks, Richard. I…"

Richard glanced at her dashboard clock and suddenly looked stricken. "I'm meeting Misty for dinner, and she's going to be furious if I'm late. Good luck with Allie." He waved goodbye and hurried off to his BMW.

Caroline buried her head in her hands on the steering wheel and groaned. "Misty."

****

Caroline had been watching out her bedroom window for Allie's car. Turns out Allie's prediction had been right; it was nearly midnight by the time she finally got home. Caroline stepped into her flip flops and tiptoed past Megan's closed bedroom door and down the hall, intent on catching Allie before she got inside their house and stumbled over any of the packed boxes lying around.

Allie quietly opened the front door to the Benedict house and carefully set her suitcase on the floor inside. As she was attempting to make her way to the table lamp near the staircase, before Caroline could warn her, she stubbed her toe on one of the boxes and squealed in pain. "What the...?" Allie said. She fumbled in her handbag for her keys and got the attached penlight to illuminate the entry hall around her. With the tiny light in hand, she stumbled over to the table lamp and flicked it on. She stared in silence until Caroline flipped on the upstairs hall light.

"Allie?" Caroline whispered.

"Yeah, it's me," Allie called back, "trying to walk in the front door until I tripped over all these boxes. What is all this?"

Caroline sighed. "I tried to tell you this morning when I called, but you wouldn't let me get a word in." She walked down to the bottom of the staircase, faced her sister, and forced a smile. "So there's news. We're moving."

Allie's eyes widened. "Moving? What? Where?" She again took in all the moving boxes and shook her head in confusion. "Why?"

"I'm so sorry. I thought I'd be able to tell you about all this"—Caroline waved her arms around at the mess—"before you saw it for yourself. Dad and Sharlene are moving in here on the first of June. That's when the lease on his penthouse is up."

Allie all but collapsed onto one of the nearby

boxes. Her gaze floated around the entry hall. The walls were bare, the bookshelves empty, decorations were missing, all packed in boxes. Slowly she got up and walked through the living room, family room, dining room, kitchen, circling back to the entry hall.

Susan came to the top of the stairs and whispered, "Allie, is that you? Where have you been? We expected you hours ago."

"I'm here now!" Allie shouted. "What in the world is going on here?"

"Caroline, didn't you tell her?"

Caroline nodded. Allie glared at both of them, hands on her hips.

Susan put a finger to her lips and pointed toward Megan's room. "Sorry about the mess, Allie. We've got most of what we're taking already packed, but…"

"Mom!" Allie interrupted. "What's going on?"

"I just told you, Allie," Caroline said. "Dad wants this house back, or really Sharlene wants it, and they want it in about ten days. Everything has just happened so fast."

"If it helps, Caroline started packing some of the things in your bedroom," Susan offered. "If you don't unpack anything from school, it should save some time in the next few days."

Allie ran to the top of the stairs and got in Susan's face. "For God's sake, Mom! Why didn't anybody tell me about this? This is so unfair!"

Susan took a step back. "Caroline wanted to call you, but I was afraid to disturb you during finals, so…"

"Actually, Mom," Caroline said, "I did try to tell her this morning, but…" She shouldn't have given up so easily. She could see that Allie was devastated.

Allie crossed her arms and glared at them both. "So exactly where are we moving?"

Susan reached out to hug Allie, but Allie backed away. Susan's arms fell limp at her side. "Emily was down from Chicago a few days ago, and she helped me find an adorable house in Rosslyn Village."

Allie's mouth dropped open. "Why Rosslyn Village?"

Susan offered a crooked smile. "Well, that's the good news. I got a teaching job at Rosslyn High School for next fall."

Allie narrowed her eyes at her mother. "So, great. Commute. And by 'adorable' do you mean small? What about my piano?"

Caroline and Susan exchanged glances.

"There's no room for the piano, Allie," Susan said. "It has to stay here. We're taking a few things with us, but the new house is just too small for everything."

"Then where am I supposed to practice? I can't just quit for the entire summer! When I get back to school next fall…" Allie scrutinized her mother's face. "What else aren't you telling me?"

"Allie, we just don't have any money for private education. Your dad… Well, there was a loophole in the divorce settlement that only requires him to pay for public-school expenses."

"Loophole? Mom!"

"I'm so sorry, Allie. I didn't listen to Sara when she tried to tell me. When I signed the divorce papers, I was very upset and not paying attention."

The color drained out of Allie's face, and she took a step back, catching herself before she tripped on the top step. "I'm not going back to school? At all? I know

Sharlene kept complaining to Dad about my expensive 'hobby,' but..."

Susan shook her head. "Not to Bryce, anyway. But I've been checking around and it seems Ball State University has a nice music department. They would be willing to accept you as a transfer student."

The blood drained from Allie's face. She slowly collapsed onto the top step and put her head between her knees, breathing deeply.

Susan sat down next to Allie and rubbed her neck. "I know this is a shock, and it's true that Caroline, Megan, and I have all had a couple of weeks to adjust to the news."

"It's not just you, Allie," Caroline added. "Megan has to leave Willowby Hall and attend public school, too." And then there was her own problem, something she'd been wrestling with ever since her mother had told her about their new financial situation. "I've got to do something about my job..."

"Public school?" Allie mumbled, lifting her head. "Ball State? But I love Bryce. I've never even visited a public school." Tears came to her eyes, and her chin began quivering. Not saying another word, she shuffled down the stairs directly to the piano in the formal living room, tied her long, straight black hair into a ponytail and sat down at the bench, feeling for the pedals. She scrunched up her brow and began feverishly playing Mozart's *Turkish Rondo.* The frenetic pace of the music was in direct contrast to the somber mood in the room.

Caroline and Susan tiptoed downstairs, watching silently while Allie played. "It's like she's playing for the last time," Caroline whispered. "You go on back to bed, Mom. I'll talk to her."

Susan nodded and started upstairs. She looked back at her daughters and opened her mouth to speak, but instead shook her head and went up.

Caroline walked into the living room, sat down on the piano bench next to Allie, and waited patiently until Allie finished the piece and dropped her arms in exhaustion. Caroline put her arm around Allie's shoulder, gave it a gentle squeeze, and said, "We'll get through this as a family, I promise."

Allie nodded. Finally she put her head on her sister's shoulder, tears spilling from her eyes. "Why is he doing this to us, Car?"

Caroline sighed. "Dad doesn't seem to have any backbone where Sharlene's concerned."

"It's not fair!" Allie looked her sister in the eye. "And you sure didn't try very hard to tell me."

"You're right. I shouldn't have chickened out. I'm so sorry."

Allie sobbed for a minute. Then she sat up, wiped the tears away with the back of her hand, flexed her fingers, and started playing again, this time more quietly. Caroline hugged Allie's shoulder once more and headed back to bed.

Chapter Four

"Mom, you have *got* to be kidding! *"* Allie threw her handbag on the floor of her bedroom, tears of frustration welling up in her eyes.

Susan and Allie had just gotten back from a tour of their new house. Now Susan surveyed her middle daughter's bedroom in their soon-to-be former home, and it was a wreck. Items were divided into either packing boxes, bags designated for charity, or things to be thrown into the trash, and the boxes Allie had brought home from school were stacked everywhere. There was barely enough room to walk from the door to the bed.

Susan felt completely helpless. "Allie, you've got to calm down. I know this is hard, but…"

Allie waded through the boxes, kicked aside a few bags of giveaways, and unearthed her laptop from under a pile of clothes on the bed. She sat down on top of everything, opened it and started typing furiously.

"What are you doing?" Susan asked, peering over her shoulder.

"I sent Brittany an email telling her about that tiny house." Allie looked up at her mother and scowled. "How do you expect us to downsize from five thousand square feet to eighteen hundred?"

Susan sighed in frustration, but it dawned on her that there might still be hope. Allie's close friend

Brittany Martin, Emily's niece from Oklahoma, might be a voice of reason in this fiasco. "Did Brittany reply?"

Allie groaned and turned her attention to the computer. "Yeah, she says, 'I'm so sad about all this— Aunt Emily emailed me. Why don't you come up to Chicago and visit sometime this summer? I'm going to be staying with Aunt Emily and Aunt Sara most of the month of July while my parents are off on a cruise to Greece. Some kind of second honeymoon thing.'" Allie lifted an eyebrow. "Brittany's going to spend part of the summer in Chicago? Usually she stays home, working at that boutique to earn money for college."

Susan felt like she'd just been thrown a lifeline, at least as far as Allie was concerned. "You should go. To Chicago, I mean. Spending time with Brittany away from all this might be just what you need."

Allie shook her head. "I just left a few days ago, and you know how I hate all that urban congestion. I can't even think about going back." She heaved a sigh. "This is all Sharlene's fault."

Susan shook her head and picked her way across the cluttered room to the door. "Partly, but I'm also to blame. At least give Brittany's offer some thought, okay?"

Allie slammed her laptop shut and collapsed face down on her bed. Susan slipped out of the room.

****

Caroline rapped lightly on Richard's open office door. He was studying something on his computer and frowning.

"Come in." He motioned for her to enter and pointed to his screen. "I just had a message from

Sharlene about our recently blended families." Richard was blushing, and Caroline thought it must be embarrassment at his sister's antics. It had to be, because it wouldn't have anything to do with her. Would it?

"What does she say?"

Richard blew out a puff of air. "She wants me at her house—your house—Daniel's house—moving day. I have no idea what for, since as she says, she's got 'people' to do all the actual moving." He shoved his chair away from the computer, leaned his elbows on his desk, and rubbed his temples. "I still can't believe my sister is married to your father."

Caroline came all the way into his office and eased into a chair opposite his desk. "It's so, I don't know, like on that soap opera Mom watches all the time; everyone's related to everyone else by marriage or something, and it gets so convoluted." She gave him a rueful smile.

Richard laughed. He reached out for her hand resting on his desk but quickly drew back. He sat up straight in his chair and cleared his throat. "Now what can I do for you? And why are you still here at this hour?"

Caroline fiddled with the pencil holder on Richard's desk. Being this close to him, joking around, was as wonderful as it was uncomfortable. "I had a few last-minute ends to tie up."

Richard shifted uncomfortably in his chair. "You should go home. I'm sure you have packing left to do." He moved the pencil holder back where it was, and then just started randomly moving items around on his desk. "How are Allie and Megan handling all this?"

Caroline stood up and was about to place her hands on Richard's to slow his nervous energy, thought better of it, and instead moved closer to the door. "Not too well, actually, but it's nice of you to ask. This is really hard on Allie, and bewildering for Megan."

"She's a tough kid, and I'm sure she'll adjust. If you need any help...I mean, if your family needs any help..." Richard turned away, blushing again. After a moment of silence, he gave her a polite nod and said, "Well, have a nice Memorial Day weekend."

"Thanks. You, too." Caroline closed the door behind her and breathed deeply, willing her queasy stomach to calm down. She gave her desk a quick straightening before heading out the front door.

"Lucy! What are you still doing here?" Caroline asked when she reached the reception desk. Lucy was engrossed in a romance novel and didn't even look up.

"Too much traffic. Besides, I have to come to work to get some rest, what with two helpless guys at home. And one of them isn't even in diapers." Lucy looked up and winked, making Caroline giggle. "I'll leave in about half an hour after the traffic dies down."

"Do you have plans for the holiday weekend?" Caroline asked.

Lucy turned a page in her book. "Jonathan and his brother have tickets to the Indy 500, so I'll be home chasing after a toddler." She looked up from her book. "Is there anything you need?"

Caroline shook her head. "No. Just wondered."

Lucy shrugged. "Maybe you just need a little TLC." She reached across the waist-high reception desk, stretching as far as her growing belly would allow, and gave Caroline's shoulders a quick squeeze.

"Don't let Sharlene get you down, Caroline. That one's a handful."

Caroline smiled. "You're a good friend, Lucy."

Chapter Five

"Emily Martin! It's so good to see you here in Indianapolis again." Frank Kinley beamed as he shook Emily's hand and ushered her and Susan into the conference room.

"You too, Frank." Emily plopped her briefcase on the conference table.

"And this must be Susan Benedict, our homebuyer." Frank turned and politely shook her hand, and then held a chair for her. "You come highly recommended from our sorely missed colleague here. Emily was our top saleswoman before she allowed herself to be lured to Chicago."

Susan laughed. "Nice to meet you, too, Frank. I have to admit I miss having her here in town, but she's managing to keep your office up there pretty busy."

"Not to mention the killing I made on that downtown brownstone Sara had her eye on." Emily winked at Frank.

"How is Ms. Whetstone anyway? Still running that law firm with an iron fist?"

Emily's wife, Sara Whetstone, was a partner in the Chicago firm of Moreland, Kurtis and Whetstone, and licensed to practice in both Indiana and Illinois.

"Slight exaggeration, Frank."

Frank folded his arms and leaned against the wooden cabinet adjacent to the table. "Well, she's got that reputation as a tough lawyer to maintain."

Susan laughed. "Did you ever hear how they met, Frank? Sara stepped on Emily's foot."

Frank looked puzzled. "Stepped on her foot?"

Emily shrugged. "Well, it was summer and I was wearing shorts and sandals. Sara was with a client and had on a suit and spike heels."

"Ouch!" Frank winced.

Emily got down to business. "So are we going to close this house today, Frank?"

"Yes, but unfortunately, I have another appointment, so I'm going to turn this over to Jared McIntyre. He's young, but he's a capable mortgage loan officer." Frank picked up the phone on the wall near the corner cabinet. "Jared, we're ready for you." He turned to Susan and smiled at her once more. "It's nice to finally meet you, Susan. Good luck."

"Am I going to need it?" Suddenly Susan's confidence flagged. This was a big step, both financially and emotionally. She fidgeted with one of the many pens lying on the conference table, fumbled it, and then watched it hit the floor.

"Don't worry, Susan, you'll be fine." Emily picked up the pen, put it back on the table, and plopped down in one of the chairs. "I already told you, federal money is set aside for teachers in the public sector."

"I guess they figured most of those teachers would be young," Susan said with a sigh.

Emily laughed, shook her head, and began taking the closing papers out of her briefcase. "Courage, dear. You've bought houses before."

Susan could swear she actually felt the adrenaline coursing through her veins. "Not on my own. And certainly not without a down payment. The monthly mortgage payment is going to be a stretch on a teacher's salary."

"And Megan's child support. Don't forget about that," Emily reminded her.

Susan nodded. She was grateful that, thanks to Emily, Sara Whetstone had agreed to be her attorney during the divorce three years ago. As it was, details about her future finances had somehow slipped by her as she numbly signed the divorce papers in all the places Sara indicated. It wasn't till later that she actually read them and realized the ramifications of what she'd agreed to. She vaguely remembered Sara trying to warn her, but at the time Susan was too shell-shocked to pay any attention to the details.

Susan sighed. "It's been three years since the divorce, Emily. And I'm still so unsure about all this." She shuddered just as the conference room door opened. Emily and Susan both looked up, expecting to see Jared.

"Caroline!" Susan exclaimed. She stood up and hugged her daughter. "What brings you here?"

"Well, Meadows Advertising is only down the hall, Mom. I was on my way to the post office, but I thought I'd stop in and see how it was going."

"Hopefully we're about to finally get started." Emily stood and gave Caroline a quick hug as the door opened. "You must be Jared."

An attractive man in his late twenties walked in. He was medium height with sandy blond hair, but from his broad shoulders and slim frame, it appeared he exercised regularly. He wore an expensive business suit with a silk tie and carried a stack of papers for the closing that he placed on the conference room table with a thud. He took a seat across from Susan and Emily, grabbed a pen off the table and scribbled on scratch paper to make sure it had ink.

"Ladies, shall we begin?" He was all business until he looked up and caught sight of Caroline. "Uh, aren't you...?"

Caroline blushed as Jared stared at her. "Yes, I'm Caroline Benedict, from down the hall. But I'm not staying. I just stopped in to congratulate my mom on her new beginning." She kissed Susan on the cheek, waved at Emily, and hurriedly left.

Emily winked at Susan. "Yes, indeed, we are making new beginnings today."

****

Susan yawned, stretched, and glanced at the clock on the stove. "Moving day. And it's not even six a.m. yet." But she was too keyed up to sleep, so she might as well get busy.

As she stood for the last time in the kitchen of her Belford home, memories of raising her children here came flooding back. Everywhere she looked were reminders: the hash marks on the kitchen door where she'd measured Caroline's, Allie's and Megan's growth every year; the backyard swing still attached to the old oak tree; the front yard where Caroline and Allie had played kickball with the neighbors while Megan cooed in her stroller. All their childhood milestones were here, and now everything was packed into boxes, ready to move to a much smaller house miles away in Indianapolis. Susan sipped a cup of freshly-brewed coffee from the yet-to-be-packed Keurig and surveyed the mess.

"Good morning." Emily, dressed in old jeans and a faded Chicago Cubs t-shirt, was navigating her way through the boxes cluttering the kitchen floor. She opened and closed several empty cabinets until she finally found one unpacked coffee mug, a packet of sweetener, and then made herself a cup of coffee. "Are you ready for this?"

Susan snapped out of her memories and sighed. "I can't believe this day has actually come."

Emily blew on her coffee. "When do the movers get here?"

"About nine. I hired one of those local moving companies that charges by the hour to move the heavy furniture, but the girls and I are moving as much of our own stuff as possible. It'll save money."

"Well, that's why I'm here, too, you know. Shall we get going?"

Susan nodded and swallowed a big gulp of her own coffee. "I guess I have to. My life is waiting." She walked out of the kitchen into the dining room. There was still a lot to do.

Emily sat down in a chair next to a heavy box, propped up her feet, and sipped her coffee. "Hey, Susan," she called through the house, her voice echoing, "What furniture are you actually taking?"

Susan looked around at the disarray and shook her head. She and Caroline had walked through the house a week before, trying to decide what would fit, but now Susan had qualms about their decisions.

Caroline, with her usual pragmatism, had asked, "What do we absolutely have to take?"

"Well, I just bought this sofa and loveseat three years ago, right before..." Susan had looked wistfully at the royal blue microfiber sofa with matching loveseat she'd admired so much during happier times. "And since we have to have something to sit on in the—what shall we call that room in the new house?"

Caroline had shrugged. "I guess it's a family room." She started making a list. "Then we'll also need a coffee table and end tables to fill out the room. Which ones?"

"We'll take these." Susan pointed to the refurbished antique cherry-wood coffee table and their two matching end tables. "I'm sure if we don't take them, Sharlene will have them on the trash heap before we even pull out of the drive."

"Lamps?"

"Let's just take the two floor lamps that are in the corner by the bookshelf. Which has to stay here because there's no room for it in the Rosslyn house. No room for that overstuffed chair and ottoman either. And forget about the dining room set. The dinette in the kitchen will have to do." Susan had sighed.

Caroline had nodded in agreement. "Now what about the bedrooms?"

"We must take Megan's bedroom furniture. She's had to give up too much already. Do you think it will all fit in her new room?"

"It'll be tight, but I think so. What about your bedroom furniture, Mom?"

"The king-size bed is way too big. I guess I'll just take the queen-size bed from the guest room. The smaller dresser and one nightstand from the master bedroom's about all I have space for." Susan had frowned. "And there's really no room for yours and Allie's bedroom sets, either. Sorry you and Allie have to share a room, Car."

"Don't worry about it, Mom. As soon as I get my finances in order, I'm going to find my own place. In the meantime, what if Allie and I take the furniture out of Megan's old bedroom, the one you turned into an office? You know, the twin beds and two dressers, and put them in our bedroom? Also, we can take the computer desk, since it isn't very big and should fit under the window."

Susan called to Emily from the formal dining room. "Caroline and I settled on a few things. Hope everything fits."

Time flew by as Susan and Emily finished up the last-minute details, but Caroline came downstairs after about an hour and jumped in to help as well. The movers arrived on time and set to work hauling large boxes and furniture to the van, which they had parked blocking the walkway in front of the ornate, double-wide wooden door. Emily and Caroline sealed boxes and carried both packed and unpacked items to their cars, parked at the edge of the circular driveway, out of the way of the moving van. Caroline finished taping up boxes of last-minute items and labeled them with magic marker: kitchen, bathroom toiletries, cleaning supplies, and bed linens. Emily got the vacuum out and started to go over the floors and carpets, but Susan waved her off; let Sharlene's cleaning crew swoop in and re-clean everything.

Susan stood by the front door with a clipboard and check-off list given to her by the movers. "Emily, can you ask Megan to make sure everything is out of her closet and bathroom?" She flipped through the pages on her list and checked off the loveseat as two men maneuvered it through the front door.

Emily shook a dust rag out the open door. "Sure, if I could find her. I haven't seen her since she ate a bowl of cereal earlier and left her dirty dish in the sink."

"Allie," Susan called out from the hallway, "can you *please* come help us?"

Allie was loudly playing the piano, one tune after another, ignoring the noise around her. Mostly it was Mozart or Shubert, but then she started playing Beethoven's "Moonlight Sonata," a mournful tune at best.

Susan started to get up, but Caroline held up her hand. "Let me."

Susan nodded and went back to her check-off list.

Caroline leaned into the archway of the music room. "Allie, if you won't help us, could you at least play something more upbeat? Mom's frazzled, no one's seen Megan, and you're driving me crazy!"

Allie didn't reply, but instead began playing a version of the pop culture song "Home."

Caroline lifted her shoulders to tell her mother, *I tried.*

Susan rolled her eyes.

****

Sharlene sat in the study in Daniel's penthouse, working hard on her to-do list. She had so many ideas about how to redecorate the Belford mansion that she could barely get them down on paper fast enough.

"What are you working on?" Daniel looked sideways at her list as he carried another packed box into the room.

Sharlene looked up. "Daniel, darling, you don't need to do that. We have *people* for that."

He shrugged. "I like the exercise. So what is it that you're writing?"

"Just a list of things I need to remember to do once we get settled into the house. Now about the piano..."

Daniel dropped the box and its contents rattled. "What about it?"

Sharlene winced, hoping the brand new and very costly designer glass vase in that box wasn't in pieces. "Well, obviously the piano has to go, dear. It's right in the middle of my—our—formal living room, or at least it will be once the contractors knock that wall down to open up the space. And entertaining will be impossible with that monstrosity in the way."

"Monstrosity!" Daniel's mouth dropped open. "It's an expensive grand piano. And it belongs to my daughter. Or have you forgotten?"

Sharlene's eyes narrowed, but she composed herself. "No, of course not, darling, but really—just how often will Allison find time to play it now? Surely she'll be getting a job for the summer. Why don't you just sell it?"

Daniel stared at her and then shook his head. "No. I've let you make all the decisions about the house up till now, but I have to put my foot down about this. The piano stays."

Sharlene gritted her teeth and went back to her list. *Get rid of piano.*

****

"Knock knock! Sharlene? Are you here?"

"Richard?" Caroline knew it was possible that Richard would stop by today—after all, he told her Sharlene had insisted—but with all the commotion she wasn't sure if she'd actually heard his voice. She came out of the kitchen, a half-eaten slice of pizza in her hand, took one last bite, and tossed the rest of it into a bulging heavy-duty trash bag wrapped around a nearby door handle. She was wearing jean shorts which fit loosely on her petite frame, a white t-shirt with a blue Colts insignia on its front, and flip-flop sandals. She looked down in embarrassment at the dust smudges on her shirt and shorts, swiped at the pizza sauce on her nose and smiled self-consciously when she saw Richard standing in the hallway. "I thought I heard your voice. Sorry I'm such a mess."

"Here, you've got a little..." Richard started to reach toward the sauce on her nose but quickly retrieved his hand.

Caroline blushed and quickly finished brushing it away herself, wiping her hand on her pants. "Dad and Sharlene aren't here yet, but you're welcome to wait. Emily ordered in pizza. There's plenty left if you want some."

"No thanks. Is there anything I can do to help?" Richard looked around at the mostly empty rooms. "I guess I'm a little late, huh?"

"For moving, yeah, but actually, you could help me find Megan. Emily was looking for her earlier. She didn't show up for pizza, and if she won't eat that means she's really upset. I've looked everywhere I can think of, and I know she's not outside, so she's got to be hiding somewhere." Caroline watched Richard watching her, and it sent her pulse racing, but she figured he was staring because she didn't look like her usual put-together self. Right?

"She won't come out for me, but maybe if you go upstairs and look around—well, you know she's always liked you, ever since that summer I interned at Meadows Advertising and Megan was about thirteen."

Richard nodded. "You brought her with you to the office because…"

Caroline laughed. "You can say it, she was driving Mom crazy."

"Well, we did bond over our mutual love of art. Does she still want to be an architect?"

"Oh, yeah, more than ever." Caroline did a visual search of the entryway. "I just don't know where she's been all morning. I wonder if this is her way of sticking her head in the sand." Caroline hadn't actually thought about that until it popped out of her mouth, but now it made sense. Megan didn't want to move, and being just a kid, she probably thought hiding would make it all go away. Caroline bounded up the stairs, Richard close on her heels.

"Megan?" Richard called as he reached the second-floor landing. "Hey, kiddo, where are you?" He checked all the near-empty bedrooms one-by-one and even peeked in a few closets. He went back out into the hallway to find Caroline standing with her hands on her hips, a puzzled look on her face.

"What about her bedroom?" Richard asked. "Did you check in there?"

"A few times." Caroline shook her head. "Nothing, but that doesn't mean she hasn't sneaked in and out when I wasn't looking."

Caroline followed Richard as he walked into Megan's empty bedroom, the afternoon sunlight streaming through the open blinds. There were stains on the walls where posters had been removed, an extension cord left plugged into an outlet, and indentations in the plush carpet where her furniture had stood for years. The closet door was ajar.

He smiled, pointed, and whispered, "Caroline, I think I've found that missing item you're looking for."

Caroline nodded, tiptoed across the room and peeked in. "Megan?"

"Go away."

"Megan, come on out, okay?" Caroline slowly pushed the closet door the rest of the way open. There sat Megan curled up in the corner, dressed in khaki shorts and her Willowby Hall spirit t-shirt, clutching a large book.

"Hi, Megan!" Richard looked over Caroline's head as he peeked into the closet.

"Megan, come on out and let's talk," Caroline said.

"No way. This is my room. It's always been my room. And now Sharlene's gonna turn it into a closet!"

Richard exchanged glances with Caroline. "A closet?" he whispered.

Caroline lowered her voice. "Yes."

Richard shook his head but turned back to Megan. "What's that book you're holding?"

Megan was tightly clutching a coffee-table book with pictures of historic Indiana architecture. "I *love* this book!" Megan sniffled. "Mom gave it to Dad for Christmas a few years ago. Remember how disappointed Dad looked when he saw that book, Caroline?"

"Yeah, I remember. Dad just didn't appreciate it like you do."

"Can I see it, Megan?" She reluctantly handed it over to Richard. He thumbed through a few of the exquisitely photographed pages, complete with pictures of both interiors and exteriors of some of Indiana's oldest homes, and then handed it back to her.

"Dad just set it down and went on opening other presents, but I picked it up and spent ages looking at the gorgeous houses. I can't leave it here!" Megan wiped her tears on the hem of her shirt, smearing mascara everywhere on her face and t-shirt, and clutched the book even tighter. "I use it for inspiration in my drawing. Mom says it has to stay here because it's Dad's."

Caroline winked at her sister. "Well, I say we just take it with us. Dad won't miss it, and Mom probably won't notice it in all the mess in the new house. If she does, we'll just tell her it got packed by mistake."

Megan seemed to perk up a little. "You think?"

"You know, Megan," Richard said, "I've got some great art books at the office that you might enjoy. What if I send some of them home with your sister, and you can keep those as long as you like?"

"Really?" Megan smiled at him and finally stood up and walked out of the closet, still clutching the book.

Caroline hugged her sister. "Thank you," she mouthed over Megan's head.

Richard smiled, blushed, and turned away. "I think I hear Sharlene."

****

The front door flew open, and Sharlene made a grand entrance, followed by Daniel loaded down with suitcases and her handbag. "Hello?" she called out. The nearly empty house echoed back her greeting. *Nothing left.* She smiled to herself in satisfaction. *Except for that!* Sharlene frowned as she heard Allie pounding the piano keys. "Allison, dear," she called out, "could you hold that down, please?" The music played on and Sharlene groaned.

Richard peered over the upstairs railing, waved at his sister in the entry hall, and came downstairs to join her. He gave her a quick hug, shook hands with Daniel, then took one of the overstuffed soft-sided suitcases from him. "I guess this goes in the master bedroom, huh?" He didn't wait for an answer but took it directly up the stairs.

Caroline passed Richard on the stairway just as Megan ran down the hall and locked herself in a bathroom. Caroline sighed. "Hi, Dad." She walked down the rest of the stairs to kiss her father on the cheek and mumbled, "Sharlene."

Susan and Emily came out of the kitchen. Daniel shifted his footing, looked up at the chandelier dangling from the cathedral ceiling, put Sharlene's oversized Gucci handbag on the bottom step of the staircase, and then stepped out of the line of fire between his current wife and his ex-wife.

"Caroline, darling, lovely to see you," Sharlene said with an air kiss. "Can't you get your sister to stop that racket?"

"That 'racket,' Sharlene," Caroline said through gritted teeth, "is Mozart."

"Daniel, you're looking well." Susan slowly turned her back on Sharlene and faced her ex-husband. "We're just about out of your way here. Caroline was rounding up Megan a few minutes ago, and I guess you can tell where Allie is."

"Hello, Daniel," Emily said, an amused look on her face.

Sharlene was getting quite annoyed at all the

useless small talk. She had lots to do and was itching to get started on the makeover of this house. "Susan, dear, it's lovely to see you again. And your friend, too. Please don't let us keep you any longer than necessary." She waved her hand to dismiss them. "Our movers will be arriving shortly and goodness knows this place needs some updating, so I have to call the decorator right away. Besides, I'm sure you have unpacking to do in your new little cottage. Where is it again? Oh, yes, Rosslyn Village. How quaint."

"Daniel always liked the decorations in this house," Susan shot back.

Daniel coughed and shifted nervously from one foot to the other. "Hey, what's a guy got to do to get a beer around here?"

Sharlene looked from Daniel to Susan and then back again in bewilderment. She saw Susan as a mousy housewife and boring school teacher, so what Daniel had ever seen in her was beyond comprehension. Despite her fancy college education, Susan had nothing to offer. As far as Sharlene was concerned, Susan was never the kind of wife Daniel needed for his rightful place in society. *He certainly traded up when he married me.*

"Now where is my brother? I'm sure he's just as impressed with this house as Grandmother will be, once I've got it all set to rights."

In truth, Sharlene doubted Grandmother would be fazed by the opulence in this house. She and Richard had been raised mostly by their widowed father and his opinionated mother, herself a widow. Sharlene had resented Grandmother Adele's interference in her social life at school. Adele wanted her to get involved in clubs and athletics, and Sharlene only wanted to attend parties and dances. The more lavish the party, the better she liked it. Back then her friends pretty much assumed she was the life of every social event. Sharlene briefly attended community college until her father asked her to work at Meadows Advertising. Even without a degree, Sharlene proved to be a natural advertising saleswoman, bringing in lucrative business from around town and the surrounding counties.

"Susan, dear, I don't want to keep you. If I find anything you've left behind…" Sharlene glanced at her husband and bit her tongue before she blurted out that she'd throw it out. "Of course I'll see that you get it back."

Richard came back down the stairs with his arms free of baggage, noticed the tension in the room, and grabbed his sister's arm. "Come on Sharlene, let's go look at the garden."

"I've seen the garden, Richard," Sharlene said as she jerked her arm away, "and I'm aware of how much work needs to be done out there."

Richard threw an *I tried* look at Caroline, who smiled and shrugged her shoulders.

"Emily, are you ready to leave?" Susan turned on her heel and reached for the box of bed linens Caroline had left by the front door.

"Beyond ready." Emily flashed Sharlene a wicked smile as she picked up an expensive designer lamp on the entryway table.

"Emma, dear, are you sure you want to take *that* lamp?" Sharlene lunged for it, but Emily ducked out of her reach and marched triumphantly out the door with it.

"Daniel…" Sharlene whined.

"Where's Megan?" Daniel asked Caroline, ignoring his wife. "I haven't seen her in days."

"Or possibly weeks," Caroline muttered.

Sharlene narrowed her eyes at Caroline. "Isn't that a bit harsh, dear? Your father's a terribly busy man."

"Megan?" Daniel called out. His voice echoed in the empty stairwell.

Megan appeared at the top of the stairs. She was now wearing an oversized hooded sweatshirt with her khaki shorts, a noticeable bulge in its middle.

"Hi, Dad." Megan dejectedly walked down the stairs, dragging each foot on the way.

Daniel put his arm around her shoulders and gave her a tentative hug. Megan pulled away, hugging her arms tightly around herself.

"Megan, darling, how nice to see you. Aren't you a bit overdressed for the heat?" Sharlene tossed an exasperated glance at her other stepdaughter. "And Caroline, really, what is so funny?"

Daniel tried again to hug Megan, but she backed away from him. "Hey, Megs, what if you and I have dinner one night soon? Just the two of us."

Megan brightened up. "Okay. When?"

Sharlene stepped between them. "Daniel, you know that isn't possible right now," she said. "We have dinner commitments already lined up, and of course you're out of town on business next week. Maybe after we're settled in here, but really it's not a good time right now."

Daniel shrugged and took a few steps toward the living room. "Allie?" he called. "Allie, can you leave off that playing a minute? I haven't seen you in months."

The music stopped, and Allie appeared in the doorway, sheet music clutched in her arms, her jaw set tight and a glum look on her face. Daniel held out his arms, inviting her to come give him a hug. Instead, Allie walked right by him and toward the door, never making eye contact.

"Allie?" Daniel tried again as she swept by him.

She stopped in the open doorway and turned to face him. "Take care of the piano, Dad. It needs tuning."

"Allie, listen, hon. You're welcome to use the piano any time."

Sharlene wanted to scream, but again she calmly reminded him, "Daniel, that isn't going to work either. The contractors will be here, and the piano will just have to be covered with a tarp and moved aside until they're done. I don't see how Allison could possibly practice under those circumstances."

"Well, then, Allie, how about when the renovations are done?" Daniel asked. "Allie?"

Allie grabbed Megan by the arm and stormed out the door.

Sharlene smirked. *Mission accomplished.*

****

Susan looked around the new house. Boxes were stacked everywhere, furniture left sitting askew, and at that moment it didn't seem possible that order would ever be restored. The house had just the one family room, an eat-in kitchen, a small master bedroom with full bath, two other tiny bedrooms and a hallway shower/bath for the girls' use, and finally a screened-in back porch that needed the piles of leaves swept out.

It's going to be an adjustment, that's for sure. At least the previous owners had completely renovated it, with all new kitchen cabinets and appliances, fresh paint and laminate flooring, and new bathroom fixtures. The plumbing and electrical systems had been updated in the fifty-year-old house, and there were some lovely large trees in the fenced backyard.

Maybe we can get a dog. Daniel had always hated dogs, and Megan had always wanted one.

Emily found Susan gazing at the backyard. "Maybe you can adopt a dog."

Susan laughed. "It's like you can read my mind." She gave her best friend's shoulders a squeeze. "Emily, I can't thank you enough for all your help these last couple of days."

Emily smiled. "That's what friends are for."

"I imagine you'd like to be on the freeway headed to Chicago about now. You're welcome to stay the night, but this isn't the mansion of yore. I do have a free sofa, though."

Emily chuckled. "Truthfully, I was thinking that if I got started right away I could be home in time for a late supper with Sara. Would you mind?"

"Of course not." Susan hugged her friend again, then went back to staring at the boxes stacked everywhere in the small family room.

Emily watched her in silence for a moment. "What's wrong?"

Susan sighed. "I'm really worried about Allie. She usually spends her summers taking private music lessons, but now, well... Caroline will be fine, you know how strong she is, plus she has a job, sort of, and Megan will adjust. But Allie." She shook her head. "I don't know."

"Say, listen, I've had an idea about Allie. A former client of mine lives near here in the Meridian-Kessler neighborhood. He's a music professor at Bradley University, and he also gives private lessons in his home. I know he has a piano because the house I found him had to be large enough to accommodate it. I'm wondering if he'd be willing to take Allie on as a student for the summer."

Susan gave that some thought. "How much would that cost me? You know I'm on a tight budget."

"I'm sure you could work something out. His name's Brandon Phillips, and he's a great guy. Let me give him a call tomorrow and see what he says."

Susan wasn't sure how Allie would react to yet another change, especially one arranged by her mother and Emily. "What's he like? Old and stodgy?"

Emily laughed. "Heavens no. Actually Brandon's young to be a tenured professor."

Susan took a deep breath as she mulled over Emily's suggestion. "Well, give him a call and see what he says."

"I'm sure he'll want to get in touch with you—and meet Allie."

"Just one more debt I owe you, Emily. If it weren't for you…"

Emily held up her hand. "I know, Susan. You don't have to say it."

Susan smiled, opened a box, and started unpacking it. "How did I end up with this?" They both laughed as she held up Daniel's beer mug embossed with his fraternity's letters.

Emily pulled her cell phone out of her jeans pocket

and pushed speed dial #1. "Hi, Sara. It's me. Yeah, we're done. I'm coming home tonight after all. Sure…" Emily walked off into the kitchen, and Susan gladly gave her some privacy.

Chapter Six

Caroline glanced into Richard's office and quickly turned back to her computer when he looked up and their eyes met. She blushed and was trying to focus on work, when her attention was diverted by a text from Lucy.

—*Red alert!*—

Before Caroline could reply or ask what that meant, Richard motioned for her to come into his office. She got up from her desk and walked in.

He was beaming. "Caroline, I have those art books I promised Megan. They're sitting on…"

Then Caroline heard the dreaded click-click-click coming down the hall and cringed.

"Richard! Richard Meadows, where are you?"

Richard groaned. "That would be Misty. I'd know those stilettos anywhere."

Misty Peterson waltzed down the hall toward Richard's office, and suddenly Caroline understood Lucy's message. Misty was wearing a bright red camisole, a white skirt with red polka dots, red high-heeled sandals, a mauve headband around her frizzy bleached blonde hair, and way too much ruby red lipstick. Caroline turned her face away to avoid laughing.

"Richard, thank goodness." Misty brushed past Caroline with a dirty look as she swept into his office.

"I've got a *ton* of things to talk to you about. Our wedding's less than three months away, and I'm positively crazed! Let me show you these invitations." She plopped the sample books on top of his desk, scattering his work papers everywhere.

Caroline watched the two of them, wondering yet again what the attraction was. Richard looked chagrined as he glanced over at Caroline but quickly turned back to his fiancée.

"What's going on here?" Misty demanded, looking from one to the other.

"It's just that we were working, Misty, and we didn't know you were coming." Caroline sighed as she leaned down to pick up Richard's papers off the floor. It galled her to be polite to the woman, but for Richard's sake she had to fake it.

"See here, Caroline, I'll drop by whenever I like. Richard is my fiancé."

"Yes, I know." Caroline bit her tongue.

She might have wondered how a classless woman like Misty ever snagged a great guy like Richard, but she already knew. She'd heard some of it from Richard, some from his grandmother, and some of the story from Jack, who had helped facilitate the whole thing. If Caroline were prone to violence, she'd throttle Jack. True, he thought he was just being a friend to Richard, but his involvement allowed Misty to make her sneaky move. Caroline understood why Richard had gotten sucked into the plan. But she'd never understood what was in it for Misty, who didn't even seem to really like Richard. Yet the wedding plans were in full swing.

Misty was the spoiled daughter of coffee magnate Merrill Peterson, which gave Caroline pause every time she bought a Peterson's coffee. Misty mostly spent her days shopping, going to spas, and spending money however she pleased, all with her father's credit cards of course. Then one day last summer, Caroline and Richard were having lunch at an outdoor café near their office and Misty, who was out shopping with her best friend Krystal McAlister, spotted them. The two of them stopped by the table, supposedly just to say hello. But then Misty sat down, squeezed herself between Caroline and Richard, and pointed to a chair for Krystal to sit, too. Misty monopolized the conversation, going on and on about how she hadn't seen Richard in ages, reminding him they were high school sweethearts, and what would his mother think if she knew he'd neglected her, yada yada yada. Caroline had to stop eating her salad, because Misty's whole performance made her nauseous.

Later that day, Misty called Jack at work. Lucy patched the call through, but since his office was adjacent to the lobby, Lucy could easily hear the whole conversation, at least Jack's side of it. Mostly it centered on who Richard had been having lunch with.

According to Lucy, who gleefully dished to Caroline, Misty must have told Jack that seeing Richard again brought back all the old feelings she had for him.

"Old feelings?" Caroline asked. "Seriously?"

"Well," Lucy continued with a gleam in her eye, "Misty must have been pumping Jack for info about his girlfriend, aka you, because Jack told her you were just an employee. So then I heard Jack agree to set up some kind of get-together."

The rest of it Caroline got secondhand from Adele Meadows, Richard's grandmother, who called the next day, fuming about how disgusted she was over the whole thing. Misty was able to talk Jack into going along with the whole setup, so she and Krystal met Jack and Richard at The Village Bar & Grill in Rosslyn Village. Apparently Misty got Richard drunk and then played the guilt card, the one where she reminded him of his dead mother's dream of seeing him married to the daughter of her best friend, Tildie Peterson. Adele told Caroline that Richard barely even remembered the next morning that he'd proposed. But then a few days later Misty showed up at his office, sporting a five carat diamond engagement ring she'd bought for herself. She flounced in, flashed the ring at Jack, Lucy and Caroline, smirking as she walked into Richard's office.

When Richard saw the ring he'd been incredulous. "Your *father* paid for your engagement ring? How does that make me look?"

"Never mind, Richard," Misty had said. "You can pay me back in other ways."

Caroline had almost gagged and had to leave the room.

And now, here was Misty again, interrupting their business day, forcing Richard to weigh in on wedding invitations of all things. Caroline leaned against the door jam and did a slow burn.

"Misty, can't you see I'm busy?" Richard gently patted her arm until she moved it off his desk. "We can do this later."

"No, we can't, Richard, not and get the invitations out on time. These wedding preparations have taken too long as it is."

Richard stood up and walked to the window, staring out. "We've only been engaged for a year."

"Well, if you hadn't been dragging your feet, and Sharlene insisting on this big society wedding, we could've been married months ago."

Richard turned to face Misty. "Dragging my feet?"

Caroline cleared her throat, causing both Richard and Misty to remember she was still in the room. "Don't you two have a wedding planner? Why not let her do this?"

Misty scowled at Caroline, but turned back to Richard and said, "Do you think you can make a decision about the invitations before dinner tonight with my parents?"

Richard visibly cringed. "I'll see what I can do."

Misty threw her red bag over her shoulder and pushed past Caroline. "Sharlene, Daniel, and Adele will be there tonight, too, Richard, so try not to be late." And with that she walked out the door.

"Caroline, I..." Richard said, at the same time Caroline said, "Richard, what about..."

They both laughed. "You go first," Richard said.

Caroline stepped back into his office and studied Richard's face. "I was just wondering about Adele. I know she didn't really approve of your..."

"My engagement?" Richard nodded and stared up at the ceiling, using his fingers to make air quotes. "'Don't give up on love, Richard,' is what she said." Richard sighed and dropped his arms to his sides. "According to Grandmother, the love that was Adele and Rich Meadows could've inspired romance novels, and I should be looking for the same thing, not settling for Misty."

Caroline couldn't agree more, but it wasn't her place to say so. At least Mrs. Meadows was aware of what a big mistake Richard was making, and he'd be more likely to listen to his grandmother than to her. She nodded and closed Richard's office door behind her. "He's *engaged!*" she whispered to herself for the millionth time.

****

"Mom, what am I supposed to do?" Allie demanded as she stormed into the kitchen. "I take private lessons during the summer, on *my* piano. That's what I do, that's what I've always done."

Susan was unloading the dishwasher and trying yet again to get everything to fit into the smaller kitchen cabinets, when Allie came in and started, or re-started, the same conversation they'd been having for a couple of weeks now. "Have you tried asking Sharlene about—"

Allie put up her hand. "Don't go there. Total waste of time. Sharlene just makes one excuse after another."

Susan put her hands on her hips and stared at the open cabinet. The dishes and glassware just didn't fit right. Maybe she'd brought too much from the Belford house, since the kitchen there was nearly twice the size of this one. She groaned and started rearranging things, again. "Remember I told you Emily was going to talk to her former client, Professor Phillips?"

Allie reached around her mother and took one of the drinking glasses out of the cabinet where her mother had just so carefully placed it. She went to the fridge and pulled out a bottle of diet soda, checked the freezer for ice, scowled, and closed it. "Well, did she call him yet? It's June and I'm wasting valuable time."

Susan turned her back on Allie and exhaled slowly, hoping her daughter didn't see her frustration. "I don't know, Allie. I'll give Emily a call this evening."

Allie took both the half-full bottle of soda and the glass and, without another word but with a loud groan, went back to her room and closed the door.

The doorbell rang, and glad for the distraction, Susan left the cabinet doors wide open to go answer it. There stood an attractive man of about thirty, dressed in khaki pants and a green polo shirt with the Bradley University logo on it. He was tall, blond, clean-cut, and had a charming smile.

"Hi, I'm Brandon Phillips. We have a mutual friend, Emily Martin? She told me…"

"Yes, Brandon, of course, come in. Emily's told me so much about you." Susan held open the screen door for him. "I wasn't sure if Emily had gotten a chance to call you yet."

"Hope it's okay that I dropped by unannounced," Brandon said with a smile. "Emily explained your situation, and she insisted I meet your daughter right away. I understand she's quite gifted."

Susan beamed. "Yes, in my slightly biased opinion, she is. Let me get her for you."

Susan went down the short hallway to the bedroom Allie shared with Caroline and knocked twice. Allie didn't answer, so Susan opened the door. There sat Allie on her unmade bed, listening to her iPod at such a volume that Susan could hear the Mozart blasting through the earbuds, and thumbing through a fashion magazine. She'd carelessly set the moist liter bottle and glass on the nightstand, causing a wet ring. Susan decided the stain would have to wait. "Allie? You won't believe. That music professor I just told you about is here. Can you come out and meet him?"

Allie shrugged her shoulders, removed the earbuds, and followed Susan into the family room.

Brandon stared at her way too long, but he finally managed to mumble, "Nice to meet you."

She was dressed in sweats, her hair up on top of her head in a knot, wearing no makeup, yet Brandon stood there speechless. Susan had seen lots of guys fall instantly for her daughter. After all, Allie was striking—tall, slender, long black hair, and carried herself like a model. So it didn't surprise her that Brandon seemed awestruck. However, Susan had to wonder if that was a good beginning for a working relationship.

"Uh, Professor Phillips. Hello?" Allie snapped her fingers in front of his face.

Brandon recovered himself and stopped staring. "Oh, sorry. Your mother's friend Emily tells me you have some free time this summer and need a place to practice."

"Aren't you kind of young to be a music professor?"

"Allie!" Susan said.

Brandon grinned. "That's okay, Mrs. Benedict. Or can I call you Susan?" She nodded. "I know I'm young, but that just means I've got more energy than those old guys!" He turned his smile to Allie. "And I do own a piano. During the summers, my private students aren't around much, and I'm only teaching one summer session at Bradley. Lots of free time for you to make use of my instrument."

"We can't pay you much," Susan admitted, "but it would be wonderful if Allie could use your piano occasionally."

Brandon waved that notion aside. "Oh, no, you don't have to pay me anything." He sneaked another glance at Allie. "I'm happy to let Allie have the use of my piano for practice as often as she likes."

Allie shrugged. "Okay," she said, and started back toward her room.

"Allie!" She turned around when Brandon called after her. "Uh, I'm always getting free tickets to concerts around town, if you ever want to go. Tomorrow night's Symphony on the Lawn performance is Mozart. Emily says you're particularly fond of his music."

"Whatever." She turned to walk off.

"Allison!" Susan was incredulous at her daughter's rude behavior.

Allie turned back around. "What, Mom? It's not like he's asking me out on a date." Allie rolled her eyes and went back to her room.

Susan blinked, mortified. Finally she said, "I apologize for my daughter's behavior. She can be a little headstrong, and this whole move has been hard on her. It was so kind of you to come over and make her such a generous offer. About the piano, I mean."

Brandon shrugged and reached for the door. "I know all about temperamental artists. Just tell her to give me a call when she wants to come over."

"Let me get your contact information." Susan grabbed her phone off the coffee table, handed it to Brandon, and waited while he keyed in his number. "Thanks for coming by, Brandon." Susan held the door for him. "I'll have Allie call you tomorrow and set up a practice schedule." *After I have a talk with her about her manners.*

Chapter Seven

"Can you take a look at this, Richard? I can't figure out what Mr. Hamilton is trying to say here." Caroline laid this week's Hamilton Hardware ad on his desk, the one she'd just printed off from her email.

Richard looked at the jumbled up mess. He stood up, scrutinized it, paced back and forth in front of his desk, crossed his arms, and then picked it up for a closer look.

Sumer sail starts Sat. get your boat supplys at huge discontd! (Richard—put picture here! Thanx from Howard Hamilton)

Richard laughed. "Well, he's either got sailboats at a discount, or he's selling discontinued boating supplies."

Caroline also laughed. "And the picture we use will depend on what this week's special really is. Mr. Hamilton is such a good customer, but his spelling...Well, maybe one day you can convince him to let *us* write the ads."

Richard nodded. "Until then, I guess you'll have to call him and ask which it is."

"I'll get right on it." Caroline picked up Mr. Hamilton's ad and was just leaving Richard's office when Misty appeared in the doorway, blocking her way. She stifled a groan, but nodded politely.

"If you don't mind, Caroline, I need to speak to Richard—privately!" Misty marched into the office and glowered while Caroline slid past her and quietly closed the door on her way out. She could hear Misty shouting and Richard's bewildered tone, but she couldn't quite make out what they were saying.

Caroline returned to her desk and immediately heard her phone ping with a text message. It was Lucy.

—*What's all the drama?*—

Caroline responded,—*Something about the wedding I guess.*—

After several minutes of Misty's loud, angry-sounding words from inside the office, Misty emerged and flounced off down the hall without so much as a backward glance. Caroline watched her go in dismay.

"Sorry, Caroline," Richard said, stepping out into the hall. "That was rude of her."

Caroline waved away his concern. Rude was Misty's trademark. "Is there a problem?"

Richard cleared his throat. "Well, apparently Misty had a disagreement with Sharlene about some wedding detail. I need to talk to my sister, I guess. Can you get her on the phone?" He went back into his office, this time leaving the door open.

"Of course." Caroline picked up her desk phone and dialed Sharlene's cell phone, a number she'd unfortunately committed to memory. "Sharlene?" she said when Sharlene picked up. "This is Caroline at the office, and Richard needs to speak to you. Okay, please hold," she said before calling out, "Richard, I have Sharlene on line one."

Richard put his sister on speakerphone while he

logged onto his computer. "Sharlene, Misty was just here and angry about something to do with…"

"Richard, darling, it's just that neither she nor that wedding planner has any taste whatsoever. That's why *I* chose the flower arrangements for the ceremony, and I expect you to back me up."

Richard sighed. "Just do whatever you want, but please don't stir Misty up anymore. I have actual work to do here." He paused, then added, "Unless you'd like to come back to the office and handle some of the clients you left dangling?"

Sharlene snorted. "Richard, don't be absurd. You know I don't have time for that now."

"I didn't think so."

Caroline was busy at her computer by the time Richard hung up the phone, finished checking his emails, and came out of his office. She'd called Mr. Hamilton and solved the ad problem, and was planning to go to the printer after lunch.

"You forgot these yesterday," Richard said as he handed her several heavy books, "and with all the commotion from Misty, I forgot to remind you."

Caroline juggled and almost dropped them. "Oh, are these the books you promised Megan?"

Richard reached over to help her with the load, and their hands touched for a moment. He blushed as he unloaded the books onto her desk. "Yeah, and yesterday when Misty…"

"Megan will enjoy the books," Caroline told him, trying to put a cheerful spin on this uncomfortable conversation. "And I understand about Misty. Planning a wedding must be stressful." Caroline almost gagged on that sentence but stopped and forced herself to return to a professional demeanor. "If you don't mind, Richard, I'll just go ahead and put these books in my car, go to lunch, and then to the printer."

"Well, sure," he said, flustered.

Not looking at him, Caroline shoved the books into her oversized handbag and hurried to the front door.

"Problems?" Lucy asked, stopping Caroline in her tracks.

Caroline shifted the bag to her other arm, both shoulders drooping. "I'm taking an early lunch, hoping to distance myself from Richard and his wedding plans." She folded her arms and studied a spot on the floor. "What in the world does he see in Misty anyway?"

Lucy pulled her headphones off and tapped them thoughtfully on the reception desk. "Must be her sweet disposition." They both laughed. "Listen, girlfriend, Jonathan won season passes at work to this season's Symphony on the Lawn up in Belford, and I was thinking…"

"Won them?" Caroline said. "Cool."

"Yeah, some sales competition. But the last thing I want to do tonight is sit on the ground in the summer heat." She patted her expanding belly. "I was thinking you could use the distraction. Why don't you and your sisters go instead?"

Caroline's mouth dropped open. "Are you sure? That's so generous."

Lucy nodded as she put the headphones back on. "I'll have Jonathan drop them by here this afternoon. We can always go next week if the weather cools down." She pushed a button on the phone. "Meadows Advertising. How may I help you?"

****

"Did you get my text?" Caroline asked Allie. "You never answered. Are we going to the symphony tonight or not?"

"I got it," Allie said. "And we're going. Megan, too."

Caroline nodded and then dropped the stack of books on her bed in their shared bedroom.

"What's all that?" Allie asked.

"Art books, books on architecture, classic art, modern art, you name it. Richard sent them for Megan. He started to give them to me yesterday, but we got interrupted by Misty and her crisis *du jour*. And then she came back for an encore today."

"So Misty's still getting you all riled up, huh?"

Caroline sat down on her bed, dejected. "No. Well yes, but it's because she's so inconsiderate of Richard's time."

Allie lifted an eyebrow. "Isn't it maybe time for you to move on? Seriously, Caroline, you work for Richard, but you have some pretty unprofessional feelings for him."

Caroline picked up one of the art books and flipped through the pages. "No I don't."

"Oh, please, Caroline. You've been carrying a torch for the man ever since you first laid eyes on him."

Caroline sighed, shut the book, and let her shoulders slump. "Maybe once, but that was before he got engaged."

Allie slapped her forehead. "He got engaged after a drunken night in a bar when Misty brought up his dead mother and promises made before the two of them were even out of diapers! It's not an engagement, it's a guilt trip."

Caroline nodded. "Maybe, but he could've broken it off and he didn't. So guilt trip or not, he's getting married."

"Then forget Richard," Allie said, sitting down on the bed next to her. "It's time for you to find your own man."

Caroline shrugged, got up, and started pawing through her side of the closet. "Sounds good in theory, but no one ever asks me out anyway."

Allie got up and followed her. "You're young, attractive, educated; any man would be lucky to have you. What about that guy in the office down the hall from Meadows?" She reached into the closet and pulled a dress out of her side and held it up, checking the look in the mirror.

Caroline's eyes widened. "If you're referring to Malcolm Atwater, he's gay."

Allie reached over and playfully poked her sister's arm. "Not him, Car. The blond guy you said was staring at you when—is he a lawyer, or maybe he's one of the realtors? I forget, but it doesn't matter. You need to get out and find a man who's unattached."

"Says the single girl." Caroline pulled a pair of emerald green capris out of the closet and got a white cotton t-shirt from inside the dresser. "And Richard's so..."

"Engaged?"

Caroline ignored her sister's remark as she started changing out of her work clothes. "So serious, so career-minded, so..."

Allie also started changing clothes, out of her sweats and into the sundress. "So...nothing. Wake up,

Caroline! Richard has a lot of good qualities, I'll admit, and he's not bad-looking either, but the bottom line is—he's getting married, aka off the market!"

Caroline stepped to the mirror, pulled her ponytail holder out, shook her hair, and tied it back again. "But Misty's all wrong for him. How will he ever be happy with her? Maybe if I just wait…"

Allie wiggled into her dress and zipped it up the back. "No more waiting! I'm sorry, Caroline, but if he's determined to marry that woman, you need to accept it and get on with your own life."

"Oh sure, no problem." Caroline sank onto her bed. "Except I have no life."

"Then get one!" Allie put her hands on her hips and frowned at her reflection. She kicked off the flats she'd chosen and stepped into a pair of low-heeled sandals instead. "Hello? Are you listening to yourself, Caroline? Mooning over an almost married man! Here's what you do. First, go get a new job—away from Richard—and then take control of your social life!"

Caroline sighed. Here she was, twenty-four years old, working at a job she loved for a salary she couldn't live on, pining for a man she could never have, and sharing a tiny bedroom with her college-age sister. Allie had made some good points, if only she could find the strength to follow through. "I wasn't planning to live here with Mom forever. But I'm just so conflicted about the job and I can't…" Caroline paused and looked over at her sister when Allie didn't interrupt her. Allie was now wearing a very pretty flowered sundress with various shades of pink, purple and green set against a white background, her dark hair pushed back with a white headband, and pink sandals with tiny spiked heels. "You're kinda dressed up for a night of sitting in the grass, aren't you?"

Allie shrugged and grinned. "You never know who you might meet at one of those concerts. You've got the tickets, right? Megan and I have already packed the picnic supper."

Caroline nodded. She looked down at her casual pants and nondescript t-shirt. "Should I change?"

Allie looked her over and nodded. "Tonight's as good as any to start your new social life."

Caroline took off her t-shirt and changed into a crisp multi-colored blouse. "Mom tells me you met Professor Phillips."

Allie scrunched up her face. "Yeah, and he acted really weird. He just kept staring at me, all speechless or something."

Caroline winked at her. "So he noticed you're attractive?"

Allie shrugged. "It just seemed odd."

Caroline stood up and smoothed a wrinkle from the back of her blouse. "Well, don't worry about it. Emily vouched for him."

"But he's, like, old!"

"Old? I thought Mom said he was about thirty," Caroline said.

"Well, I'm only twenty-one, so being ogled by a thirty-year-old man creeps me out."

"I'm sure he wasn't 'ogling' you. You're attractive and men notice. If Emily said he's a good person, then he is. Besides, you desperately need a place to practice this summer, right?"

Allie looked dubious.

"Has Sharlene relented about the piano?" Caroline asked.

Allie shook her head.

"Then accept Brandon's offer. It's not forever, but it'll keep you busy till you decide about school in August."

Allie gave that some thought. "So either I don't practice at all this summer, or I let an old guy stare at me while I do." She cringed when Caroline frowned at her. "Okay, I'll call him tomorrow to set up a schedule."

Caroline and Allie stepped to the mirror, surveyed their look, high-fived each other and called for Megan. Caroline decided Allie was right. She needed to jump start her social life, and tonight might just be the night.

****

"It's too crowded here," Megan fussed. "We're never going to find a place to sit. Why did you two drag me to this thing anyway? I *hate* Mozart."

"Quit whining, Megan. It's not like you had anything else to do tonight," Allie shot back.

"Ladies, please," Caroline said, "no squabbling. We're here to have fun. We've got a blanket, picnic supper, and free tickets, so let's just enjoy ourselves." She looked from one to the other of her sisters, waiting.

Allie blew out a puff of air and took in the gathering crowd, but nodded in agreement with Caroline. "Megan, didn't you bring some of those art books Richard sent?" She looked over at the satchel slung over Megan's shoulder. "You can look through those during the concert."

"Yeah, and I've got way too much stuff in my hands. It's getting heavy," Megan whined.

Caroline shifted the picnic basket to her other hand and began to scout out a place for the three of them to sit. It really was crowded, but that was to be expected for the first night of the summer season. The Indianapolis Symphony Orchestra played every weekend in Belford from mid-June until Labor Day. The "lawn" was actually a large grassy hill with an amphitheater on top, and people were camped everywhere she looked. Some came prepared for a simple picnic, while others had elaborately laid out tablecloths, candles, wine, and gourmet dinners. Children played, people milled around, and adults talked, read, or just quietly ate their meals.

Caroline pointed to an open spot at the top of the hill, left of the stage. "I think that's the only spot we're going to find."

Megan stomped her foot. "No way! I'm not climbing up that hill lugging all this stuff in this heat!"

"Here, let me take some of those books," Caroline offered. Megan handed over her satchel, nearly weighing Caroline down. "Great. So can you at least take the picnic basket?"

Megan took the basket from Caroline. "Seriously, can't we find somewhere that doesn't involve hiking?"

"Caroline's right, Megs, there's no place else," Allie said. "Besides, that's where the view is the best." She started walking toward the hill. "Come on, the concert's going to start soon, and I don't want to miss a moment of Mozart."

Caroline hurried ahead of her sisters. The empty spot they'd seen was already filling with symphony-goers, so she needed to hurry if she wanted to stake out a spot. Caroline started walking uphill as fast as she could, considering all she was carrying. She got up there, scouted around for a spot, and tossed her sister's satchel down to hold it. Once it was secured, she turned around to see where Allie and Megan were. Still at the bottom of the incline, bickering. Caroline sighed, but waved at them to signal she'd found a place to set up. Allie waved back and started up the hill, Megan grudgingly following behind.

And then it happened: with Allie looking ahead of her instead of where she was stepping, her stylish pink sandals caught in some undergrowth. She stumbled over a hole in the grass and fell, twisting her ankle.

"Ahhh!" she yelled, as the blanket and her handbag fell down beside her.

Caroline gasped. She was too far away to get to Allie's side, and there were too many people between her and her sister, so all she could do was call out, "Allie! Are you okay?"

Caroline watched helplessly as Megan rushed over to her sister as quickly as her picnic-basket-laden arms would allow, but already a crowd was gathering, blocking Caroline's view. "Excuse me, pardon me," she said, making her way back down the hill and pushing through the people staring at her injured sister.

"Miss, are you all right?" asked an elderly gentleman.

"No, my ankle," Allie moaned.

"Allie!" Caroline reached her and kneeled down to have a look at Allie's swelling ankle.

"Can you stand?" asked another voice from the crowd.

Allie winced and put her hand on her forehead to shield her eyes from the early evening sun as she looked for the source of the voice. Caroline followed her gaze and saw a very handsome man stepping toward Allie, looking concerned. He appeared to be in his early twenties, tall with light brown hair, muscular, and dressed in designer jeans and a Ralph Lauren shirt. Allie opened her mouth to speak, but between rubbing her aching ankle and gaping at the attractive guy, she couldn't seem to get any words out.

The young man reached for Allie's arm. "Here, let me help you up."

"I don't think I can," Allie sputtered.

"I'm her sister," Caroline told him as she pulled out her phone. "I can call…"

"Caroline, what do I do?" Megan cried.

"What's your name?" the young man calmly asked Megan.

"Megan Benedict," she said, tears coming to her eyes. "That's my sister Allie, and my other sister Caroline. What should I do?"

"It's okay, Megan," Caroline said, "take the picnic basket and go wait at the spot I just found," she said, pointing up the hill. "I'm calling 9-1-1."

"That won't be necessary," the young man said. "I can take her to the first-aid tent."

"Are you sure?" Caroline asked, putting her phone away.

Megan sniffled but did as she was told, and the young man helped Allie up onto her good foot. When he ascertained she really couldn't walk on the injured ankle, he easily picked her up. "By the way, I'm Mark Townsend," he told Allie with a winning smile. Caroline could see that Allie was already smitten.

"Nice to meet you," Allie said as Mark carried her

down the hill to the first aid tent, Caroline trailing behind. He carefully eased her onto a chair inside the tent and told the attending nurse what had happened.

"I'm so embarrassed," Allie said.

"No need," Mark assured her. "Accidents happen. And maybe this one happened for a reason." He winked at her.

Caroline lifted an eyebrow as she watched Allie grimace in pain while the nurse examined the ankle, and then blush as Mark Townsend hovered over her.

"I think you have a rather nasty sprain here," the nurse told her. "I can give you an ice pack, but it really should be seen by a doctor. Is there someone who can drive you to the emergency room?"

"I can do that, if we can just get a golf cart," Caroline told the nurse.

"I'll just take the ice pack for now," Allie said. Caroline frowned and started to object, but Allie held up her hand in protest. "Caroline," she said without taking her eyes off Mark, "I promise to call Dr. Li in the morning, but we got these concert tickets for free, and I'm not about to miss it."

Caroline didn't think for a minute that Allie was nearly as interested in Mozart as she was in her heroic rescuer.

"Suit yourself," the nurse said. "Do you want to borrow some crutches for the rest of the evening?"

"Yes, please."

"Let me help you stand up." Allie nodded her assent as Mark placed his arm around her waist and got her onto her good foot.

The nurse brought over the crutches. "Keep that foot elevated and the ice pack on it. Okay?"

"Okay, thanks." She took a few steps leaning heavily on the crutches.

"Do you need some help with those, Allie?" Caroline asked.

Allie shook her head.

Mark stepped aside and let Allie hobble out. "A gentleman would never leave a lady in distress, so let me make sure you get back up the hill safely."

"Oh, no, that's not necessary," Caroline protested.

Allie shot her sister a dirty look.

"No trouble. Besides, my friends and I were sitting fairly close to where your sister fell. I'm going that way anyway."

Caroline rolled her eyes as Mark helped Allie slowly make her way back up the incline on crutches to rejoin his four friends. "I'll just go get our stuff," Caroline told them, but knew neither Allie nor Mark was paying any attention to her. Caroline hurried up to get Megan. The two of them gathered their belongings, and returned to join Mark and his friends. The group happily welcomed Megan and Allie, leaving Caroline feeling like a fifth wheel.

Mark made introductions. "These are some old friends from college: William, Pete, Sam and his wife Georgia. This is Allie Benedict. Where do you go to school, Allie?"

"Bryce An..." Allie broke off. "Well, at the moment, I'm sort of between schools."

"Between schools? Is that code for lost your scholarship?" Mark teased.

Allie smiled. "Something like that."

Georgia offered Allie a glass of wine. "Bryce. Would that be Bryce Anthony Music Conservatory?"

Allie nodded, taking a sip of the white chardonnay. "It would be."

"Wow!" Georgia gushed. "You must be talented or you wouldn't have gotten in there. And rich, because that school's expensive from what I hear."

"Allie's the best piano player you ever heard!" Megan exclaimed.

Allie blushed. "I do have other interests besides music."

"Like what?" Mark asked.

He was extremely good-looking, and as Caroline sat on the sidelines watching all this, she knew Allie was succumbing to his charms. But they didn't know anything about this guy and that bothered her. Allie and Mark talked all through the first half of the concert, the intermission, and the second half. They discussed literature, theatre, pop music, classical music, and art. In fact, everything that Allie was passionate about, Mark claimed to also enjoy, although Caroline was dubious about his sincerity.

"Mark, are you in school?" Caroline asked.

"I just graduated from Ball State University this spring, but I'm planning to go back for my MBA in the fall," he replied, never taking his eyes off Allie.

"Hmm. Ball State. Small world," Allie said, an attractive pink glow spreading across her cheeks. "That's where my mother wants me to transfer next year. We had to move recently. My dad's new wife wanted the Belford house, so now we live in Rosslyn Village."

"In a tiny house," Megan interjected, pouting.

Mark nodded. "I know what you mean about downsizing. My family lost a lot of money in the recession of '08, and well, let's just say old money doesn't go as far as it used to. But your dad, isn't he…"

Suddenly Allie slapped her forehead. "Didn't you go to Willowby Hall Prep, and graduate two years ahead of me?"

Mark look startled. "I guess I did." They both laughed, and then Mark added, "Imagine that: we attended the same high school at about the same time, but never knew each other."

Allie sighed and looked down at her swollen ankle, reaching over to massage it. "I'm wondering how I'll make the adjustment from a small music conservatory to a big university. It's pretty overwhelming."

"Don't worry. It's a great school, and I know you'll like it once you've been up there for a visit. What if I show you around campus? After your ankle heals."

Allie nodded enthusiastically. "I'd like that."

Caroline groaned inwardly. *I'll bet you would.*

The sun sets late in June, so it had barely gotten dark as the concert ended, the stars just bright enough to afford some light as people quickly cleared out. Caroline didn't think Allie had listened to a note of the Mozart pieces she'd been so eager to hear.

Mark got Allie to her feet, helped Megan and Caroline gather their belongings, and told his friends he'd join them in the parking lot.

Caroline was concerned as she watched Allie hobble on her crutches, visibly favoring her right ankle. "I think we're going to need a golf cart to get Allie to the car," she said, scouting around for one. But all she saw was hundreds of people dragging picnic remnants and their personal items to the crowded parking lot. "I guess I'll have to go ask the nurse to call for one."

"I'll wait here with Allie," Mark told Caroline, "till you and Megan get back." Immediately his attention was on Allie again. "And speaking of calling, give me your cell phone." Allie handed it to Mark, and he programmed his number into it.

"There." He placed it in her hand with an affectionate squeeze. "Promise you'll call me after you see the doctor tomorrow."

Allie giggled. "Okay."

Caroline hadn't planned to leave Allie alone with this guy, but she didn't want to be rude. "Come on, Megan," she said, and started walking to the first aid tent.

Chapter Eight

Susan walked into the family room with a basketful of laundry. "Anyone want to help? No?" She shrugged and sat down on the floor to fold clean clothes.

Allie was sitting on the love seat in the family room watching TV, her bandaged ankle propped on a pillow, the crutches nearby, while Megan, sprawled on the other sofa, poked at her phone.

"I'd help, Mom, but this ankle…"

"How's it feeling today?"

Allie held up her hand to stop Susan from talking as she listened intently to the conversation on the television. Finally it went to commercial. "Mom, did you know there's nothing on TV during the day except talk shows and soap operas?" she asked. "I had no idea. And boy, are they addictive!"

"Really?" Susan grinned. "As a matter of fact I did know, but I guess you've never had much time to just sit around watching daytime TV before. Is that *All My Tomorrows*?"

Allie nodded.

"What's Elsa up to today?" Susan glanced up from the towels she was folding.

"From what I can tell, her fiancé is supposedly working with some attractive woman and they kissed."

The two of them watched the next scene for a minute. "So how is the ankle?" Susan asked.

"I think it's getting better, but Dr. Li said to stay off it for at least a week. I'll be pretty addicted to the soaps by then."

Megan picked up the remote off the coffee table and aimed it at the television. "Then why don't we watch something else?"

"Don't you dare!" Allie and Susan both exclaimed.

"Geez." Megan shrugged and put the remote down.

Susan started folding a pile of t-shirts. "By the way, Allie, did you ever return Brandon Phillips's phone call about setting up a practice schedule? It's rude to keep ignoring his calls. He's doing you a favor after all."

Allie winced. "I know, but I've sort of had my mind on other things."

"M-aaa-rrr-kkk!" Megan sang out.

Allie blushed just as her phone rang. She fumbled for it in the pillow cushions, retrieving it just before it went to voice mail. "Hello?" she said. "Oh hi, Brandon. I'm sorry I haven't called you back." She rolled her eyes. "I sprained my ankle at the concert the other evening, and I'm following doctor's orders, staying off it and keeping it propped." She made the motion with her hand indicating Brandon was talking too much. "What? Oh, sure, I do still want to use your piano, but with this ankle... Can I call you when I'm feeling better? I promise it won't be more than three or four days." Allie drummed her fingers on the sofa as Brandon talked. "Thanks, Brandon, you're great. See you then."

"Aren't you being a little hard on the guy?" Susan asked.

Allie rearranged the pillow under her foot and

shifted her weight with a grimace. "Yeah, maybe, but he's so…insistent. And anyway, I wasn't kidding about my ankle. I couldn't possibly operate the foot pedals till it heals."

Allie settled herself back into the cushions just as there was a knock at the door. She looked over to see Mark smiling at her through the screen meshing. He'd been by the house every day since they met at Symphony on the Lawn, solicitously checking on her progress and ingratiating himself with the family. Well, at least Susan and Megan liked him. Susan wasn't so sure about Caroline.

"How's the patient today?" Mark asked, letting himself in.

"A little better," Allie said.

"I was wondering if you felt up to a late lunch. I promise to get us a booth where you can prop your foot." Mark nodded politely to Susan, winked at Megan, and then turned his attention back to Allie. "Have you been to that little bistro down on College Avenue? It's got great food."

"No, but I'd like to try it," Allie said. Mark helped her up onto her crutches and held the screen door for her as she shuffled across the floor.

"Enjoy your lunch," Susan said.

Allie smiled at Mark and hobbled out the open door.

"Must be true love," Megan giggled.

"We'll see." Susan sighed and went back to folding the laundry.

A few hours, more laundry, and three episodes of *House Hunters* later, Susan heard a crash in the family room and raced from her bedroom. "Megan? What happened?" She followed Megan's gaze across the room.

Megan had flung her cell phone, hitting a lamp and knocking it over. "Mom! I'm bored!" Megan sat on the floor in front of the TV and began channel surfing, her arms folded across her chest.

Susan understood Megan's frustration with their new environment but didn't condone her petulant behavior. She calmly checked the lamp for broken pieces and finding it still intact, set it upright on the table. She handed Megan's also-unscathed cell phone back to her. "Do you want to talk about it?"

Megan rolled onto her stomach to face her mother. "What am I supposed to do all summer? I don't live in Belford anymore where all my friends are, and there's no one in this neighborhood but old people."

Susan winced. "You're right, Megs, and I feel awful about it. So what would you like to do?"

"Something! I usually go swimming or to the mall or movies or, or… something. But sitting around this tiny house watching TV all day is so boring!"

Susan sighed. "Megan, I get that you're at loose ends, but please suggest something I can actually do about it." Susan thought for a moment. "Why don't you call one of your friends in Belford, and I'll drive you up there."

Megan resumed her position on her back. "I tried that. They're all 'too busy.' Which means they don't want to associate with someone going to a public school."

Susan didn't doubt that some of Megan's friends were snubbing her, but she felt sure there was still someone she could count on. "What about Annabeth

Walton?"

"Gone to Lake Michigan for the summer. Remember?"

"Oh. Well, anyone else?"

"Mom! You just don't get it!" Megan stormed off to her bedroom.

"And it's only June," Susan muttered to herself. The guilt washed over her again. So Susan did the only thing she knew to do to relieve stress. She went back to her bedroom, changed into her running clothes, and went out the front door, closing it quietly behind her.

****

Caroline came home from work and collapsed onto the family room sofa. It was hot outside, and her car had barely cooled down on the five-mile drive home from Meadows Advertising. She thought about going to the kitchen for some iced tea, but the ceiling fan blowing on her felt refreshing, and she didn't want to move. She closed her eyes, enjoying the hum of the fan and the cool breeze, and just before she drifted off, the front door opened. Susan came in dressed in shorts, t-shirt and athletic shoes, glistening with sweat.

"Where have you been in all this heat?" Caroline asked.

"Out for a run on the Monon Trail, sweating out my frustrations. Since I can't afford a gym right now, it's convenient that we live close to a free hiking trail." Susan went to the kitchen and got a bottled water from the fridge. "Can I get you anything?"

"I was thinking about grabbing some iced tea, but I couldn't get myself to move." Caroline sat up and stretched her neck. "What are you so frustrated about?"

Susan returned with the tea and water and sat down

next to her daughter. "Megan. I don't know what to do."

Caroline took a long swallow of the cool, sweet tea. "Do about what?"

Susan held the cold bottle of water to her forehead. "Megan's Willowby friends are snubbing her, I guess, or else they just can't make time for someone living thirty minutes away, but she's got nothing to do except watch TV and complain. So I need ideas on what to do with her all summer. With little or no money, of course."

Caroline thought about that. She remembered that in summers past her mother had had a hard enough time keeping Megan occupied when things were fairly normal. Now... "That's a tough one. I don't suppose Dad..." Caroline looked over at Susan who shook her head. "Well, I could take her to the mall or a movie or something on the weekends."

"That would help, but Megan doesn't have any direction at the moment. She's too young for a job, and there aren't any kids her age in this neighborhood. I don't even know where to suggest she go to meet them. I feel bad for her."

Caroline went to the kitchen to refill her glass of iced tea, and then she remembered something. "What happened to the idea of getting her a dog? She's always wanted one. Remember that picture she drew years ago? It was pretty good."

"Well, art class was always Megan's favorite," Susan said. "When she was in elementary school she had an assignment to draw the family pet, but of course we didn't have one, so Megan drew a yellow puppy and named it Honey."

Caroline said, "You put the *A* paper on the refrigerator next to Megan's other artwork."

Susan frowned. "Your dad wasn't too impressed." She lowered her voice to mimic Daniel's. " 'We're not getting a dog.' "

Caroline stifled a giggle as Susan smiled at the memory of the artwork. "Well, I *have* thought about getting a dog, now that we have our own place. Do you think she can handle the responsibility?"

Caroline went to the kitchen, plopped fresh ice cubes into her glass, and jiggled them around to cool down the tea. "I think if you let Megan choose the dog, she'll be more inclined to want to take care of it. But Mom, adopt one from a homeless pet shelter. It's less expensive, and it saves a life."

Susan nodded. "Good advice as always, Caroline. I'll speak to Megan first thing tomorrow about adopting a puppy."

****

Susan was waiting for Allie when she returned from Brandon Phillips's house. She wanted to hear all the details of her daughter's first time practicing on his piano. Allie had left hours ago with a bag full of sheet music, but she returned without it. "How'd it go at Brandon's?"

Allie shrugged, tossed her purse on the coffee table, and sat down to massage her still-sore ankle. "Okay. He's got a grand piano in a room acoustically designed for it, and he let me leave all my music there, so I don't have to cart it back and forth."

"That was nice of him," Susan said.

"I started to say no. I told him I didn't want to leave clutter all over his house. Mom, seriously, it looked like some fusty old lady lived there instead of a young bachelor."

Susan lifted an eyebrow. "Would you prefer it was a mess? Maybe he has a housekeeper."

Allie sprawled herself on the sofa, propping a pillow under her foot. "He says her name is 'Mom.' I guess whenever his mother visits she always straightens up."

"So he's probably not the neat freak it appears," Susan said. She hoped Allie wasn't looking for ways to avoid Brandon. His offer was her only option if she wanted to keep up with her piano practices. "So do you go back tomorrow?"

Allie shrugged. "I don't know. I've got a date with Mark tonight, and then tomorrow he's driving me up to Ball State University to show me around the school."

Susan crossed her arms and tapped her foot. "You're still not sold on the idea of going there, are you?" Allie didn't answer. "I'll bet if Mark weren't planning to go to grad school there, you wouldn't even have considered it."

"Probably not. But he is and I am." Allie closed her eyes as if she was about to doze off, so Susan left her alone. As much as Susan wanted Allie to apply for a transfer to a state school her father would pay for, and one she'd have a shot at being admitted to this late, Susan didn't think Allie's heart was in it. But if she didn't go back to school in August, Susan didn't know what the future held for her daughter. Music was her life, and Daniel—or rather Sharlene—had ripped it away from her.

The next morning, Susan poked her head into Allie's bedroom. Allie was studying her reflection in the mirror, checking all sides to make sure her khaki walking shorts and white eyelet blouse looked right. She had her hair pulled back into a sleek ponytail at the nape of her neck, and was wearing pearl ear studs.

Allie waved her mother in as she applied more mascara and lip gloss. "What do you think? Sandals or sneakers?"

"Depends on how your ankle feels," Susan said.

Allie tried on a pair of low-heeled slip-on sandals and then immediately stepped out of them. "Ouch. Sneakers it is. It's a big campus, and I'm pretty sure I can't do a lot of walking today in slip-ons, cute as they are."

The doorbell rang, and Allie followed Susan into the living room. Susan opened the door wide and smiled as Mark stepped in. "I'm so glad you're giving this a chance, Allie," Susan told her.

Mark beamed at Allie as he squeezed her hand and held the door for her. "I think she'll like what she sees," he told Susan. "I'll have her home by supper time."

"No rush. You two have fun."

Allie colored as she gazed up into Mark's handsome face, her reddened cheeks highlighting her dark hair and eyes, and allowed him to lead her out the door.

****

"How'd it go at Ball State?" Susan asked Allie that evening.

Just as Mark had promised, he brought her back home around six p.m., walked her to the door, kissed her goodbye, and waved as he got back into his sports car and drove off.

Allie looked both love-sick and confused, if that

108

was possible. Susan patted the spot on the sofa next to her, but Allie didn't sit down. Instead, she went to the window and craned her neck, watching till Mark was out of sight. "It's an hour's drive up there, the town is tiny…"

"But that should work for you," Susan interrupted. "You never did like Chicago."

"…and the campus is huge. I don't know how I'd fit in." She shook her head and collapsed onto the loveseat across the room from her mother. "He told me about some professor who inspired him during his undergrad years and encouraged him to get his MBA. Mark said she was what convinced him that he could be successful on his own, despite his dad's financial problems."

"Well, you've got that in common, I guess. And if Mark could overcome his problems, you can, too."

Allie shrugged but didn't answer.

"So what do you think?" Susan asked after a few moments of silence. "I know it's a huge change, but I'm sure you'll adjust once you get there."

"It's okay. I'll get online and start filling out the application. Mark's so enthusiastic about the school, and it'd be cool for us to be there together…" Her voice trailed off.

"But it's scary," Susan finished for her.

"I have to go to school somewhere, so it might as well be there, as long as Dad's willing to pay for it." Allie picked up her bag and opened the front door. "I'm going to Brandon's. I need to feel the piano keys under my fingers."

****

Caroline was leaning on Lucy's reception desk,

chatting and laughing, when Misty blew through the front door of Meadows Advertising, ushering in a gust of hot air. They both stared open-mouthed as she waltzed right by the two of them without a word, her arms loaded down with manila folders, and stormed back toward Richard's office.

"Uh-oh, now what?" Lucy whispered.

"I don't know, but Richard's in a meeting with a client, so I'd better try to head off Hurricane Peterson." Caroline walked briskly down the hall after Misty, overtaking her just before she barged in on Richard's meeting.

She planted herself in front of Richard's closed office door, hands spread wide across the doorway. "Misty, Richard isn't available at the moment."

Misty scowled and tapped her foot. "It's late in the day, and time he stopped working anyway."

"He's with a client and asked not to be disturbed."

Misty huffed. "I'm his fiancée, not a disturbance, and if I don't show him these wedding invitation mockups right now, they'll never get back from the printer on time."

But Caroline was just as determined that Misty not disrupt yet another business day. "It'll have to wait, Misty; he's with an important potential client."

"This is important, too!" Misty was shouting now. "And you're ruining all my plans, so back off!"

"Aren't you being a little dramatic? Wedding invitations aren't life or death, Misty."

"Oh! I hate you, Caroline Benedict!" Misty reached around Caroline and opened Richard's office door.

"Sorry, Richard," Caroline said, "I tried…"

Richard stood up and shook hands with the man in his office. "Caroline, if you'd see Mr. Forsythe out."

Caroline stood there speechless for a moment, then nodded. "Certainly." She gave Misty a dirty look and turned to walk the client down the hall.

Chapter Nine

Caroline stormed into her bedroom, frowned, and then slumped listlessly onto the bed. "I'm frustrated," she told her sister.

Allie looked up from her phone and wrinkled her nose. "What happened?"

Caroline sat up and looked over at Allie. "How was the grand tour?"

Allie tossed her phone aside. "Ugh, Caroline, why do you do that? You start to say something important about yourself, and then suddenly you're concerned about everyone else. What happened to upset *you*? My news can wait."

Caroline leaned back on the bed pillows, reliving the scene with Misty at the office earlier. Caroline sat back up, angrier than before. "Misty Peterson happened. That woman's driving me nuts! She's so *rude*. She interrupted an important meeting, and Richard was totally embarrassed. I can't take one more minute of her!"

Allie put her hands on her hips. "So are you mad enough yet to do something about it?"

Caroline picked up her bed pillow and tossed it on the floor in anger, thought better of her behavior, reached for the pillow and replaced it carefully on the bed. "Like what?"

"You've got to put some distance between you and

Richard Meadows, that's what. Start job hunting. And what about your promise to start meeting single men?"

Caroline fluffed the pillow. "You're right about the job," she said, "but the idea of dating makes me nauseous, even though Lucy keeps telling me the same thing."

Allie let out a loud, exasperated sigh. "There's medicine for the nausea, Car. And Lucy's right."

"So what do I do?" Caroline pleaded, desperate for a practical solution to this mess.

"You need to have the guts to tell Richard how you feel about him."

"OMG!" Caroline moaned as she buried her head in the pillow. "I can't tell Richard. That would seem so pathetic, me pouring out my heart to a nearly-married man."

Allie gave her sister's shoulders a sympathetic squeeze. "Here's an idea. Let's go out tonight, just you and me. We can go to that restaurant on 86th Street. You know, the one that has live music outside. The music's free and single men are everywhere." Allie held up her hand to stop Caroline's objections. "Come on, it'll be fun."

"I'm supposed to pick up a man?" Caroline shook her head, dubious.

"No, silly, just mingle. You know, see and be seen. How hard is it to chat up a few handsome guys?"

"Well, okay, I guess that wouldn't hurt."

Allie high-fived Caroline. "It's a date."

****

The restaurant was hopping, mostly with the twenty-something crowd. People were mingling both inside the restaurant and outside on the patio, listening to music and flirting with significant others or potential dates. Inside it was stifling because all the patio doors had been flung wide open, letting in the hot, humid air. Caroline and Allie decided to stay outside, hoping to get a better view of the band and also catch what little breeze there was.

They wiggled through the knot of people collected near the makeshift bar and stage, but they finally found an open spot to stand and listen to the music. Allie drank her beer, and Caroline sipped her diet soda while she took in the whole scene: the musicians—a three piece acoustic band with a reggae singer—and the young professionals who had come straight from work in their business attire.

Allie tugged on Caroline's arm. "Ooo, look at that guy over there. Isn't he cute? Maybe you should…"

Caroline shook her head. After another tug on her arm, she reluctantly took a quick glance at the man Allie was indicating. "Yeah, he's okay I guess."

Allie pulled a face. "No, he's not Richard, but he *is* hot. Come on, Car, get with the program!"

Caroline obligingly looked around, noticing a number of nice-looking men, but none she was interested in. Then suddenly she blinked, wondering if she was seeing things. "Allie," she said, "look over there across the patio. No, don't stare, act casual."

Allie followed Caroline's gaze. "Lots of guys there, Car. Describe him."

"No, not a guy. Do you see her?"

"Her?"

Caroline turned her back to avoid being seen. "It's Misty Peterson. Look and tell me if Richard's here, too."

Allie looked. "Nope, no Richard."

Caroline took another peek. Sure enough, it was Misty, surrounded by lots of attractive young men and women, all of them laughing and enjoying the summer evening.

Then Allie gasped. "Ohmigod Caroline, there's Mark! Over there with Misty. Come on, let's go say hi."

Caroline started to object, but Allie was already making her way toward the group. The last thing Caroline wanted was to run into Misty in a social setting.

"Mark, hi," Allie called out.

The color drained from Mark's face, but he quickly recovered and leaned down to kiss her on the cheek. "Allie! What a surprise."

Caroline didn't think Allie's sudden appearance was a pleasant surprise to Mark, but she kept that to herself. She did a quick study of all the people standing and chatting with Misty, including Mark. "Misty, where's Richard?"

Misty waved that question away like it was a buzzing fly. "Said he had some business thing."

Caroline didn't have a clue what Misty was talking about. "He told *me* he had his weekly basketball game tonight."

Misty turned her back on Caroline and resumed her conversation with Krystal McAlister, the friend who'd helped Misty trick Richard into the marriage proposal last summer. There was an awkward silence among Misty's friends. Allie looked lovingly at Mark who shifted from one foot to the other, alternately stuffing his hands in his pockets and then shaking them loose.

Misty said in a stage whisper to Krystal, "Why don't we move over there where the air's fresher?"

Caroline got the hint and took Allie's arm. Trying to sound breezy, she told Mark, "We have to go. Work night and all. Have a nice evening." Despite Allie's resistance, Caroline dragged her to the parking lot.

When they were out of earshot, Allie pulled her arm loose. "Caroline! Why did you do that? I wanted to talk to Mark."

Caroline didn't like the whole scene she'd just witnessed, but for Allie's sake she tried to be diplomatic. "Mark was with friends and wasn't expecting you. Besides, you spent all afternoon with him."

"So?"

"Allie, something just didn't feel right."

"To you, maybe, but I was just starting to have fun. You didn't even give it a chance. We see people we know and pfft—you're outta there." Allie let out a huge puff of air as she stormed off to the car. Caroline sighed and followed her.

****

Richard was in his office working at his computer. Caroline could easily walk in and hand him her résumé, but it was easier on her conscience to communicate with him electronically. That way he couldn't see the look of anguish on her face as she told him she was trying to find a new job elsewhere. But since he'd made no move to renegotiate her part-time salary, she couldn't wait any longer. Neither her finances nor her heart could afford to stay at Meadows Advertising. She sat down at her computer and started composing the hardest message she'd ever written.

Richard,

I've attached my updated résumé for your opinion, following up on our discussion last year of my career objectives. Can I count on you for a reference?

Sincerely, Caroline

Then she couldn't resist adding a less-than professional P.S.

Saw Misty last night at that bar on 86th. She said you had a business thing? Did you need my help? How was your basketball game?

Caroline pulled the ponytail holder out of her hair and twisted it nervously while she awaited his reply. When she heard it ping, she pulled her hair back up and opened the email.

Caroline,

How will I manage without my right-hand man, uh, woman? Yes, I'll look over your résumé and of course I'll be a reference. What's this about Misty? I went home last night after the gym and watched Late Night with Darren.

—R

Caroline sighed as she read the message. Leaving Meadows Advertising was the last thing she wanted to do, but since Richard didn't seem to object to her proposed job search, she had to face reality and get on with it.

Her mind drifted back to her encounter with Misty at the crowded restaurant last night. Misty sure hadn't behaved like a woman about to be married. *Maybe she's having second thoughts?* "I can only hope," she muttered. And why did the woman make up that story about Richard having a business meeting? Caroline shook her head just as the phone rang, and she prayed it wasn't Misty.

"Good morning, Richard Meadows' office," she said, and then exhaled when she saw the caller ID.

"Good morning, Caroline, this is Adele."

"Good morning, Mrs. Meadows. Richard's in his office on a conference call. Do you want to hold?"

"No, dear, I have a Red Hat Society luncheon to get ready for, and I'm in a rush. I don't suppose he's broken his engagement yet?"

Caroline gasped. "Uh, Mrs. Meadows, I…uh, um, well…." Even though she was flustered, she had to admit Richard's grandmother had a wicked sense of humor.

"Well, hope springs eternal," Adele said with a lilt in her voice. "Never mind, dear, just ask him to call me."

Caroline giggled as she stared into the dead phone and then replaced it on the cradle. With Richard not objecting to her job search, Caroline decided she might as well log onto a job search site. She typed in the keywords *copywriting* and *marketing* and awaited the results.

Her office intercom buzzed. "Yes, Lucy?"

"Your sister's on the phone. Allison. Says it's urgent."

Caroline rolled her eyes. More angst about Mark, she assumed. But she was having trouble concentrating on her job search and Richard was still on his conference call, so she picked up. "Hi, Allie, I…"

"Caroline," Allie blurted out, "I've left Mark three messages this morning already, and he won't call me back. Do you think he was mad that I left so suddenly last night?"

Great. Trouble in paradise. Here we go again, Caroline thought. "No, Allie, I don't think that's it at all." She could hear loud piano music. "Where are you, anyway?"

"Brandon's. Why won't Mark return my calls?"

"Allie, take me off speaker phone." Caroline waited till she had her sister's full attention. "Okay, I don't know why Mark's not calling back, but quit leaving him so many messages. It smacks of desperation."

Allie's voice caught, emotion flooding in. "Well, Brandon thinks Mark's being disrespectful, but…"

"I agree with Brandon. Listen, Allie, I'm working. Can we talk later?"

"Yeah…oh, wait! Mark's ringing in now. Hold on."

Caroline groaned, set her phone down, and turned back to her computer. A few minutes later Allie clicked back in.

"Caroline? You there? Okay, crisis averted. He wasn't mad about last night. He's been working for his dad all day. He says his dad can't afford to hire extra help in his architectural firm, so Mark's doing bookkeeping and payroll."

Oh, good, no crisis, Caroline almost said aloud, with a touch of sarcasm, but what she did say was, "I guess that makes sense."

"Oh, and I asked him how he knew Misty Peterson. Said he met her Memorial Day weekend at the Race, up in the Suites. Mutual friends, that sort of thing."

"Hmm, small world," Caroline replied. "I guess they got to know each really fast, judging by how friendly they looked last night."

"Caroline, really!" Allie exclaimed. "Must you always see the worst in everyone?"

Chapter Ten

Caroline stepped into the elevator and pushed the twelfth floor button to take her to the offices of Charing Cross Marketing, a large company with offices in several major cities. She had summoned every ounce of courage she had to force herself to apply for the open position in copyediting she found online, and then Margaret Smithson, head of Human Resources, had called her to interview for it. The office building was located in a fast-growing business corridor not far from Meadows Advertising, so Caroline rationalized that the drive to and from work would be nearly the same.

As the elevator doors parted, Caroline hesitated and almost didn't get off. *You* have *to do this.* She set her jaw, walked down the short hallway, opened the heavy double glass doors, and strode purposefully into the office.

"Good morning," she said to the receptionist. "I'm Caroline Benedict, and I have an appointment with Ms. Smithson."

The receptionist pushed a button on her headset and announced Caroline's arrival. "Please have a seat. Ms. Smithson will be right out."

Caroline sat down on the leather sofa in the plush waiting area, nervously flipped through one of the business magazines on the mahogany coffee table, and looked around at what she could see of the offices from that vantage point. The company handled mostly corporate clients, unlike Meadows Advertising, which dealt with small businesses. Caroline saw the irony in the fact that this would have been the perfect agency to handle Truitt's ad campaign, the one her father had so cavalierly handed over to Sharlene while under her seductive spell.

The office was remarkably quiet, with assistants in business suits bustling around and speaking in hushed tones. *Do I really want to join Corporate America?* The answer was that this was the only response she had gotten to her many job applications, and if she was hired, it would pay well and come with full benefits. And distance her from Richard and his wedding plans.

A slender African-American woman in an impeccable two-piece business suit and black pumps emerged from a wood-embossed corridor. Caroline briefly wondered how the woman could walk wearing that tight pencil skirt, but forced herself to refocus.

"Ms. Benedict?"

"Yes." Caroline stood to shake her hand.

"Please, follow me. I think you'll find Charing Cross to be quite different from Meadows Advertising, but with your qualifications, I'm sure you'll fit right in here." Ms. Smithson led Caroline down the hall to her private office. Caroline tried to swallow the lump in her throat before stepping inside.

****

Caroline returned to her office at Meadows after the nerve-wracking interview and checked her email. To her surprise, Allie had loaded up her inbox. "I don't have time for all this drama," she groused, but opened the first one anyway.

Car,

Brittany and I have been emailing back and forth, so I'm forwarding them to you for your opinion. She wants me to come up to Chicago to visit. I feel guilty for putting her off, but my relationship with Mark is going so well and I don't want to be anywhere but with him. Besides, you know I hate Chicago. Too many memories of school and it's too soon, even if I wanted to be parted from Mark, which I don't. Besides, when was the last time Brittany was in love? She just doesn't get it.

Caroline moaned. In love? She reluctantly opened the forwarded exchange between Allie and Brittany.

Allie,

I'm leaving for Chicago tomorrow to spend the entire month of July with Aunt Emily. There's only so much shopping I can do (okay, not entirely true). When are you coming? I'm sure Mark can spare you for a few days. Please? Nordstrom's is calling my name!

Brittany

Brittany,

Yes, but Mark is so gorgeous, and sweet and lovable and—you get the idea. I just can't tear myself away right now! The last three days alone we've been to a museum, a boat ride on the Canal, and an outdoor classic movie. I'm falling in love! :)

Allie

Caroline couldn't believe her eyes. *Allie thinks she's falling in love with Mark? They've only known each other a few weeks.* She shook her head and deleted the email, clicking on the last one from Allie.

Caroline,

I told Brittany I'd ask, so can you spare a few days in July to drive me up to Chicago? Feel free to say no.

:)

Caroline replied, rather tersely if she was being honest.

Allie,

Why are you emailing me? We share a very small bedroom, and I'm busy right now—working. Talk to me tonight.

"Caroline, darling, you look nice today. Why are you all dressed up?"

Caroline had just hit send on that email to Allie when she looked up to see Sharlene standing over her. It grated on her nerves that Sharlene called her "darling" or "dear" like she was so much older. Caroline had dressed carefully for the interview in a gray pinstripe pantsuit with a white camisole, black pumps, her hair tied neatly back with a clip. She'd given special thought that morning to looking professional, but Sharlene's implication that she usually didn't hit home. Caroline made a mental note to start dressing more appropriately, even if Meadows Advertising was a business casual environment.

"I had a job interview this morning."

"Job interview? Interesting." Sharlene tried to hide her smirk. "Where was your interview? Maybe I can put in a good word. You know I'm acquainted with all the right people at all the right agencies in town."

Caroline groaned inwardly, but since Richard and everyone else in the office already knew, she replied, "Charing Cross Marketing."

"Wonderful, Caroline! I must say it's certainly time you moved on with your career. Why, just yesterday I said the same thing to your father when…"

Caroline braced herself for more of Sharlene's self-congratulatory monologue, but with perfect timing, Richard came out of his office and saved Caroline from ennui. Richard and Caroline exchanged shy smiles. Sharlene narrowed her eyes and grabbed Richard's arm to get his attention.

"Richard, dear, I've got one o'clock reservations at the Skybridge Club downtown, and they won't hold the table for us. Misty's meeting us there. We've got lots of wedding details to discuss," Sharlene said as she tossed a menacing look at Caroline, "including the rehearsal dinner and the guest list."

Caroline blushed and tried to appear busy, organizing paper clips, rubber bands, pens, and post-its in her desk drawer.

"Between you and Misty, I'm never sure who's actually planning this wedding," Richard protested. "Don't we have a wedding planner?"

"My poor brother. So wrapped up in his work he hasn't paid any attention to the details. In case you've forgotten, brother dearest, Daniel and I are giving the rehearsal dinner, and I'd like at least nominal input from you and your lovely fiancée." Richard gave Caroline a look that said *what can I do?* and allowed his sister to nudge him down the hall.

"Have a nice lunch." Caroline turned back to her computer in anguish.

But Sharlene had one last parting shot. "Caroline, you and your sisters must come up to Belford and have dinner with your father and me one evening."

"When?" Caroline challenged her.

Sharlene hedged. "Well, I can't give you an exact date right now, dear, because we're still in the midst of redecorations, plus all these wedding preparations…"

"Uh huh."

"No really, Caroline, I intend to have you girls up for dinner as soon as possible. I'll call you." She threw her an air kiss and walked off down the hall on Richard's arm.

Caroline shuddered. *Yeah, right. Dinner with "us girls."* She knew it would never be arranged.

****

"I see Misty's already at our table." Sharlene waved to her as she and Richard got off the elevator. The Skybridge Club, a private dining club atop an historic downtown skyscraper, was accessible only by private elevator with a key, which was only distributed to members in good standing. Sharlene had used Daniel's membership continuously since her marriage and quite a few times before that, so she was practically on a first-name basis with the wait staff. *If* that had been appropriate.

"Hi, Misty," Richard said, kissing her lightly on the lips. When she didn't kiss him back, he shrugged, held the chair for his sister, and sat down opposite his fiancée.

"Richard, why are you late? You're always so late to everything." Misty snapped her napkin open and spread it on her lap.

"Oh, Misty, dear, don't be angry. It was all my fault," Sharlene told her. "We couldn't find a decent place in the parking garage—at least not one close to the door. These shoes…"

"New?" Misty lifted the white linen tablecloth to get a look at Sharlene's feet.

"Well, of course, dear. You didn't expect me to go through a second summer wearing last year's shoes, did

126

you?" They both tittered.

Richard rolled his eyes but brightened when the waiter handed them their menus and started listing the day's specials. Sharlene waved him away.

"Just bring three Cobb salads and three iced teas. We have business to discuss."

"Very good, Mrs. Meadows-Benedict." The waiter walked over to the service station and returned immediately with their tumblers of tea.

"Richard," Misty cooed, "please tell me you've spoken to your best man and arranged for groomsmen. We're running out of time, honey."

Richard grabbed a roll out of the basket in the center of the table and absent-mindedly slathered it with butter. "Well, Jack already agreed to be best man. And I'm going on the GGG next week, so I'll talk to the rest of the guys then."

"And just what is the GGG?" Misty demanded.

Sharlene put her fingers to her lips in a silent reminder. She didn't want to insult her very wealthy future sister-in-law, but sometimes Misty could be a bit, well, inappropriate. Like yelling at her fiancé in a nearly deserted restaurant.

"Guys' Golf Getaway," Richard told her. "I thought you knew I went to Vegas around this time every summer for a week's golf outing."

"How would I know that?" Misty took a loud slurp of her iced tea. "And what am I supposed to do while you're golfing?"

Richard looked perplexed. "I thought you had shopping to do, or something. Didn't you say you were looking for a trousseau?"

Sharlene decided to intervene before the two of

them had a spat. "Really, Richard, this golf outing is poorly timed," she scolded. "We have so much left to do, and we haven't even started discussing the rehearsal dinner."

Richard scowled. "Sharlene, it's a tradition, one Dad started when I was in high school. Remember? Besides, I don't think you need my input on any of this." Turning to Misty, he added, "And if it helps, I'll use the time to line up the groomsmen."

"Well, my goodness, what do we have here?"

Sharlene, Richard, and Misty all looked up to see Adele Meadows standing next to their table.

Richard stood up and greeted her with a hug. "Grandmother, what a pleasant surprise. What are you doing here?"

"Joining Polly Henderson for a late lunch, but she stopped to powder her nose, so I'll just join the three of you while I wait." Richard held out the fourth chair for her. "What do you young folks have your heads together about? As if I didn't know."

"The wedding, of course, Adele," Misty growled. She poured yet another sugar packet into her tea and stirred it vigorously, clinking the spoon against the glass.

"We're trying to settle some details about the rehearsal dinner, Grandmother," Sharlene said. She reached over and put a steadying arm on Misty's wrist. "So far, all that's been decided is that it'll be at the Belford Country Club. Do you have any suggestions?"

"I suggest you rethink the whole thing!" Adele looked first at Misty squeezing too much lemon into her tea, Richard back to scraping butter off his roll and reapplying it, and Sharlene drumming the table with her well-manicured fingernails.

Sharlene huffed, "Grandmother, please. We have so many loose ends to tie up and very little time left, so unless you have constructive ideas…"

Adele sighed. "I'm sure you'll arrange all the wedding minutiae, Sharlene, with your usual impeccable taste." She confronted Richard. "What I'm wondering about is the marriage."

Richard cleared his throat, tossed the roll on its plate, and took a big swallow of iced tea. Misty busied herself rearranging the silverware next to her plate and didn't make eye contact with him or his grandmother.

Adele glared first at Richard and then Misty. "Will you two be writing your own vows?"

Richard nearly choked on his iced tea. "Uh, I hadn't thought about it." He looked helplessly at his fiancée.

"That's another thing to consider," Sharlene replied, when Misty said nothing. "I suppose we could have the wedding planner compose them."

Adele sat up straight and leveled her gaze at each of them. "Wedding ceremonies should be about your love. You know, your grandfather and I wrote our own vows, and back then it wasn't even a popular thing to do like it is nowadays. Rich spoke so eloquently it brought tears to my eyes, and still does every time I remember it. What will you be saying to your bride, Richard?"

Sharlene wanted her grandmother gone before she ruined everything. "Thank you for your help, Grandmother, but I think we can let the happy couple decide this on their own." She stood and reached over to help Adele out of her chair and out of their business.

Really, her grandmother was the most infuriating old woman.

Adele patted Richard's arm. "I suppose you young folks will have to excuse me now. I see Polly waving at me across the room."

Richard stood politely as Adele got up and walked briskly across the dining room, leaving the three of them alone in an awkward silence.

Chapter Eleven

"Oh, it's you."

Caroline came in the front door, kicked off her pumps, and untucked her white crepe blouse before taking a seat on the sofa. "Gee, thanks, nice to see you, too, Allie," she said.

"Sorry. Mark's supposed to be here, and he's running late."

"Traffic's terrible."

"That's kind of what I hoped—thought," Allie said. "No big deal, as long as we get there in time for the opening credits."

Caroline began thumbing through the mail on the coffee table. "Where are you going?"

Allie was peering out the front window, watching for his car. "That new Sandra Bullock movie, then dinner. Romantic pre-July Fourth evening."

That got Caroline's attention. "Why *pre*-July Fourth? What's wrong with spending the actual holiday with him?"

"He has plans with his family tomorrow afternoon—cookout or something—but we're meeting tomorrow night at the Belford Independence Day Festival to watch the fireworks." Allie got a dreamy look on her face.

Caroline winced and sat up straight. "I know that look, Allie. I've seen it before, plenty of times."

"What look? I don't know what you're talking about." Allie turned back to the window, indignant.

Caroline thought for a minute, wondering if she should just bite her tongue, but Allie needed to hear it and maybe then she'd see the big picture. "It's just like Spencer in eighth grade. Edward in tenth grade. Senior year it was Felix. You get so wrapped up in your romantic notions that you don't realize when the relationship has, well, soured."

"Caroline, you can't compare high school crushes to *this*. I'm in a real relationship with Mark."

"Allie, are you sure? You've only known Mark a short time."

"Caroline!" Allie fairly shouted. "You are so impossible! Can't you just be happy for me, for once?"

"I'm just concerned. I'm not willing to watch you go through more misery, or put the rest of us through three days of migraines."

Allie opened her mouth to argue back, but just then Mark's car drove up and instead of waiting for him to come to the door, she ran outside and hopped in the passenger side. Mark peeled off down the street.

****

Allie stormed through the front door, slamming it behind her. Caroline came out of the kitchen, surprised to see her sister back so soon. Allie's eyes were red and puffy and it was obvious she'd been crying.

"Allie, what in the world?" Caroline began, but Allie pushed past her to the freezer, took out a pint of ice cream and grabbed a spoon from the drawer. Double chocolate chunk. "Uh-oh, the good stuff. Bad news?"

"Leave me alone." Allie flipped the lid off the carton and tossed it on the kitchen counter.

Caroline picked up the sticky chocolate lid and laid it in the sink. She rummaged through the counter and pulled out a bowl, setting it on the table in front of Allie. "You haven't even been gone half an hour. What happened to the movie and dinner? And where's Mark?"

Allie sat down and began eating ice cream straight from the carton, shoving the bowl aside. "Mark had someplace to be," she said between mouthfuls.

Caroline watched Allie blink hard to fight back tears, and her heart went out to her sister. "Did you two have a fight?"

"No! *Yes*! I don't want to talk about it!" Allie shoved another large spoonful of ice cream into her mouth.

Caroline sat down at the kitchen table across from Allie and reached for her hand. "Judging by the way you're gorging yourself, this must be serious. What happened?"

Allie jerked her hand back. "Mind your own business!" She jumped up from the chair, grabbed her handbag, and marched to the front door. She slammed out, leaving the ice cream on the table with the spoon still in it.

Caroline ran to the door after her. "Allie, wait! Where are you going?"

"To Brandon's," Allie called over her shoulder. "I need to practice! Now!"

Caroline watched dumbfounded as Allie sped off down the street. She was still staring in disbelief when Megan and Susan returned from a walk.

"Hey, ice cream!" Megan grabbed Allie's spoon and scooped some ice cream into the clean bowl still sitting on the table.

"What's going on?" Susan asked Caroline.

Caroline took the carton from where Megan had pushed it aside, grabbed the sponge off the sink, and wiped up some chocolate that had dripped down the side of it. "I have no idea. Allie and Mark had a date that was over before it began. They must have had some sort of fight. She wouldn't tell me what about, but she stormed out the door again saying she was going to Brandon's." Caroline looked up at the wall clock. "I hope he's expecting her at this hour."

"Brandon won't care. He's got a thing for Allie, in case you didn't notice," Megan said with a mouthful of ice cream.

"I wonder what Allie and Mark fought about," Susan said. "Well, hopefully it'll all blow over soon. They seem so right for each other."

Caroline opened the freezer and put the thawing ice cream back inside. "Do they, Mom? Really? I don't know, it just all seems too fast." Caroline folded her arms and leaned against the kitchen counter. "Sort of fits her pattern, though, which means it probably won't end well."

"Yes, it is fast," Susan agreed. "But if it helps, I think this time her feelings are genuine."

"It doesn't help. Something's not right, but I just can't put my finger on it."

"Better get out the Excedrin Migraine," Megan giggled.

Caroline frowned. "Eat your ice cream, Megan."

Megan rolled her eyes at her sister but went back to eating the softening ice cream. Susan handed her a paper towel. "I hope you're wrong this time, Caroline, but you need to stay out of it. Let your sister handle her own relationship."

Caroline took a spoon from the nearby silverware drawer and helped herself to a bite out of Megan's bowl. Megan scowled at her as Caroline slowly nibbled, thinking about what her mother had said.

"Guess what, Caroline. Mom's going to let me pick out a dog at the pet shelter after the Fourth."

"Really? A dog?" Caroline looked directly at Susan and gave her the thumbs-up sign behind Megan's back.

"I've told her, Caroline, and I hope you'll back me up," Susan said, winking back at her, "that this dog will be Megan's responsibility, not mine."

"*Mooommmm*, I know! You've said it about a thousand times, and I'm old enough to take care of a dog. I'm nearly sixteen!"

"Not for another five months!" Susan reminded her.

Caroline hugged her sister and whispered in her ear, "If you need any help with the puppy, just call me." Megan giggled and nodded as she put her dirty dish in the sink.

Caroline turned back to her mother. "Seriously, Mom, if Allie gets her heart broken again—on top of losing her piano, her home, and her school—I don't know what she'll do."

"Oh, chill, Caroline." Megan danced off to her room.

"I'm certainly trying," Caroline called back.

Chapter Twelve

"Mom. Hurry up and park the car. We're going to miss the Fourth of July parade!"

"Megan, we've never missed Belford's Independence Day Festival since you were a toddler, so just let me...A*ha*!" Susan spotted an open parking place near the town square's gazebo, right under a large shade tree, and zipped into it. "See? No problem, ladies."

"Let me out. I'm meeting some kids from Willowby." Megan jumped out of the front passenger side before Susan had even turned off the engine.

Susan rolled down the window and called after her. "Megan, call me or Caroline when you're ready to leave! Megan...!" She shook her head, because Megan was already disappearing into the holiday crowd.

"I'm sure she heard you, Mom," Caroline said as she unfastened her seatbelt and opened the back door. Allie was already bounding out of the other backseat door, cell phone pressed to her ear.

The hot, cloudless day was perfect for the Independence Day Festival and the parade set to start at noon on Main Street, in the middle of Historic Old Town Belford. With the Belford High School marching band, civic leaders in convertibles, various floats, clowns, and school clubs with matching t-shirts carrying banners, the parade was always exciting and usually stretched into the early afternoon.

"What's the plan, ladies?" Susan squinted in the bright sunlight and pulled her sunglasses out of her handbag. "Allie?"

"I'm off to find Mark." Allie started visually searching the crowd.

"Do you even know if he's going to be here?" Caroline asked her.

Allie pulled a face. "No, but everyone in town's here, so I'm sure I'll run into him if he can sneak away from his family. I sent him a text but haven't gotten an answer yet."

"Well, call me if you don't find him, and you can join Mom and me."

Caroline watched Allie as she hurried away, her fingers flying over the keypad of her phone. "Do you think he's really going to meet her, Mom? He's not answering her messages."

Susan was beginning to be as doubtful of Allie's relationship with Mark as Caroline was. "I wish I knew, Car." She thought Allie might have a difficult time locating Mark today, even if he did respond to her texts, since it appeared the whole town had turned out. Families strolled through the town square, hordes of teens sat on the edge of the fountain dipping their toes in, and off in the distance faint strains of music drew crowds. There was nothing she or Caroline could do about Allie and Mark right now anyway, so she took a deep breath and said, "I say we just enjoy the day. What shall we do? Go watch the parade or listen to the band—under a shade tree?" Susan fanned herself her with her hand, and Caroline laughed as they walked in the direction of the gazebo.

Two hours later, the sun was directly overhead and

the day had gotten extremely hot. Caroline stretched herself after sitting for too long on a cement bench. "I wonder if Allie found Mark and if Megan met up with her Willowby friends," she said.

"I hope so." And Susan hoped one or both of her other daughters would text once they were happily situated with friends. "I'm dying of thirst. Lemonade?"

"Sounds great. It must be over ninety degrees out here," Caroline said, sweat glistening on her brow.

Booths were scattered all around the town square, some selling souvenirs and others offering food or cold drinks. "Whoever owns this stand is probably making a fortune," Susan remarked as they drew near the lemonade stand. "Look how long the line is."

While they waited in the queue, Caroline scouted out the crowd. "Uh-oh. There's trouble."

Susan followed Caroline's gaze. Off in the distance she spotted Daniel, dressed in khaki shorts and a golf shirt, and Sharlene, way overdressed for the outdoor event in a polished cotton sundress and high-heeled sandals. Her oversized hat nearly dwarfed her head, and a designer handbag was slung over one shoulder.

"Do you think they saw us?" Caroline asked, quickly turning her head away.

But before Susan could answer, a voice behind them caught them both off guard. Caroline turned to see Richard and Misty standing in the lemonade line behind her.

Richard pulled off his sunglasses and smiled at them. "Great to see you, Caroline, and Susan, too, of course."

Susan watched Caroline alternately blush and fumble for words. Her daughter was so obviously pining for this man who was unavailable, and it broke her heart. "Nice event, isn't it?" Susan said.

"It's too hot," Misty complained, "and now we have to stand in this stupid line just to get something to drink. Richard, I *told* you this was a bad idea!"

Richard turned to her impatiently. "It's July, Misty, and you knew it would be hot outside. If you like, I can take you home."

"No, just get me the lemonade. I'll be waiting over there under that shade tree." Misty fanned herself with a cardboard advertising fan one of the vendors was handing out, and made a big show of brushing leaves off the bench before sitting down under the sprawling oak.

Caroline visibly relaxed once Misty was out of earshot. "I guess the heat makes some people cranky."

Richard folded his arms and frowned. "Some people don't need heat to get cranky."

Caroline bit her lip as she and Susan exchanged amused glances. "Is everything okay?" she asked him.

Before he could answer, a voice called out, "Yoo hoo! Richard!" It was Sharlene, walking over to join them, her arm linked through Daniel's. "Richard, where's Misty? I know I just saw her." She shaded her eyes and looked around. "Oh, there she is, under the tree. Don't forget you two are coming over this evening for the barbecue cookout."

Daniel gave Caroline a quick hug, then spoke awkwardly to Susan. "Are you enjoying the holiday?"

"Very much, thank you," Susan responded, and was relieved that it was finally her turn to order lemonade. She stepped up to the window, Caroline right behind her, attempting to make polite conversation with her father and his trophy wife. Susan again felt the injustice of it all.

"A party tonight?" Caroline asked her father. "Does that mean the house reno is done?"

"We're, uh, having some people over this evening," Daniel mumbled. "We would have invited you girls…"

"Uh-huh," Caroline said, with a barely perceptible lifted eyebrow. "Mom's grilling burgers this evening, and we've got some friends coming over, so even if Allie, Megan and I *had* been invited…"

"That's lovely, dear," Sharlene interrupted. "It works out well for everyone."

Daniel frowned at his wife but turned back to Caroline. "Friends? Anyone I know?"

"Oh, Daniel, darling, of course not," Sharlene said.

"Brandon Phillips, friend of Emily's." Caroline turned to Sharlene, hands on her hips. "He's a music professor at Bradley University, and Allie's been using his piano this summer, since hers has been covered with a tarp for weeks. And Brandon's bringing a colleague."

Sharlene dismissed Caroline with the wave of her hand. "I never was very interested in academia, dear. However, some of Daniel's business and social contacts…"

Susan held up the two cups of lemonade like prizes and she and Caroline walked off, leaving Sharlene in mid-sentence.

****

"Daniel, wait!" Sharlene called after her husband.

Daniel strode toward the shade tree near the gazebo stage, where they'd left a blanket and cooler on the grass. He sat down in disgust, rummaged in the cooler for a beer, twisted off the lid, and gulped half the bottle in one swallow. Sharlene trailed behind him, breathlessly trying to keep up in the heat. She would have cursed herself for wearing these high-heeled sandals if they weren't so cute, not to mention expensive, but they certainly made walking in the grass difficult. She eventually caught up to him and plopped herself down next to him, seductively rearranging her low-cut sundress.

"My goodness, Daniel, why the rush? It's too hot out here to do all this running." She rummaged in the cooler and pulled out a chilled bottle of water.

Daniel glanced sideways at his wife. "Once again, Sharlene," he said as he lowered the beer bottle from his lips, "you've snubbed my daughters."

"Snubbed? How?" Sharlene plastered an innocent look on her face, hoping he'd buy that she hadn't deliberately left his daughters out.

Daniel took another long pull from the bottle. "By not including them in the barbecue you're having tonight. And by discussing it in front of Caroline. That was rude, Sharlene."

"*I'm* having? You mean *we!*"

"No, I mean *you*. You never consult me when you decide to have one of these parties." Daniel finished off his beer and opened another one.

Sharlene smiled sweetly and took a dainty sip of her water. "Well, darling, I didn't invite them because I just didn't think they'd fit in. It's going to be all adults, you know."

"Caroline and Allie *are* adults," Daniel reminded her in exasperation, "and I see very little of my daughters as it is. It's time you realized the divorce was from Susan, not them!"

Sharlene patted Daniel's hand. "Daniel, darling, as you pointed out, it would be rude to invite them now, but perhaps we can have them over for dinner later this month."

Daniel glared at his wife as he twisted the cold beer bottle between his fingers. "You keep saying that, but..." He shook his head, stared off into the distance, and sipped his drink.

Sharlene knew how to bring her husband to heel. She batted her eyelashes and cooed, "Well, darling, I've been giving this some thought. What if I ask one of the girls to be a bridesmaid in Richard and Misty's wedding? It can't be Caroline, of course, since she's so obviously smitten with my brother, and Allie is probably too busy with her music, so I could ask Megan. What do you say, Daniel? Won't she look adorable in one of those dresses Misty picked out? I'll speak to her right away."

Daniel shrugged in resignation, finished the beer, and tossed the bottle in the grass.

****

Megan ran across the Belford town square, threw herself into Susan's arms, and burst into tears. "I *hate* those girls!"

Susan was totally taken by surprise. She held Megan at arm's length and looked her in the face. "Who? What happened?"

"My so-called friends! At first it was great, seeing everyone again. But when I told them where I was going to school next year, they acted like I was, I don't know, contaminated or something. Then they just went off and left me." Megan sobbed even louder.

Megan had loved going to Willowby Hall, especially in elementary school. But in sixth grade when her parents divorced, Susan knew Megan felt like a pariah in a school where hardly anyone's parents ever split up. In eighth grade Megan began getting into arguments with her teachers, fights with her peers, and her grades plummeted. The Headmaster of Willowby Hall called Susan into his office and threatened to expel Megan, who sat slumped in a chair, a scowl on her face.

"Mrs. Benedict, Megan cannot continue in this fashion," Dr. Miller had said. "She's disrupting the educational process, and it's completely unacceptable. Perhaps public school…"

At the time, that idea caused Susan to blanch. "Please, Dr. Miller, Megan's never been in any school except this one. It's true she's having a hard time adjusting to the divorce, but I'm sure she can do better."

Megan had stomped a foot on the floor. "I'm sitting right here, Mom."

Dr. Miller was firm. "Unfortunately, today has seen yet another outburst of Megan's temper in class."

Susan had wanted to slide under the chair. Neither of her other two daughters had ever caused a single problem at that school, but she was now a frequent visitor to the offices of administrators and guidance counselors, thanks to her high-strung youngest.

"Megan," Susan had said, "do you want to stay here at Willowby? Because if you don't stop these arguments, you're going to have to go to Belford Middle School."

"But I like the art program here!" Megan had whined.

"I'll give you one last chance, Megan," Dr. Miller

told her. "You are now on probation until the end of the semester. One more disruption and you'll be expelled. If you prove yourself worthy, Willowby will then be pleased to invite you to stay on for high school."

So Megan had attempted to improve herself by focusing on her art classes, and she made an even bigger effort to ignore the teenage whispering about her family. Unfortunately, Willowby was a small school, gossip was hard to avoid, and Megan continued to get into scrapes with her peers. Miraculously, Willowby had allowed her to enroll in high school on a probationary status. It didn't hurt that her father was CEO of a large corporation and paid the tuition in cash.

Now Susan was drowning in guilt, her heart bleeding for Megan, knowing how she'd looked forward to attending the July Fourth festivities in Belford, and getting to spend time with girls she previously thought of as friends. However, she couldn't help but hope that Megan would soon have an opportunity to meet new kids in a new school, and experience more diversity than she would ever see at Willowby. "Megs, I'm sorry you were treated badly." Susan gave her shoulders a squeeze. "It's time for us to head home now anyway. Our dinner guests are coming at seven."

"But it's so *unfair!*"

"It is. But hey! Remember, tomorrow we're going to pick out a dog." Susan hoped that letting Megan choose the long sought-after pet would help cheer her up.

"Yeah, I guess. Anyway, I'm beyond ready. Let's go."

****

Dinner was almost ready. Susan flipped the burgers off the grill onto a serving platter with the warmed buns. Potato salad and coleslaw were chilling in the fridge, and Megan had baked the brownies last night. Caroline began bringing out the food to the picnic table in the backyard. It was cheerfully set with a red-and-white checkered plastic-backed tablecloth, and Susan had bought festive Fourth of July decorative paper plates and matching napkins.

The doorbell rang just as Caroline was taking the salads out of the fridge. "Mom, my hands are full. Can you get the door?"

Susan walked through the living room and opened the front door. There stood Brandon Phillips, a bottle of chilled sparkling cider in his hand, and beside him was a very handsome man. Of course Susan knew Brandon was bringing a colleague, but she'd expected a stodgy old professor, not someone so dashing. For a moment she forgot to speak. "Oh, sorry, please come in."

"Susan, thanks for asking me," Brandon said, stepping inside. "I'd like you to meet Patrick Williams. He teaches classic literature at Bradley."

Patrick didn't look like a college professor, or Susan's image of one anyway—bearded, pipe in his mouth, wearing a blazer with elbow patches. She shook that cliché right out of her head. Patrick was medium height, dark-haired with streaks of gray, late forties, and dressed in jeans and an Old Navy July Fourth t-shirt. He shook her hand and smiled, and she liked him immediately.

"Literature? It so happens I'm a high school English teacher." Susan nervously pushed a stray hair out of her face. "Or I will be, once school starts next month."

Patrick grinned. "Thanks for letting me tag along, Susan. All my family lives in Texas except for a sister who lives in Louisville, so I'm sort of on my own for most holidays."

Susan couldn't help noticing his marked Texas drawl. "Texas? I'm from Oklahoma, practically neighbors." She led them through the kitchen and out into the backyard, where Caroline was putting serving spoons into the potato salad and baked beans.

"So how'd you end up in Indiana?" Patrick asked, sitting in the folding chair Susan indicated for him.

She found the sound of his voice soothing, like being with someone from back home. "Sort of roundabout, I guess. After I graduated from college, my husband took a job in Belford, and I've been a Hoosier ever since." Susan blushed as Patrick smiled at her, and his drawl felt like home.

"Where's your family now?" Patrick asked her.

Susan sat down in a lawn chair and pulled it up closer to Patrick. "My parents moved to Boca Raton, Florida, a couple of years after I moved to Indiana."

"Do you see them often?" Patrick leaned in closer.

Susan wasn't sure if it was really hot out this evening or if she was blushing in the presence of this fascinating man. "I usually take the girls to visit my parents in the winter. It's too hot to go to Florida this time of year."

Patrick grinned. "Same reason I don't visit Texas in the summer!"

"But what about you?" Susan asked. "Indiana's a big change of scenery from Texas."

"My wife was from Terre Haute and all her

family's still there, so moving to Indiana after grad school was a given."

Susan didn't know about a wife. In fact, she knew very little about Patrick Williams other than he and Brandon were colleagues. Was Patrick married? She didn't see a wedding ring, but some men didn't wear them. Just in case, she scooted her chair back a safe distance. "I didn't know you had a wife, or I certainly would've invited her…"

Patrick moved his chair closer to where Susan had just moved. "She had breast cancer. It's been nearly two years now." He shook off the somber mood. "Since then I've tried to make her death count for something, so I've gotten involved with breast cancer fundraising events."

Susan was surprised that Patrick was a widower, and such a young one. "I'm so sorry for your loss, but I've actually volunteered at some of those events myself. I even walked in the 5K race last April."

"There were about eight thousand people participating, but if I'd known you were there…" Patrick didn't finish his sentence.

Susan blushed again.

Caroline stepped out the back door, her cell phone to her ear. "Okay, Allie, I'll tell Mom, but Brandon's going to be disappointed. And you're missing out on Mom's famous potato salad. Yeah, we'll save you some. Bye. Hey, Mom," she called out, "Allie's not coming. She still hasn't met up with Mark, but they have a date to watch fireworks at ten, so she's staying up in Belford. I guess he'll bring her home."

****

Megan and Caroline went for a late-evening walk

on the Monon Trail after dinner. The hiking and biking trail stretched for miles along an abandoned railroad line, both north of Rosslyn Village to Belford, and south all the way to downtown Indianapolis. As the sun set, a warm pleasant breeze felt refreshing after the heat of the day. The trail was full of walkers, joggers and bike-riders. Caroline had invited Susan, Brandon, and Patrick to join them, but the three of them had preferred to stay in the backyard and talk.

"If we walk far enough, maybe we can see the fireworks in Belford," Megan said.

"I don't think so, Megs, it's pretty far and there are a lot of trees."

"Did you see the way Mr. Williams was looking at Mom?" Megan giggled. "Sort of the same way Brandon looks at Allie. Who knew old people could get crushes?"

Caroline focused her eyes on the pavement beneath her so Megan wouldn't see her laugh. Once she'd recovered control, she asked, "Do you like him? Patrick I mean."

"He's nice, I guess."

"I feel bad for Brandon. He looked so disappointed when Allie called and said she wouldn't be home." Caroline glanced at her watch. "I hope by now she's met up with Mark and ended all this angst."

Off in the distance, somewhere in nearby Rosslyn Village, someone was shooting off firecrackers. Caroline's phone rang. She pulled it out of the pocket of her white shorts, checked the caller ID and frowned. "Allie, what's up? Allie? I can barely hear you."

Allie was sobbing, but she had to practically scream over the Belford fireworks accompanied by the high school marching band. "Caroline, Mark never showed. Can you come get me?"

This was Caroline's worst fear, that Mark and Allie were over and Allie wasn't accepting it. "Of course, I'll be right there. Allie, I'm really sorry. Allie?"

"Just hurry, okay?" Allie disconnected the line.

Chapter Thirteen

*Melting ice cream. Wet and sticky, running down her fingers...*Caroline woke with a start and blinked at the bedside clock. Six a.m. She groaned and started to turn over, when she realized the wet sticky feeling was actually Megan's new dog, Honey, the one her mom and sister had adopted from the shelter on July fifth. Honey licked Caroline's fingers again, so Caroline reached down and patted the dog on the head. "Do you need to go out?" she whispered. She glanced over at Allie's bed, but Allie wasn't in it. In fact, it didn't look like the bed had been slept in at all. Caroline climbed out of bed, picked up the dog, and carried her into Megan's bedroom.

"Psst, Megs," Caroline whispered next to her ear. "You have to take the dog out."

Megan pulled the pillow over her ears, moaned, and rolled over to the wall. Caroline tapped Megan's shoulder, but she didn't move, and now the dog was getting wiggly. She sighed and tiptoed down the hall, her sister's new dog—the one Megan swore she'd take responsibility for—in her arms. She checked to see if Allie was in the bathroom, but the door was open and the light was off. Caroline wondered where Allie was as she crept past her mother's room and headed through the house. But in the family room, there was Allie asleep on the sofa, the TV still on but muted, her cell phone clutched in her hand. Caroline set the dog down, tried to shush the exuberant animal, found the remote under the coffee table, and turned off the television.

"Huh?" Allie mumbled.

"What are you doing out here?" Caroline asked.

"Sleeping," Allie growled.

Caroline knew without asking that Allie was waiting for a phone call from Mark, but she decided not to mention it. "Go back to sleep."

"I thought that was Megan's dog." Allie punched the throw pillow and closed her eyes again.

Caroline scrutinized Allie while keeping a close eye on Honey. "Supposed to be, but she was in our room, and I couldn't get Megan up to let her out."

Just then the dog sniffed a likely spot near the leg of the coffee table, but before Caroline could get to her, Megan swooped into the room, snatched the dog up right before she squatted on the carpet, and hurried to the backyard with her. "I told you I'd take care of her, Caroline!" Megan called as she let the screen door slam.

Caroline lifted an eyebrow and started to go back to her room, but now she was fully awake. She had to go to work in a few hours anyway, so she went to the kitchen to make coffee. Allie wasn't asleep, either, despite pretending to be.

Megan and Honey padded back through the family room. "Sorry I snapped at you, Car," Megan said. Honey trotted happily alongside as Megan went back to her bedroom.

"Allie," Caroline said, "why don't you go get into bed? You aren't going to get any sleep out here."

Allie nodded, stood up with a stretch, checked her

phone for messages, and exclaimed, "Yes! Finally!"

Caroline pushed Brew on the coffee pot and poked her head into the living room. "Mark? What's he say?"

"*'Sorry missed 4th—in Chicago for job interview.'* What the…?" Allie mumbled.

Caroline didn't buy it. Who goes for any kind of interview on a national holiday? "Wasn't a Chicago job interview something he would have mentioned?"

Allie rubbed her eyes and looked again. "I need to sleep on this." She stumbled down the hallway.

Caroline wondered why the guy didn't just end their relationship. Or had he?

****

Caroline was scrolling through the email messages that had piled up at work over the holiday when she saw one from the advertising firm where she had interviewed last week. The idea of a new position was exciting, but she dreaded the thought of having to leave Meadows Advertising. While she was hesitating, she heard her cell phone ping with a text.

—Thar she blows!—

Caroline smiled at Lucy's humor, but when she looked up and saw Misty barreling down the hall, she wasn't amused anymore.

Misty stopped just inches from Caroline's desk, her arms folded, puffing from exertion. "Caroline, I have to speak to Richard!"

When have you ever asked my permission? is what Caroline would have liked to say, but what she did say was, "I think he's on the phone."

"I don't care." Misty threw open Richard's door and marched in. She stood just inside the doorway tapping her foot impatiently.

Richard looked up, finished his phone conversation with what Caroline thought was a deliberately slow pace, scribbled a few notes on a legal pad next to the desk phone, and finally turned to his fiancée. "Good morning, Misty."

Misty stomped her foot like a petulant child. "I have nothing to wear!"

Richard's mouth dropped open. "You came all the way over here to tell me that?" He turned back to his computer and resumed working. "So I guess you're going shopping."

"You don't understand, Richard. I'm so frustrated! I've been to three malls and all over downtown Indianapolis, but this city doesn't have enough upscale stores. I can't find anything, and I desperately need new clothes for all the pre-wedding parties and our honeymoon!"

Caroline felt sick when Misty mentioned the upcoming nuptials, not to mention the honeymoon, but if she felt bad, she saw Richard visibly cringe.

"So do you want me to come with you?" he offered.

"Of course not. You'd just be in the way. I came to tell you I'm going to Chicago for a few days. At least I know I can find decent fashion choices there! I'm leaving this afternoon."

Richard opened his mouth, closed it, shook his head and said, "Have a nice…"

But Misty didn't even let him finish before she flew out, leaving Caroline dumbfounded. "What was that all about?" she asked after Misty was gone.

Richard shrugged. "Just Misty being Misty." He picked up the desk phone and dialed out.

Caroline admired his patience with her, but she knew something was up. Misty could go to Chicago and be back in day if that's what she wanted to do. The thing Caroline couldn't figure out was why Misty wanted to marry Richard at all, since she never wanted to spend time with him. She was certain Misty had some kind of hidden agenda and obviously Richard couldn't see that, but Caroline had promised herself to stay out of it.

She sat back down at her computer, and with trepidation, opened the email.

Dear Ms. Benedict,

After our meeting the other day, I reviewed your impressive résumé and I'm pleased to offer you a position at Charing Cross Marketing as a copy editor. The salary would be the top dollar we discussed, which includes full medical benefits and an opportunity at a later date to buy into our 401K program. We'd like to have a response from you by early next week.

Sincerely,

Margaret Smithson

Human Resources Manager

Caroline sighed. She couldn't afford to turn down such a great offer. She gathered her courage and tapped on Richard's still-open door. He looked up from his computer and smiled at her.

"Richard, I've had a job offer."

The smile melted from his face. "Did you accept it yet?" She shook her head no. "If you can hold off a few days, I need some time to…"

Caroline waited for him to finish that sentence, but he leaned back in his chair and tapped his forefingers together, lost in thought. She sighed. "They said they want to hear from me by the first of next week."

What if Richard made her a counter-offer? He couldn't match the offer she'd just gotten, and her rational side questioned the wisdom of continuing to work at Meadows Advertising when she had such deep feelings for him. And such a dislike for his soon-to-be wife. Caroline didn't have an answer for that dilemma. It was already past one p.m. so she decided to take a late lunch away from the office, think it through, and hopefully get some perspective.

When she returned she saw an email from her sister. Caroline rolled her eyes as she opened it. More Mark drama, she assumed.

Hey Car!

Remember I wanted to go to Chicago to spend time with Brittany? Can you drive me up there this weekend?

Caroline didn't think for a minute this sudden desire to go to Chicago had anything to do with Brittany.

What about Brandon and your promise to practice every day?

Caroline hit send.

Allie replied within minutes.

Poor Brandon, he's been so patient. I'll send him a thank-you note, but I really need to go to Illinois. I already told Brittany we were coming, and she's alerted Emily and Sara. Please? I'm desperate!

Caroline suspected Allie was planning to fix her relationship with Mark while she was in Chicago, which was probably not going to work. But Caroline had her own reason for wanting to get out of town for a couple of days, so she replied:

It's weird, because there are a lot of desperate people off to Chicago for the weekend. I'll explain later. Yes, I can drive you up on Friday, but you owe me.

Chapter Fourteen

Caroline dug through her overnight bag to make sure she hadn't forgotten anything. This last-minute trip came up so fast, she'd barely had time to pack.

"You're going to get stuck in Chicago rush-hour traffic. You should have started earlier in the day," Susan said as she tossed Allie's bag into the trunk of Caroline's car.

"It's my fault, Mom," Caroline said, tossing in her own bag and slamming the trunk shut. "I just couldn't get away from the office any earlier." Caroline knew she should start distancing herself from Meadows Advertising and think seriously about the offer from Charing Cross, but any time Richard asked her for a favor…She shook her head and gave her mom a quick hug. "Any message for Emily and Sara?"

"Tell Emily I'll call her early next week, and give them both hugs for me. And thank them again for taking you both in like this on such short notice." She turned to her other daughter, who was already in the passenger seat, impatiently tapping her foot. "Allie, did you remember to tell Brandon you'd be out of town for a few days?"

Allie concentrated on fastening her seat belt. "I'll call him from the road, Mom. As you've already pointed out, we need to go."

Susan leaned into the open window. "Did you ever

hear from Mark?"

"Yes, Mom."

"Well? What did he say?"

"He said he's in Chicago for a job interview."

Susan's eyes widened. "So *that's* why you're going to Chicago?"

Susan looked at Caroline, who shrugged. "Allie, what's going on with you and Mark?"

Allie stared straight ahead. "I don't want to talk about it."

Susan sighed and whispered to Caroline, "See if you can get to the bottom of this."

Caroline nodded, backed out of the driveway, and headed north on Meridian Street.

Once they were northbound on I-65, Caroline slipped a CD into the player. She checked the gas gauge and hoped she had enough fuel to make it to Chicago, since her cash flow was limited, and then glanced over at her sister who was staring out the window.

"Allie, what's the plan once you get to Chicago?"

"Spending time with Brittany, of course," Allie snapped. "I haven't seen her in a year."

Caroline adjusted the volume down. "You don't have to be so defensive, Allie. I mean what about Mark? You and I both know this trip isn't about Brittany."

"Don't start, Caroline." Allie reached over and turned the music up.

Caroline glanced over at her sister, who was slumped in the seat, looking glum. "I'm worried about you, that's all. Ever since the Fourth, you've been in a funk. Is Mark meeting you in Chicago?"

"I sent him a text."

So that answered the question. Allie didn't even know if Mark would see her while they were there. "I really wish you'd tell me what happened between you two." Caroline put on her turn signal to pass a slow-moving pickup truck.

"It was just a stupid argument, and I'm sure Mark and I can work it out. So back off." Allie pulled a Jane Austen novel out of her bag, flipped open a page, and pretended to be engrossed.

Caroline sighed, noticed the construction signs, and focused on her driving. It looked like a long, bumpy road ahead.

Mom was right about the traffic, Caroline admitted to herself. It took two and a half hours to drive to the outskirts of Chicago from Indianapolis, and then another two hours to drive to Emily's downtown condo. Friday evening rush-hour was gridlocked. Caroline was exhausted and hungry when they finally arrived. Allie jumped out of the car the minute Caroline had it in park.

A barefoot Brittany, her auburn hair pulled back in a ponytail, wearing running shorts and tank top, ran outside to greet them. "You're here!"

Caroline turned off the engine and stretched her shoulders as she got out. "Chicago traffic was awful, and then when I finally got to this neighborhood, I had to circle the block three times to find a parking space."

Brittany nodded and gave Caroline a quick hug, but had to stand on tiptoes to hug Allie. "Well, we're so happy you're here. Emily and Sara have something cooking that smells divine. Where are your bags?" Caroline popped the trunk, and Brittany yanked both bags out and then just as quickly dropped them on the sidewalk. "Geez, did you pack everything you own?"

Allie pulled her phone out and started walking to the front steps, texting the whole way.

"Here, let me help you, Brittany." Caroline eyed her sister who was being impossibly rude, reached for her bag, slung it over her shoulder, and followed tiny little Brittany, who was lugging Allie's bag.

Brittany set Allie's bag on the front step. "Sara said to put you both in the guest room, and there are fresh towels in the adjoining bathroom."

"Great." Allie didn't even look up from her phone, all but ignoring Brittany.

Caroline sighed, took both bags, and headed up the steps of the Chicago brownstone.

"So what's this about Mark? Allie?" Brittany waved her hand in front of Allie's face. "Hello?"

Allie stuffed her phone in a jeans pocket. "I'll tell you about it later. He's just being weird, but I plan to see him later so we can talk."

Brittany looked dejected. "And here I thought you came to spend time with me."

Allie gave Brittany a quick hug. "Of course I came to see you. How could I not come visit my best friend?"

Brittany looked at her askance. "Really, or was I just an excuse?"

Caroline felt bad for Brittany. Both of them had easily seen through Allie's ruse, yet her sister continued to pretend this trip was just a visit with a friend. Caroline sighed. "'Fess up, Allie. How many times have you called Mark this afternoon?"

"I only left one voice mail, just before we left home, and I just texted him telling him we're here."

"Do you even know where he's staying?" Caroline

asked.

"No. With friends, I guess."

"Oh, Allie, this doesn't sound good," Brittany said, shaking her head. "Maybe you should give him some space."

Emily stepped out the door and smothered both Caroline and Allie in hugs. "It's so good to have you both here. How's your mom?"

"She's great. She said to tell you she'll call," Caroline said. "I'm starved, and something in the kitchen smells delicious!"

****

On Saturday morning it was a luxury getting to sleep in. No barking dog, no ringing phones, no loud TV, just peace and quiet. Caroline could smell the fresh-brewed coffee as she came downstairs. Emily had put out blueberry muffins and was sitting at the kitchen table, reading the newspaper.

"Good morning," she said as Caroline walked in.

"Good morning." Caroline yawned and poured a cup of coffee. She noticed with surprise that Emily was dressed in business attire. "Are you working today?"

"I've got a client from Houston wanting to do some serious house-hunting. Sara's still asleep. Her law firm's handling a big case, and she's been in court all week. What do you ladies have planned, or should I even ask?" She winked at Caroline.

"Shopping, of course." Caroline laughed, before thinking logically. "Really just window-shopping, though, because Allie and I are on a tight budget. One pair of designer shoes could set us back a month. But there's no place better than Chicago to look at the latest fashions, and we can enjoy advising Brittany."

"Brittany's out for her morning run," Emily said. "I guess Allie's still asleep?"

"I guess." Caroline sipped her hot coffee slowly, mulling over Allie's behavior the last few days. "Emily, something about this business with Mark Townsend just doesn't sit right with me. Why would he act like he's falling in love with her one minute, then stand her up for a date the next? After that, nothing except a text about some bogus job interview."

"You're asking *me* to explain men?" Emily laughed.

Caroline laughed too. "I guess not." Still, the whole situation was making her very nervous. "Maybe shopping will take Allie's mind off him for a while. Do we have any dinner plans?"

"Actually, Sara and I would like to take the three of you to a new restaurant downtown. All the young people your age hang out there." Emily winked at Caroline. "Our treat of course."

"You're too good to us!" Caroline hugged Emily, grabbed a muffin and started toward the stairs. "I'll just see if I can drag Allie out of the bed."

Upstairs, she found Allie awake, checking her messages. "No word from Mark?"

Allie shook her head. "I'm texting him, letting him know exactly where I'll be today. Maybe he can meet me for lunch or something. *Something*."

Caroline's heart was breaking for her sister. She could only nod, bite her tongue, and tell her sister about their dinner plans.

****

Caroline thought the restaurant Emily and Sara had chosen certainly lived up to its hype. It was definitely *the* trendsetting establishment for the twenty- and thirty-something crowd. Valet parking and a hostess in evening clothes added to the ambiance, as did the extensive wine list and gourmet menu. Emily had made eight-thirty dinner reservations, but even then their table wasn't quite ready when they arrived, due to the many reservations ahead of them. Still, it was worth the wait, because the food was excellent and the service was impeccable. Waiters in semi-tux attire hovered endlessly, refilling water or wine glasses unbidden, and bringing extra baskets of bread and olive oil for dipping.

"Thanks for picking up the tab, you two," Caroline said to Sara and Emily. Any restaurant that didn't post its prices on the menu meant if you had to ask, you couldn't afford it.

Sara smiled at Caroline, put her credit card inside the black leather folder with the restaurant logo embossed in gold, and shoved it to the end of the table. "Our pleasure."

Once dinner was over, Brittany said, "Let's go into the bar. There's dance music and lots of hot guys!"

Emily and Sara were agreeable, Allie was indifferent, and Caroline wasn't interested in that idea at all. But Brittany was itching to dance, so the five of them left their table and went into the bar. Or at least they tried to go in. It was even more crowded than the restaurant. Young adults, dressed to impress, mingled everywhere, drinks in hand, laughing and chatting with good-looking members of the opposite sex.

Brittany playfully elbowed Caroline and tilted her head in the direction of a couple of attractive guys standing by the bar. "Single guys everywhere, girlfriend!"

Caroline winced but turned to Emily as she tried in vain to see anything above the shoulders of the crowd. There was a DJ on a platform, loud music with a steady beat, and way too many people crammed onto the tiny dance floor. Florescent lights gave an eerie purple cast to the room, and naturally it was so loud, conversation was out of the question. "Is this a good idea? Maybe we should go somewhere quieter," Caroline shouted.

"I'm going to try to make my way to the bar," Emily shouted back. "Anyone want anything?"

"I'll go with you," Sara said in loud lawyer voice. "Ladies? Anything?" She turned to Allie, Caroline, and Brittany.

"White wine for me, if you can get there," Brittany shouted. "Need any help?"

"No, we can manage," Emily called back.

Judging from the number of people milling around the bar flirting with potential dates, and the difficulty squeezing by them just to place an order, Caroline figured Sara and Emily would be a while. There was nothing else to do but people-watch from their location near the entryway. And people of all shapes, sizes, and fashion statements were there to watch.

Brittany could hardly stand still. "Caroline, Allie, come on! Let's dance!"

Caroline shook her head. No way was she venturing out among all those strangers. "Allie, you and Brittany go ahead. I'll wait here for Sara and Emily."

Allie pulled a face. "It's too crowded, and there's no one to dance with."

Brittany stood on tiptoe and searched the room. "Come on, you party-poopers, there are good-looking guys all over the place. Hey, check out that one over there!" Brittany tugged on Allie's arm as she pointed to an attractive young man already on the dance floor. "He's *hot!*"

Allie looked in the direction Brittany was pointing. She blinked her eyes and looked again, shouting into her sister's ear. "Caroline! Mark's here!"

Caroline looked, sure her sister was mistaken, yet when she stood on tiptoe she was stunned to see Mark Townsend. He was enjoying himself on the dance floor, dancing closely with some woman wearing a too-tight red cocktail dress whose face she couldn't see. Before she could stop Allie, her sister was pushing her way through the crowd, headed toward him.

"Allie!" Caroline called after her, but it was too loud for Allie to hear, or maybe she didn't want to hear. Caroline pushed her way through the crowd to catch up to her sister, reaching out to grab her arm just as Allie got close to the dance floor.

"Mark! Mark!" Allie called out, breaking free of Caroline's grasp and shoving her way close enough to tap him on the shoulder. "Mark! Ohmigod, why haven't you returned any of my messages?"

Mark gazed at Allie for a moment as if he had never met her, calmly turned back to his dance partner, and whispered something in the woman's ear. The woman laughed, nodded, and pulled Mark in close as they resumed dancing. Allie stood there, stunned by the rejection.

"Allie, come on, let's go." Caroline took her arm and tried to lead her away from the dance floor, just as Mark's dance partner turned around.

"Misty!" Caroline exclaimed. "What are you—?"

Misty seemed just as surprised to see Caroline, and they stood glaring at each other in silence for a tense moment. But Misty quickly recovered her composure, turned her back on Caroline, and threw her arms around Mark. And now it was Caroline's turn to be shocked as he pulled her in closer.

Allie jerked her arm away from Caroline, shoved her way through the throng of people, and didn't stop moving until she was out of the bar. Caroline tried to go after her, but she couldn't get through the knot of people quickly enough.

Brittany stopped a breathless Caroline. "What happened? Where'd Allie go?"

"Mark Townsend's a jerk," was all Caroline said as she chased after Allie.

Brittany hurried along behind Caroline, and they arrived at the entrance to the restaurant just in time to see Allie jump into a cab and speed off.

Chapter Fifteen

Caroline was frantic, pacing the floor at Emily's condo as she checked her phone yet again. "Why won't Allie answer?" she asked. "Every phone call goes to voice mail, and she's not responding to texts either."

Brittany peered out the front window one more time. "It's like Chicago just swallowed her up, like she vanished into thin air."

Emily stifled a yawn. "I just made a pot of fresh coffee, ladies, and I don't want to make light of this situation, but it's three a.m. and I'm falling asleep." She was headed for the stairs when a cab pulled up in front of the building.

"Thank goodness! There she is." Caroline ran outside as Allie stumbled out of the taxi.

"Currlyne," Allie slurred, "I'm outta cash, and I told thish nice man you'd pay 'im."

Caroline looked at the meter and sucked in her breath. "Oh, Allie, that's a huge tab, and I don't think I have enough…"

Caroline had no choice but to ask Emily. She sprinted back into the house, trying to calm her rapidly beating heart. "Allie promised the driver we'd pay him, and—"

"Say no more." Emily grabbed her wallet from her bag sitting on the coffee table and went outside to pay the fare. Caroline followed closely behind. Emily added on a generous tip and waved the cabbie away, and with Emily on one side and Caroline on the other, they helped Allie stagger into the house.

"Where have you been?" Caroline demanded. "We were worried sick!"

"Part-ee!"Allie laughed and then coughed and gagged. "Clozhed down sevrull barz."

Caroline shook her head and realized Allie would just have to sleep it off. They could talk in the morning—much later in the morning—when Allie was sober. And probably hung over.

She and Emily helped Allie up the stairs and into the guest room. Allie collapsed on the bed and was instantly asleep. Caroline looked sympathetically at her sister, removed Allie's shoes, and covered her with a blanket. Caroline didn't know if what she felt was exhaustion or relief, but when she glimpsed her pale complexion in the dresser mirror, she admitted she'd been scared out of her wits. "Emily, if you don't mind, I think I'll stay up a while longer, maybe read a magazine or something. My stomach's all tied in knots, and I doubt I could sleep anyway."

Emily nodded assent. "I'll just say good night then."

Caroline turned off the light and quietly closed the door. She couldn't help going over and over in her mind the scene with Mark at the bar earlier. *Why was Mark so cold to Allie, and why*—why?—*was he with Misty?* Suddenly Misty's 'desperate' shopping trip to Chicago made sense.

****

It was early afternoon when Caroline finally peeked into the guest room. "Allie?"

"Yeah," Allie croaked.

Caroline opened the door and stepped inside. "You look terrible."

"Gee thanks." Allie lifted herself up on one elbow long enough to peer at her reflection in the dresser mirror, and then collapsed back onto the pillow. She was pale with dark circles under her eyes, hair plastered to her head, clothes wrinkled and covered in stains from spills of tropical beverages. She blinked and looked away as Caroline opened the curtains, letting in the sunlight. "I think I drank too much."

"Ya *think?*" Caroline felt bad about the emotional state Allie was in, but she wasn't so sympathetic about Allie's bender. She handed her a bottle of water. "Here, drink this. You need an aspirin?"

"Ugh, no." She twisted open the bottle and took a couple of tentative sips.

Caroline sat down on the edge of the bed. "So just how many bars did you close down last night?"

"I lost count after three."

"All by yourself?"

"Of course not." Allie tried to smile, but then grabbed her forehead in pain. "The bars were full of men ready to buy me drinks, and I had the company of the cabdriver, too." She moaned. "Oh, my head!"

Caroline frowned at her sister. She always knew Allie could be overly dramatic, but last night's bar crawl exceeded any stunt she'd ever pulled. "That's crazy, Allie."

Allie eased herself down onto the fluffy pillow. "I got dumped and I got stupid."

"You ran up a huge bill with the cabdriver, too, which Emily paid, by the way."

Allie frowned. "Sorry."

Caroline didn't think her sister was in any condition to make amends right now. "I've got to get back to Indy. I know you don't feel well, but you need to come with me, put some distance between you and Mark Townsend." She got up and started putting her belongings into her overnight bag.

"I can't go home right now." Allie moaned as she carefully shifted her head to ease the pain.

Caroline zipped up her bag. "I'm sure Emily and Sara and Brittany would be glad to have you stay, but I don't think it's a good idea. And please don't tell me you're going to try to contact Mark again."

Allie's eyes filled with tears as she slowly sat up. "No, he made himself pretty clear last night."

Caroline felt terrible for her sister, but Allie had been so secretive about what had actually happened with her and Mark, and now she wanted answers. "All this started July third. You have to tell me what happened."

Allie grabbed a tissue and blew her nose. "He told me he thought I was getting too serious."

"That doesn't sound unreasonable."

Allie put the chilled water bottle to her throbbing temples. "I told him I was falling in love with him."

Caroline groaned, her worst fear realized. "Love? You barely knew him, Allie."

"But we'd spent practically every waking minute together since we met. He told me...or he let me believe..." Allie broke off with a sigh. "He said he was too worried about his dad's money problems to get involved in a relationship." Allie laughed a humorless laugh. "Can you believe that? Money problems? We live in a tiny house, no money, no school..."

Caroline gave that some thought. "It sounds like a lame excuse, like he wasn't really that into you."

"Starving artist—that's what he called me," Allie said with tears streaming down her face.

"Oh." Caroline was finally seeing the big picture, and she didn't like the view.

"I just thought he needed more time," Allie said with a sniffle, "but I guess what he really needed was someone to bankroll his family's debt."

"And when he heard the name Benedict, he thought that was you. Then he found out you didn't have a trust fund, so he moved on to a richer woman—Misty Peterson."

Allie wiped away tears with the back of her hand. "As strongly as we felt about each other, I still hoped..."

Caroline put up her hand to stop the rest of that thought. "I think you should've believed him when he said he wasn't ready for a commitment. And even if you *didn't* believe him, his cyber-silence spoke volumes."

"But I *know* he felt something for me!" Allie exclaimed.

Caroline reached over and patted her sister's shoulder. "Maybe. But it wasn't enough." She gave Allie a hug. "I'm sorry you got hurt, Allie, but you have to let him go."

Allie watched as her sister slung her bag over her shoulder and stepped to the door. "You're leaving? I'm upset here."

"I've got to deal with another problem now, Allie. Richard and Misty."

Allie narrowed her eyes. "At least I had a relationship with Mark," Allie mumbled. "Not like you pining over Richard and never saying a word to him about it."

Caroline's mouth dropped open. "Maybe I don't wear my heart on my sleeve like you do, but the situation is entirely different. I can't tell him. He's engaged!"

"To a woman who's cheating on him!"

Caroline sighed. "I never did think Misty loved Richard, but until last night I had no idea how far her dishonesty went."

"Now you know, so what are you going to do about it?" Allie demanded.

Every muscle in Caroline's body tensed up at the thought of either confronting Misty or ratting her out to Richard. She shook her head. "I'm staying out of it. He and Misty will just have to work this out on their own."

Allie slowly stood up and steadied herself on the nightstand. "But what if they don't? Richard has a right to know what his fiancée's been up to! With my boy—ex-boyfriend, no less." Tears came to her eyes again. "Car, admit it, you're in love with Richard."

Caroline caught a glimpse of her steely-eyed look in the mirror, and didn't like what she saw. "Believe me, Allison, if I thought telling him would change anything…"

Allie grabbed her sister and pulled her into a tight hug. "This sucks!"

Slowly Caroline pulled away. "I know." She readjusted the bag on her shoulder. "You sure you don't want to come home with me?"

Allie shook her head, so Caroline closed the door

behind her and went downstairs. Brittany was flipping through a magazine, and Emily was poring over some MLS listings on her phone.

"So what happened last night?" Emily asked.

Brittany put her magazine aside. "Yeah, is Allie okay?"

Caroline shook her head and slumped into an arm chair. "The condensed version is that Mark told Allie in Indianapolis that he didn't want a relationship with her, but she refused to believe him and followed him up here."

Emily pointed to Caroline's packed bag. "Are you leaving?"

"I have to be at work tomorrow, but Allie wants to stay. I told her okay, as long as she promises to stay away from Mark."

"Allison is welcome to stay," Emily said. "We'll take good care of her."

Brittany jumped to her feet. "Yeah, I'll take her shopping, to museums, a concert, whatever. I can cheer her up! She'll forget about what's-his-name in no time!"

Caroline smiled. "Thanks, Brittany. She's lucky to have a friend like you. Either Mom or I can come get her next weekend, or Allie can take the Megabus home if she's ready before then. Maybe a few days of shopping and sightseeing will do her good." She fumbled in her purse for her keys.

"Caroline," Emily said, "who was that woman Mark was dancing with last night? You seemed to know her."

Caroline rolled her eyes. "Don't get me started on Misty Peterson."

"Peterson? Like Peterson's Coffee Emporium Peterson?"

Caroline found her keys and pulled them out of her handbag. "One and the same. And she's engaged to Richard, my boss and Sharlene's brother. One big happy, dysfunctional family."

Chapter Sixteen

When Caroline got to her desk at work the next morning, her phone's message light was blinking. Before she could pick it up and dial into voice mail, the phone rang.

"Richard Meadows' office. May I—"

"Caroline, it's Misty."

She braced herself. "Richard's not in yet, Misty. Did you try his cell phone?"

"I didn't call to talk to Richard, I have something to say to you, you miserable b—"

"Misty!" Caroline was about to hang up.

"Did you tell Richard you saw me in Chicago?" Misty shouted into the receiver.

Caroline reluctantly put the phone back to her ear. "I haven't talked to Richard."

"And you'd better not. If you know what's good for you."

Caroline would have laughed at the veiled threats if it weren't for the fact that Misty was hurting Richard. That wasn't funny. "Richard already knew you were in Chicago, Misty, so maybe you should tell your fiancé about your 'shopping' trip yourself."

"This is none of your business, Caroline. I was out with friends, dancing, that's all."

Caroline pulled an antacid out of her desk drawer and swallowed it. "It looked pretty friendly all right, dancing so close with my sister's boyfriend."

"I *said* he's a friend! And don't play innocent with me, Caroline Benedict. I've seen how you look at Richard!"

Caroline gulped. Had she been that obvious? "Look at him? He's my boss." True, but who was she kidding? Certainly not Misty.

"Listen, Miss Smarty-Pants with the fancy college degree, just do your work and keep your eyes to yourself, because he's engaged to me!"

Caroline held the receiver away from her ear as Misty spewed verbal bile. When she thought she could get a word in, she said, "Really, Misty, why do you care? You can't tell me you love Richard, especially after dancing cheek-to-cheek with Mark Townsend!"

"Stay out of my business, Caroline! Richard could never love someone as mousy as you anyway, so don't even think about trying to break us up."

If only I could *break you two up.* But she cringed at the thought that she hadn't kept her feelings for Richard better hidden. She didn't care in the least about offending Misty, but she would never dream of making Richard uncomfortable.

Caroline reverted to her business tone. "Is there a message?"

"The message is, if you tell Richard about seeing me in Chicago, I'll see to it that Sharlene has you thrown out of that office so fast it'll make your head spin!" And with that she slammed down the phone.

"Nice talking to you, too," Caroline said into the dead line. *Could Misty have Sharlene fire me?* Or worse yet, could she convince Richard to end their friendship? Maybe.

The office phone rang again. She picked it up and checked the caller ID, and then with a sigh of relief said, "Good morning, Mrs. Meadows."

Richard arrived a couple of hours later and stopped by her desk. "Any calls?" he asked.

Caroline thought about the nasty call from Misty and nearly gagged, but said as professionally as possible, "Misty. And your grandmother."

"Thanks. Anyone else—like business? I've already spoken to Grandmother, and Misty can wait."

"I sent you an email with the rest of the messages."

"Can I talk to you a minute, Caroline?"

She followed him into his office, feeling her pulse race.

Richard closed the door and sat down on the edge of his large mahogany desk to face her. "Did you accept that other job offer yet?"

Caroline felt herself sway, so she quickly sat down in the nearest chair. "No. You asked me to wait so I, uh, was waiting…" She stopped a minute to clear her head. This was the moment she'd been dreading. "I'm going to have to respond soon or lose out on the opportunity."

Richard nervously clicked and un-clicked a ballpoint pen. "Well, I know we had an agreement to re-evaluate your position and salary, and I'm ashamed of myself for not doing this sooner like I promised, but what with the wedding…" Richard threw the pen on his desk. "I had a long conversation with Grandmother last night."

Caroline liked Adele Meadows. She appreciated her common sense approach to life, and they had a mutual dislike of Misty Peterson. "Okay…"

"You probably know that Sharlene and I each own

forty percent of this company, but Grandmother owns the other twenty percent."

Caroline didn't know that. Her pulse quickened, but her throat went dry and all she could do was nod.

"Caroline, you're such an asset to me—uh, well, to the company—and I just don't want to lose you or have to train another assistant. So I went to Grandmother, and between us we have enough stock to overrule Sharlene."

Caroline could barely contain the butterflies in her stomach. "Overrule her? On what?"

"Personnel issues, finances, that sort of thing. Anyway, I'd like to finally offer you that raise and benefits that I promised you a year ago. I—we—hope you'll agree to stay on here at Meadows Advertising."

Caroline's mouth dropped open, and for a moment she couldn't say a word as her eyes welled up with tears of joy. Then she realized Richard was waiting for an answer and she hesitated. This was what she truly wanted in her heart, but her head was telling her she was asking for trouble. Unrequited love for one's soon-to-be-married boss was not conducive to a good working relationship. But Caroline's heart overrode her head. "*Yes!* Yes, of course, I'd love to stay."

"I can offer you a salary competitive to what Charing Cross offered, full benefits and a 401K. And a real office. Sharlene's empty one." His eyes twinkled. "Feel free to redecorate it."

Caroline wanted to hug Richard, but she remembered what Misty had just said—her feelings were too obvious—so she restrained herself in an attempt to appear professional. "Thank you, Richard. When do I start—officially?"

Richard smiled the smile that Caroline found so irresistible. "Next week, at the beginning of the pay period on Monday. You'll be doing most of the same things you've been doing, but there may be a few added responsibilities to go along with the title of Executive Assistant to the CEO. Okay?"

Caroline smiled back at him. "Yes. *Very* okay."

"One more thing, just to complicate matters," Richard said as he pointed to his desk calendar. "I have to leave town on Sunday for the Guys' Golf Getaway in Vegas. From there I'm off to Los Angeles to meet with the production company that's filming that series of TV commercials for Truitt. I probably won't be back till the first week in August. That's why I have to have an assistant here who's familiar with the business. Do you feel comfortable with that?"

"Of course. I may have a few questions, but I can text or email, right?"

"Right." Richard opened the door for Caroline. He offered his hand in mock formality before she walked out, and when she returned his handshake, he held her hand a bit longer than necessary. "Welcome aboard, Miss Benedict."

****

Susan glanced at the clock on the dashboard as she drove down College Avenue.

"Mom's got a D-A-T-E!" Megan had teased her this morning as she tried to decide what to wear.

"Hush, Megan, I'm nervous enough as it is." Susan straightened her multi-colored blouse, made sure her pink capris were not creased in back, and checked her makeup one last time. "I haven't been on a date since the Bush administration—the first Bush—so I hope I remember how to do this."

"Patrick's nice, Mom. Just relax."

Relax, Susan told herself as she drove into the parking lot. *It's only lunch.*

Patrick was waiting for her inside the door. He smiled at her, that twinkling smile that lit up the corners of his eyes, the one that had so captivated her when they first met.

He extended his hand in greeting. "I don't know about you, but I'm famished. Shall we eat outside?"

Susan nodded, and followed him to a table on the patio. It was a small, casual bistro, bustling with the lunch crowd. "I guess professors are able to take leisurely lunches in the summertime," she said as a waiter led them to a table.

"That's one of the perks." Patrick held her chair for her and then sat down across from her. "The food here's good," he said as the waiter handed her a menu. "It's close to campus, so Brandon and I eat lunch here a lot."

As she looked over the menu, she couldn't quite tell if the twitters in her stomach were nerves or excitement. Either way, a light lunch was definitely in order.

"Could you bring us some iced tea?" Patrick said to the waiter. "Do you know what you'd like to eat?" he asked Susan.

She nodded and handed the menu to the waiter. "Fruit salad, please."

"Sounds good," Patrick said to Susan as he turned to the waiter, "but I'll have the burger and fries." He winked at Susan.

Susan barely knew this man, yet they had

discovered so many mutual interests that talking to Patrick was like being with an old friend. "I love that you teach classic literature. To me, that's like not working."

He moved his silverware aside as the waiter set their iced teas on the table. "Yep, everything from Austen to Wordsworth."

Susan crossed her arms on the table in front of her and leaned in. "I love Jane Austen!"

Patrick laughed as he took a swig of tea. "Spoken like a true English teacher. What's your favorite?"

Susan absent-mindedly stirred sweetener into her tea while she thought. "Everyone always says *Pride and Prejudice*, or *Emma*, but I really think I prefer *Sense and Sensibility*."

"Interesting. Why?"

Susan smiled and set the spoon on the table. "Probably it's those three daughters."

He laughed. "Your girls keep you pretty busy, I guess."

"Well, yes, at least Allie and Megan do. They're both at loose ends this summer." Susan's eyes drifted off for a moment while she thought about the emotional upheaval her girls were going through, but then she snapped back. "Caroline's pretty self-sufficient, so I don't usually worry about her."

"I haven't actually met Allie yet, but Brandon talks about her all the time, about how gifted she is."

Susan started laughing and almost choked on her beverage. "Gifted? Does that mean high maintenance? Because she is, that's for sure. Brandon's a love to put up with all her drama."

"He's a good guy, and I'm pretty sure he really

cares about her," Patrick said as he took her hand across the table. "I mean *really* cares."

Susan suspected as much, but she also was pretty sure Allie was too involved in her budding romance with Mark to give Brandon more than a cursory glance. "Believe it or not, Allie isn't the only talented daughter I have. Megan's an excellent artist, and Caroline writes beautifully when she allows herself to. She also has the ability to find any grammatical or punctuation mistake ever written. That's one reason she's so valuable to Richard."

"Hmmm, Richard. I think I remember Phillips saying something about him," Patrick mused. "Her boss?"

Susan nodded. "Caroline really admires him. More than admires him, I'm afraid." Susan shook her head but allowed her hand to stay intertwined with Patrick's. "Tell me, do you have children?"

"Here are your orders, sir," said the waiter as he set their lunches in front of them. "Do you need anything else?"

Patrick looked up at the waiter and squeezed Susan's hand before releasing it. "Thanks. I think we're fine for now." He poured a glob of ketchup onto the side of his plate next to the fries and shoved the bottle aside. He glanced over at Susan and said, "You were asking about children."

Susan stopped mid-bite when she realized her mistake. "I'm sorry. I guess I overstepped."

Patrick swirled a fry in the ketchup. "No, it's fine, it's just that it never seemed to be the right time for us to start a family. First our careers, then buying a house, fixing it up. My wife was from a huge family, and every year it seemed like one of her siblings had a new baby, so we didn't miss having our own. Then she got sick."

Susan set her fork down. "I'm so sorry, I didn't mean to…"

He looked her in the face and smiled, a trace of sorrow in his voice. "We had a good life, and I don't regret a thing."

"I guess I didn't realize how different things were for me. Getting divorced was painful, but what you went through…" Susan shook her head.

Patrick reached across the table and took Susan's hand once again. "I'm ready to move on," he said.

****

Susan's cell phone rang while she was in the backyard pulling weeds in her flower garden. "Hi, Em! How's Allie doing?"

"Not too well, actually. Brittany can barely get her out of the bedroom. She doesn't seem interested in eating, and only came out last night to watch a DVD downstairs with Brit. Then she went right back up to bed."

Susan sighed as she tossed her trowel aside. "It's only been a few days, Emily. Caroline finally told me what happened with her and Mark. Her heart's been broken, so she'll probably wallow for a while. Just give her some time and she'll snap out of it."

"Well, okay, if you think so. I'll call you back in a few days."

"Thanks Emily. Let me know if I need to come get her."

Susan had no more hung up with Emily and picked up her trowel again than the phone rang a second time.

She glanced at the caller ID. "Hi, Brandon. How are you?"

"Fine, thanks. Well, not so fine really. Susan, I've been trying to reach Allie, and she's not answering her phone. Is she coming back any time soon? I'm concerned about—about the practice sessions she's missing."

Susan could hear his real emotions in his voice. "Thanks for calling, Brandon. No, Allie probably won't be back for a week or so. She and Mark had a falling out up in Chicago, and she's mourning Allie-style. Anyway, I'll have her call you first thing when she gets home."

"Well, all right, but if you talk to her, could you ask her to call me? And Susan?" he said before she could hang up, "Is she really okay?"

Susan wished Allie could see how much *this* man cared about her.

****

Caroline picked up the ringing phone. "Richard Meadows's office."

"Caroline! I'm so happy to hear the news, that you accepted Richard's offer."

Caroline was still pinching herself at her good fortune. "I hear I have you to thank, Mrs. Meadows. I haven't told my family yet, but I'm sure they'll be pleased."

"Just a warning, dear. Sharlene and Misty are on the warpath. The two of them can be a devilish force of nature, you know."

Don't I know. Caroline hung up the phone and felt a bit queasy. She glanced at the clock and realized it was well past quitting time, so she turned off her computer, grabbed her handbag out of the bottom desk drawer, and headed to the reception area. Even Lucy had already gone home.

On the drive home, she went over and over her day—the harassing phone call from Misty, getting the job offer she'd dreamed about, and Adele Meadows's warning about Misty and Sharlene. Five miles of rush hour traffic coupled with worry didn't solve anything. She walked into the house and tossed her handbag on the coffee table. "Mom? Megan? Anyone home?" Honey came bounding in from the kitchen, her tail wagging. Caroline reached down and patted the dog's head. "Mom, I've got great news!" At least she hoped everyone would think it was great.

Susan appeared from the kitchen, a dishtowel in her hand, the smell of fresh lasagna wafting through the air. "Hi, Car. What news?"

"Mom, Richard offered me a job today!"

Susan put her hands on her hips. "You already have a job with Richard—one that doesn't pay very well. What about that agency you interviewed with awhile back? Did you hear from them?"

Caroline went to the picture window and began adjusting the curtains that were already in alignment. "Yes." She swallowed hard and turned to face her mother. "I just didn't feel comfortable there. It's so big and, well, corporate. But this morning Richard counteroffered and I accepted. I'll be his assistant with a title and office, plus salary and benefits."

Susan tilted her head to one side. "Caroline, is that wise? Turning down that other agency?"

Caroline looked away. "I don't know what you mean, Mom. I accepted the best offer I received."

"You accepted the offer from Richard."

Caroline sat down on the sofa and stared up at the ceiling. "I know how to be professional, Mom. I can do this."

"I know you can do the job, but what about the emotional baggage? Maybe you'd be better off working in an office where"—Susan cleared her throat—"where Richard *isn't!*"

Caroline's shoulders slumped. "I'll handle it, Mom. Don't worry."

"That's just it, Caroline. I do worry. This is going to be hard on you." Susan wiped away a tear on Caroline's cheek, gave her a quick hug, and whispered in her ear, "Congratulations on your new job."

Megan walked into the family room just in time to see her mother and sister hugging. "Hi, Car. Heard about your new job!"

Caroline looked at Megan in surprise. "What? How?"

"Sharlene. And she told me she already told Dad," Megan said over her shoulder as she headed to the kitchen. "When's dinner, Mom?"

"News travels fast," Susan said. "I guess the only person who doesn't know is Allie."

"By the way, have you heard from her?" Caroline asked.

"No, but Emily's keeping me up to date. I guess Allie's still grieving over Mark."

****

Susan's cell phone rang, waking her out of a sound sleep. She glanced at the bedside clock which read 2:00 a.m. before drowsily checking the caller ID. "Emily?" she said hoarsely.

"Susan, I hope I'm not overreacting, but Allie's not doing well. She doesn't eat, she's pale, and she hardly comes out of the bedroom."

"I'll try calling her again in the morning," Susan said with a yawn.

"No, don't call. You've got to come up here as soon as possible."

Susan heard the worry in Emily's voice and was instantly wide awake. "How about first thing in the morning?"

"The sooner the better."

Susan stared at the phone for a minute, then felt panic rising in her throat. This didn't sound like Allie's usual melodramatic reaction to a romantic breakup. She had to get to Chicago right away.

Chapter Seventeen

Susan was running on adrenaline. She'd never gotten back to sleep after Emily's phone call, so at first light she got up and got ready to make the drive to Chicago. She tossed her handbag in her car's passenger seat, concern for Allie's health weighing heavily on her mind. Megan followed her out, Honey skipping playfully alongside.

"Mom, when will you be back? I want to go to the mall this afternoon."

Susan gave her daughter a quick hug and got into the driver's seat. She adjusted the rearview mirror and checked the gas gauge. "Not today, Megan, unless you can get Caroline to take you. By the time I get to Chicago, get Allie loaded up and start back, I'll probably hit evening rush hour. Did you feed the dog?"

"Yes, I fed her," Megan groaned in that juvenile tone Susan hated.

"Then if there's nothing else, I've got to go. I need to get gas, which means I'll be even later getting on the freeway. If you need anything, call Caroline." Susan got into the car and waved at Megan as she drove off.

She'd left early enough in the morning that she made good time to Chicago, especially since she was driving about eight miles over the speed limit all the way. It was noontime, when most people were at their offices, so Susan easily found a parking space in front of Emily's condo building. Emily let her in with a worried look on her face.

"Susan, I'm so glad you're here," Emily told her with a quick hug, as she waved her up the stairs to the guest room.

Susan opened the door and gasped. Allie looked terrible, extremely pale and thinner than usual. But what worried Susan the most was that her eyes had that dull, glassy look she always got as a child when she was running a fever.

Susan went to her daughter and hugged her while feeling her forehead. "Allie, why didn't you call and tell me you were this sick?"

"I don't know," Allie groaned. "I didn't want to worry you." She gently massaged her right side and winced. "It's probably just the flu."

"This isn't flu season, Allie. Any other symptoms besides the pain and fever?"

Allie shook her head and lay back down on the bed with a groan. Susan wasted no time gathering up her daughter's clothes and throwing them in the open suitcase on the floor. Emily took her cue from Susan's urgency and went to the bathroom to collect Allie's toiletries.

"Emily," Susan called out, "I need to get Allie to a doctor."

"Do you want to take her to an emergency room here in Chicago?"

"Maybe I should drive her back to Belford and take her to St. Mary's where her dad's insurance will pay."

"Stop talking about me like I'm not here," Allie said.

"All right." Susan closed the suitcase and turned to

her daughter. "Do you think you can make the drive back to Indianapolis, or shall I take you to a hospital here in Chicago?"

Allie forced herself to a sitting position on the edge of the bed and slid into her sandals. "Take me home."

"Wait here," Susan told Allie. She picked up the bag and carried it out to her car, Emily right behind her. Susan locked the bag in the trunk while Emily arranged a pillow in the back seat.

"Susan, I'm really sorry. I thought Allie was just being dramatic about her breakup with Mark. If I'd known she was this sick…"

"Don't blame yourself, Em. You had no way of knowing, especially if Allie didn't want you to. I'll call you from the hospital when I get a diagnosis." Susan saw the worried look on Emily's face. "Please don't feel guilty. You've been a great friend."

Emily and Susan went back inside and helped Allie walk down the stairs, one on each side of her. Susan was alarmed at how weak her daughter appeared to be.

"When was the last time you ate anything?" Susan asked her.

"Yesterday." If possible, Allie looked even sicker at the mere thought of food. "Some soup, I think."

They got her settled into the back seat of the car, seatbelt loosely fastened, her head propped on the pillow. Susan jumped behind the wheel and waved goodbye to Emily as she sped off.

She managed to avoid the worst of the Chicago traffic getting out of town. Once she was on I-65 in Indiana, despite knowing she shouldn't use her phone while driving, she pulled it out of her bag, scrolled down the list, and found Dr. Li's office number. She pressed CALL, set it next to her on speaker, and waited for a receptionist to pick up.

"Hello, this is Susan Benedict, and I'm calling for my daughter Allison. We're driving back to Indianapolis from Chicago, and Allison is quite ill." She paused to let the receptionist pull up Allie's chart. "She has a fever, no appetite, and abdominal pain. No, I'm sorry, I didn't think to check her actual temperature. Yes, I'll hold."

She waited several minutes, trying to keep an eye on Allie sleeping fitfully in the back seat, and watch the road at the same time.

"Yes, I'm here. Okay, thank you, I'll do that."

Next she pressed Caroline on speed dial. Voice mail. With a groan, Susan left Caroline a message, telling her that Allie's illness was real and they were headed to St. Mary's Hospital in Indianapolis, expecting to arrive about five o'clock. Susan disconnected the phone and concentrated on her driving. She glanced back at Allie. The speed limit was sixty-five but she set the cruise control at seventy-three and hoped for the best.

A little more than two hours and no speeding ticket later, Susan pulled into a parking spot in front of St. Mary's Emergency Room. Her back ached, and her foot was cramped from pressing so hard on the accelerator.

"Allie, are you awake? We're at the hospital." Susan helped ease her out of the car, through the automatic glass doors and into the nearest chair. She proceeded to the reception desk and spoke to a nurse inside. "This is my daughter, Allison Benedict, a patient of Dr. Tina Li. I think you're expecting her?"

The nurse thumbed through some files on her desk.

"Yes, the doctor's office called. Dr. Li wishes to be notified as soon as Allison's been examined by the ER doctor."

Susan felt a wave of relief as the nurse got a wheelchair to take Allie back to the examining rooms. She sank into a chair, exhausted and worried, and pulled out her phone to dial Caroline again, who picked up this time.

"Caroline, hi, we're at St. Mary's and the nurse has taken Allie back to see the ER doctor. Is Megan okay?"

"Mom, just how sick is Allie? Do I need to come to the hospital? And yes, Megan's fine, just a little mad that I didn't take her to the mall."

Susan was exhausted and could certainly have used Caroline's help, but she hesitated. "Until they figure out what's wrong with her, there's really nothing you can do here. Just stay with Megan and I'll call you when I know more."

"Mom, Brandon called me this afternoon, checking on Allie again, and I told him how sick she was. He's been calling every hour since."

Susan sighed. "I don't think Allie will be playing piano for a few days, but if he calls again, tell him—well, I don't know what to tell him. Caroline, I have to go, the nurse is here."

"Mrs. Benedict, it appears your daughter has an inflamed appendix and the doctor's advising surgery. I called Dr. Li and she's on her way." The nurse paused to let the news sink in. "We need you to go around to Admissions and fill out some paperwork. Allison already signed the consent forms, so we'll be prepping her for surgery shortly."

Susan suddenly regretted telling Caroline not to

come. Right now she felt so alone and completely helpless. She walked numbly toward Admissions, took a number, and had a seat in the waiting area. Nearly an hour later, the admissions clerk finally called her to the counter.

"Hello, I'm Allison Benedict's mother, and the doctor is advising surgery. Appendicitis, I think." Susan fumbled nervously in her purse. "I don't have her insurance card with me. Can you go ahead and start the paperwork?"

"Not without your card," the woman said.

Susan tried to push down her fear and frustration. "But this is an emergency. I'm sure when I get home…"

"Ms. Benedict, we cannot admit your daughter to St. Mary's without proof of insurance. If you'd like to take her to Wishford…"

Susan cringed at the thought of taking her daughter to the hospital for the uninsured in downtown Indianapolis. "Allison's father is CEO of Truitt Wellness Corporation here in Belford. Daniel Benedict. Perhaps you've heard of him?"

The woman narrowed her eyes at Susan. "Yes, of course we've heard of him," she said. "But we can't just take your word for it. We need proof of insurance."

"Fine. I'll call him."

Susan had to stop and think a moment to remember Daniel's office number, and then she realized it was late in the day. She said a silent prayer that Daniel and his assistant were still there. Otherwise she'd be forced to call Sharlene to get Daniel's cell number, and she doubted that conversation would go well. Susan groaned as she listened to a recorded speech and was electronically offered several options to push. "Daniel Benedict please," she said, once a human finally came on the line. Some clicking noises were followed by an interminable wait as generic music played in the background. Susan tapped her foot impatiently.

"Mr. Benedict's office. May I help you?"

Susan breathed a sigh of relief, glad she didn't get his voice mail. "Chloe, this is Susan Benedict. I need to speak to Daniel immediately."

"Just a moment, Susan, I'll see if he's available," said the well-trained Chloe.

"Chloe," Susan cut in, "you tell Daniel this is an emergency. His daughter Allison is at St. Mary's in need of surgery, and they won't admit her without proof of insurance." Chloe put her on hold.

Almost immediately Daniel was on the line. "What's this about Allie?"

"Daniel, thank goodness. Allie has appendicitis and needs surgery, but *they*—" she said loudly, looking at the admissions clerk "—need your insurance information."

Susan turned to the clerk. "He wants to speak to you." She handed the woman her cell.

She saw the woman scribbling numbers on a pad and furiously entering information into her computer. "Yes, Mr. Benedict, I have it all now. Thank you." She hung up the phone and handed it back to Susan. "It's all been taken care of, Ms. Benedict. I'll notify the ER that they can move her up to surgery when they're ready. And Mr. Benedict says he's on his way."

"Thank you." Susan turned on her heel and stormed off.

Sheer exhaustion threatened to overtake her. It had

been a long, frightening day after a sleepless night, and she was bone-weary. She leaned back in the chair in the surgery waiting area and closed her eyes. From nowhere, she felt an arm around her shoulders. She opened her eyes to see Patrick sitting next to her.

"Hi," she said in surprise.

"Hi, yourself. I thought you could use some moral support."

"How did you even know I was here?"

Patrick gave her shoulders a squeeze, and Susan felt the comfort she'd been missing.

"Caroline," Patrick told her.

Susan smiled. "Caroline. Of course. Always looking out for everyone else."

Patrick looked into Susan's exhausted face. "I'm here to offer any help I can."

"Just having a friend is help enough." Susan leaned into his arms. "I've been really scared, Patrick. Allie is so sick."

"I know what it's like to wait helplessly in a hospital." He pulled her closer to him, and she rested her head on his shoulder.

****

Caroline rushed into the surgery waiting room, found her mother, and threw her arms around her. "Are you okay?"

Susan nodded. "I am now that you're here."

"I called a few people," Caroline said. "And they all wanted to come. To be here for Allie, and for you." Caroline tilted her head toward Brandon.

"Patrick's here, thanks to you," Susan said. "He just stepped out, offered to get me some magazines, like that's going to distract me." She searched the waiting room. "Where's Megan?"

"I sent her to the cafeteria for coffee and sandwiches, which Dad paid for," Caroline hurried to add. "Did you remember to call Emily?"

"Yes, I called her about an hour ago. She was concerned about Allie, but not surprised, considering the symptoms."

"So Patrick's getting reading material, Megan's gone for food, and I saw Dad heading over to the finance office." Caroline was relieved when her mother finally allowed a smile to creep onto her face. "Is there anything I can do for you, Mom?"

Susan eyed Brandon and lowered her voice. "Maybe distract poor Brandon. He looks sicker than Allie."

Brow furrowed, Brandon paced back and forth between the lounge area and the water fountain in the hall, watching anxiously every time a door opened.

Caroline went over to him and tapped him on the shoulder. "Brandon, it's okay. Allie's in good hands."

"Oh, I know," he said, but the grim look quickly returned to his face as he went back to pacing.

Caroline admired Brandon's brave face, but until they had word about Allie, there was nothing else she could do for him. So she went back and sat down next to her mother. "Dad called Sharlene," Caroline said as she stretched her legs out and rested her head on the back of the plastic chair. "She expressed as much concern as she's capable of, I guess, but only after she let Dad have it for not showing up to some cocktail party."

Caroline's cell rang and she glanced at the caller ID. "Richard?"

"Hey, Caroline, Sharlene called me. She said Allie's sick. What's up?"

Caroline sighed. "Appendicitis. She's in surgery right now. But don't worry about the office, I'll…"

"The office can wait. Take care of your family. I just wish I could be there with you, but Las Vegas is a long way from Indianapolis."

As surprised as Caroline was that Sharlene had bothered to notify her brother about Allie's illness, she appreciated Richard taking time from his vacation to check in. "Thanks for calling, Richard. I'll keep in touch." She disconnected the phone and stood silent a few moments before replacing it in her pocket.

Megan appeared, juggling several cups of hot coffee, half a dozen plastic-wrapped sandwiches, and a bakery bag. "Someone take this stuff!"

Caroline and Brandon both rushed over to help her, grabbing the drinks just as one of the cups of hot coffee was about to tip over.

"Thanks." Megan carefully set everything else down on a nearby coffee table. "I got some with cream and sugar and some black. I didn't know what anyone wanted."

"You did fine, Megs," Caroline assured her with a hug.

"There's sandwiches—mystery meat, vegetarian, whatever. They don't look too great, but I also bought some cookies that looked okay."

"I'm sure Mom's hungry, Megan, and who knows when anyone else ate. Thanks for doing this." Caroline got busy sorting out the sandwiches, cookies, and coffee, along with napkins and stir-sticks, so that everyone could help themselves.

Megan stood silently by as her sister took over her task. Finally she went and sat down next to her mother, arms folded across her chest, a scowl on her face.

After what seemed an interminable wait, Dr. Li came out. Susan hurried over, followed closely by Caroline and Brandon. Daniel ambled across the floor and leaned against the hall door.

"Allison came through the surgery just fine," Dr. Li told them, "but she's going to be in recovery for several hours. It might be better if everyone went home. It's too soon for her to have visitors anyway."

"I'm not leaving," Susan announced. "I'm staying until Allie's awake, and I can see for myself that she's okay. Caroline, why don't you take Megan home?"

"I'm not leaving either," Brandon said, planting his feet firmly, fists clenched at his sides.

"Oh, Brandon, that's not necessary," Susan said.

Brandon shook his head. "No, I'm staying."

"Do you want me to stay awhile longer?" Patrick asked, coming up behind her and wrapping his arms around her.

"You were so kind to come, Patrick, but I'll be fine." Susan gave his arm a squeeze, slowly relinquishing it.

"Well, Susan, it seems you have plenty of support, and Sharlene's texting me, so…" Daniel shrugged.

Susan eyed Daniel warily. "Thank you for helping out with…everything."

"I think I'll go on home and check back tomorrow," he said, yawning. "Caroline? What about you?"

"I'm taking Megan home, like Mom said. By the way, have you seen her?" Caroline looked around the waiting room when she realized she hadn't seen Megan in quite some time.

Daniel stretched his shoulders. "No, not for a couple of hours."

Caroline was concerned. "Where would she go?" she muttered under her breath. Her mom had enough to worry about, so she didn't mention to her that Megan was missing. Instead, she went down the hall and checked the women's restroom, but there was no sign of Megan. Next she walked down to the far end of the hall and searched the other waiting area. It was completely empty, and the TV wasn't even on, so no one had been in there for a while. She went over to the gift shop in case Megan was window-shopping, but she wasn't there either.

Caroline checked the wall clock and realized how late it was. *Where's Megan?* She sent her a text but got no reply. Caroline thought about all the chaos during the evening surrounding Allie's surgery, and realized she didn't know how or when her fifteen-year-old sister had gone missing. Just as she was about to call security, it hit her. *Patrick was there for Mom, I was consoling Brandon while he was pacing the floor, and Dad spent his time reading The Wall Street Journal. Megan must have felt scared and ignored.* Megan had a habit of hiding when she was upset and an idea occurred to Caroline.

"Dad!" Caroline caught up to Daniel as he was heading out the main entrance. "I still can't find Megan. I thought maybe..." Caroline's eyes darted around, scouting out her youngest sister. "Oh, thank goodness, there she is!" She pointed to Megan, leaning against the passenger door of Daniel's car.

"Hey, Megan, what are you doing out here?" Daniel walked casually over to his car and beeped open the doors like nothing was amiss.

Caroline wasn't surprised, but she turned her attention to Megan. "It's not safe to be out in a parking lot alone this time of night. You had me worried, Megs."

Megan turned to her father, her eyes pleading. "I wanted to know if I could go home with you. I've been waiting out here for eons."

Daniel shook his head. "Not tonight, Megan, Sharlene wouldn't be expecting you. Caroline said she'd take you home, didn't you, Car?"

Megan looked miserable, so Caroline tried to make light of Daniel's rejection. "Of course," she said, pulling Megan back as Daniel got into his car. He waved to them and drove off, leaving Caroline to walk a downcast Megan back into the hospital waiting area. "Dad shouldn't..." She sighed. "I'm sorry about Dad."

Megan shrugged.

"Are you ready to go home? Honey misses you, and she probably needs to go outside."

Megan brightened up a little at the mention of her dog.

****

After everyone had gone, Susan collapsed back into the waiting-room chair.

"Can I get you anything?" Brandon asked.

Susan shook her head and rested it on her arm.

Brandon looked tired but determined. "No, really, Susan, tell me something I can do to help, because if I just sit here I'll go crazy."

Susan looked closely at Brandon and realized he

was truly frightened. It was touching how much he cared about Allie. "Well, yes, I really could use some herbal tea," she said, hoping to make him feel useful. "And Brandon, thank you for being here and for being such a good friend, to all of us."

Brandon smiled stiffly and headed off to the cafeteria.

Chapter Eighteen

Susan had dozed off in the waiting room chair but awoke with a start when the attendant turned on the TV to the local early morning newscast. She looked around, disoriented, her brain in a fog. Then it all came rushing back to her in a matter of seconds. Allie's surgery!

Brandon had stayed until just before dawn when Susan finally convinced him to go home. Despite being bone-weary, she was too keyed up from the events of the previous twenty-four hours and couldn't relax. She'd tried reading a newspaper, then a magazine, but couldn't concentrate on the words. Then she'd tried various chairs and sitting positions, but nothing felt right. Finally she'd gotten comfortable in a chair leaning against the wall, propped her feet on a coffee table, and fell asleep for a few minutes. Now she was wide awake again.

A nurse came through the double doors and spoke quietly. "Ms. Benedict? Allison's awake. Would you like to come back?"

"Yes, thank you," Susan said. She stood and tried to stretch the kinks out of her back and neck. "How's she doing?"

"She awoke a few times in the night and experienced some pain, but Dr. Li ordered meds to be administered as needed. Allison should be comfortable enough to talk now."

"How soon can I take her home?"

"Probably in a day or two." The nurse led Susan through the double doors and down the hall to her daughter's private room. She had Daniel to thank for that.

Susan's knees felt weak when she saw her daughter lying in the hospital bed. Allie's face was ghost-white, and there were IVs, tubes, and bleeping machines everywhere. The TV was on, set to the same station as in the waiting area, the weather girl pointing to a map of hot daytime temperatures. Susan sat down on a chair next to Allie's bed and gently took her hand.

"Allie? It's Mom."

"Hi," Allie mumbled without opening her eyes.

"How do you feel?"

"Ready for a marathon."

Susan smiled. "Well, at least you haven't lost your sense of humor."

Allie drifted back to sleep. Susan watched TV on mute, read the medical literature lying around the room, strolled to the cafeteria for coffee and a newspaper, and chatted with nurses as they came and went from her daughter's room. Finally by noon, Allie woke up and asked for food.

"I haven't had anything to eat except soup for about three days," she told Susan.

A nurse stopped in to check Allie's pulse and blood pressure.

"It's a good sign that she's hungry, right?" Susan asked her.

"Just a liquid diet for today," the nurse replied. The food cart ambled down the corridor, the midday meal smelling divine even for institution food, but all they brought Allie was Jell-O and apple juice.

"Yum," Allie said, making a face.

The room phone rang. Allie painstakingly reached over to the nightstand next to the bed and picked it up with a facetious, "Post-surgical starvation room." She pointed to the phone and mouthed, "Caroline."

"It's okay, Car, Mom's here. Do whatever you need to do at work."

Allie had no more hung up the phone, groaning as she did so, than it rang again. "Hi Brittany." She chatted briefly with her, and this time Susan took the receiver and hung it up so Allie wouldn't have to stretch so far.

"No more phone calls," Allie said. "It hurts too much to reach over there." She slowly shifted her weight to face Susan. "Mom, you look almost as bad as I do. Why don't you go home and rest?"

Susan hesitated. "I hate to leave you."

"I'm fine. I've got all these nurses at my beck and call, and if you don't mind, I'd really like to nap for a while."

Susan nodded and picked up her purse from the table near the window. "This may surprise you, but Brandon was here most of the night." Susan watched for her daughter's reaction.

Allie lifted an eyebrow. "He was? Why?"

"Because he cares about you. He'd probably still be here if I hadn't insisted he go home. I'm sure he'll be back once you're up to having visitors."

Allie didn't respond but instead stared at the TV, still on mute. "Maybe I haven't given him enough credit," she finally said.

Susan fluffed the pillow behind Allie's neck.

"Well, I don't see Mark around here anywhere."

Allie nodded, and then closed her eyes and soon drifted off to sleep. Susan crept quietly out of the room. She told herself she was only going home for a quick shower and change of clothes, but once she got there, she lay down for a few minutes to "rest her eyes." She awoke hours later, found herself still in the same clothes from yesterday, now wrinkled, and her hair a tangled mess.

It was almost supper time when Susan got back to the hospital. She pushed the elevator button for the third floor, waited impatiently while it stopped on every floor, then hurried out as soon as the doors opened. "Allie!" she exclaimed.

Allie was walking up and down the corridor, escorted by a nurse and still attached to her IV. "I'm so sorry," Susan said, joining them. "I didn't mean to be gone this long. How are you doing?"

"Okay, I guess. But my stomach hurts where the incision is, and then she…" Allie tilted her head in the nurse's direction, "made me get out of bed and walk."

The nurse helped Allie back into her room and back into bed. "Ring if you need me."

Susan smiled at the nurse as she left the room and kissed Allie's forehead, relieved to see some color back in her cheeks. "Megan wanted to come, but I told her to wait till tomorrow. Caroline said something about Daniel owing Megan, so she's taking her to the mall this evening to buy school clothes. With his credit card."

Allie smiled. "That'll keep them both busy."

"Hello?" said a familiar voice.

Brandon was standing in the doorway, a beautiful

flower arrangement in his hands and a grin on his face. Allie motioned him in.

Brandon took a few hesitant steps into the room. "How are you feeling?"

"Better. Are those for me?"

Brandon nodded and came the rest of the way into the room. He set the flowers on the table near the window and adjusted them just so. "Can you see these over here?"

"They're beautiful. That was so sweet of you," Allie said with a smile.

Brandon blushed. "I'm just glad you're okay." He turned around from the window, and joked, "You have to get well because you're missing too much practice time!"

Allie started to laugh but grabbed her side in pain. "Ouch! Don't make me laugh. It hurts."

Brandon was all worried concern again. "I'll be serious then. Really, I just wanted to say a quick hello, so I'll leave you in your mom's capable hands."

"Thanks for coming," Allie said. "And thanks again for the flowers."

Susan took in the whole, brief interaction between Allie and Brandon and hoped she was seeing a shift in Allie's feelings toward him.

Allie watched as Brandon left the room. "It's like I've never really seen what a great guy he is," she told her mom.

****

Caroline logged off her company-issued laptop, straightened the desktop in her new office, and pulled her handbag out of the bottom desk drawer. It was mid-afternoon, but she was leaving early to get home and spend some time with Megan. Lucy had agreed to field Richard's business calls for the rest of the day. As she was about to turn off the lights, she heard Lucy's giggle in the hall.

"Delivery for Miss Caroline Benedict," Lucy announced loudly, walking into Caroline's office with a lovely bouquet of yellow roses.

"What in the world?"

Lucy was practically dancing with excitement. "These were just delivered! Hurry up and read the card."

Caroline couldn't imagine who would send her flowers. *Richard? Don't be silly. Dad? Unlikely.* Her curiosity piqued, she gingerly disentangled the card from where it lay nestled among the roses, and slowly opened it.

"What does it say?"

Caroline read and reread the card. "It says, 'From your secret admirer.' Huh?"

Lucy tossed her hands in the air. "That's it? No name?" She grabbed the card out of Caroline's hand. "What secret admirer?"

Caroline retrieved the card and carefully replaced it in the flower arrangement and shrugged. "Well, if I knew that, it wouldn't be a secret."

"Oh, I know!" Lucy said. "It's got to be that guy at the realty company that's always staring at you. What's his name, Jared?"

"Well if he wants to be more than a secret admirer, he'll just have to tell me so himself." Baffled, Caroline left the beautiful roses prominently displayed in their vase on her desk, turned off her lights, and closed the door.

****

Susan collapsed onto her bed in exhaustion after another long day at the hospital with Allie. It was too early to go to sleep, yet she couldn't keep her eyes open. And she needed to go back to the hospital early in the morning, so she reached over to set the alarm...

She didn't even realize she'd fallen asleep until she heard her phone ringing. In her dazed state, she had no idea where she'd left it, so she stumbled to her feet and began searching. Not in her handbag, not on the nightstand, not in the bed covers.

"Where's the phone?" she asked aloud in frustration. It quit ringing just as she realized it was on the floor next to her bed, where she must have dropped it. She checked the voice mail and smiled. Patrick.

"Hi Susan, I hope you're getting some rest. I just wanted to tell you I have a date tomorrow with not one but two very beautiful young ladies with blonde hair." Susan's eyebrow went up. "Well, of course one of them has four legs and a bushy tail, but hey... we'll all have a fine time at the Rosslyn Village Bark Park. You spend all the time you need with Allie and don't worry about Megan."

Susan laughed and disconnected the phone. *Patrick's taking Megan and Honey to the park tomorrow? How did that happen?*

She curled up on her bed and fell into a deep sleep, comforted by the knowledge that Patrick would take care of Megan.

****

Allie was sitting up in the hospital bed the next day, watching *All My Tomorrows*, when Susan poked her head in the door. She was relieved to see that Allie looked more like her old self. She was showered, had on a little bit of makeup, and had pulled her hair back into a ponytail. "How's the patient?"

Allie opened her mouth to answer, but at that moment, Dr. Li came into the room. Allie hurriedly muted the TV.

Dr. Li perused Allie's medical chart at the foot of her bed, making notations and nodding to herself as she checked off items. She replaced the chart and said, "Well, Allison, how are you feeling today?"

Allie shifted uncomfortably. "My incision is still tender, but I can walk by myself now. Can I *please* go home?"

Dr. Li examined Allie's stitches. "I think so, as long as your mother's there to help you. I don't want you pushing yourself too hard too soon."

"Don't worry, doctor," Susan said. "I'll take good care of her."

"Thank you, thank you!" Allie exclaimed, but winced in pain and curtailed her exuberance.

"I'll leave a prescription for pain meds at the nurse's station. Susan, be sure you fill it before you take her home." Dr. Li patted Allie's arm and left.

"What all shall we take with us?" Susan asked, surveying the room. A lot had accumulated in a mere forty-eight hours. There was the hastily packed bag she'd brought for Allie yesterday, filled with clean underwear, socks, and clothes to wear home; the flowers from Brandon; a potted plant from her dad and Sharlene; get-well cards from Megan, Caroline, Richard, Brittany, and one from Emily and Sara. Susan started gathering up the cards and stopped short. "Hey, when did this one arrive?"

"This morning," Allie said with a frown. "It's a generic *Get well soon* card, just signed Mark."

Susan flipped it open. "How did he even know you were sick?"

"Does it matter?" Allie asked.

Susan hated the look of hurt and disappointment on Allie's face. "Does it?"

Allie sighed. "Mark and I never had the relationship I fantasized about, Mom. He wouldn't even speak to me that night in Chicago." She shook her head, the tears springing to her eyes. "How could I have been such an idiot?"

Susan stepped to Allie's bedside and took her hand. "You weren't an idiot."

"But I was so sure it was the real thing. Even though Caroline kept warning me."

Susan gently hugged Allie, thinking what a run of bad luck her daughter had had this summer, but there was a knock on the half-open door, interrupting her unhappy thoughts.

"Come in," Allie called as Brandon pushed open the door.

Brandon looked around the room. "Going home today?"

Allie smiled and nodded. "Dr. Li just discharged me."

Susan turned her back to give them a little privacy, and took much longer than necessary to gather up the cards, flowers and toiletries, and place them on the rolling cart.

"Maybe it won't be long before you can get back to practicing the piano."

Allie slowly moved to dangle her feet off the side

of the bed and slipped into her sandals. "It's hard for me to sit up for any length of time right now, but maybe in a week or so. Besides," she sighed, "my piano career may be over."

Susan turned around in surprise. "What?" she asked at the same time that Brandon said, "Why?"

"I was in the process of applying for a transfer to Ball State when this"—she indicated her stomach—"happened. And really, the only reason I was planning to go there was because of Mark. It's probably too late to apply anywhere now, at least for the fall semester."

Susan frowned. "Allie, tell me you weren't applying to Ball State just because of Mark."

Allie looked chagrined. "Sort of. They do have an excellent music school, but I don't know anyone else there. Now I don't have a dorm room, and I don't know what classes I could enroll in so late. I'm probably just going to have to drop out until the winter term. Maybe I can find a job…"

Brandon held up his hand to stop Susan's objection, his eyes twinkling. "Did you ever consider transferring to Bradley?"

"I wish," Allie replied. "But it's too expensive. Dad's made it clear he won't pay for any more private schools."

Brandon rocked back on his heels and beamed. "I hope you don't mind, but I looked into it, and if you're interested, I know the right people in the admissions office. You know—the ones who can put your application through and bypass all the red tape."

Allie frowned. "I'd be paying back student loans until I'm old and gray."

Brandon shook his head. "That's the best part.

There's a full ride scholarship available. Of course you'd have to audition…"

"Brandon," Susan said, "what a great opportunity!" She silently crossed her fingers, hoping this miracle offer could become reality.

Allie was stunned. "You did all this for me?"

"Of course! Bradley's music department would be lucky to have you." He winked at her.

"And you wouldn't have to worry about living arrangements since you could live at home," Susan added.

Allie looked at her mom, her face glowing. "This would be perfect if it works out! Brandon, I can't thank you enough." Allie beamed at him and reached for his hand. He blushed as their fingers touched.

Susan went back to her fictitious packing. She promised herself she'd send a nice, long thank-you note to Emily. First for taking such good care of Allie, and second, for bringing Brandon into their lives.

Chapter Nineteen

Caroline had been on her "new" job as Richard's executive assistant for two full weeks. Her pay increase would show up in her next paycheck, and she'd already made up her mind to look for an apartment of her own. *I'm independently wealthy! Okay, just independent.* She laughed to herself but felt liberated all the same.

Richard was due back in the office today after his week-long golf trip and then business trip to Los Angeles. Caroline had been in constant touch with him, but she knew today would be a stressful day. With Richard out of town, Caroline had functioned efficiently on his behalf, but now that he was back, she felt the familiar butterflies in her stomach.

Business, strictly business, Caroline.

She had already checked email this morning and forwarded important messages to Richard, returned voice-mail messages he didn't need to personally handle, and was proofing a new Hamilton Hardware ad for the Sunday *Indianapolis Star*.

As if the day wasn't already busy enough, Caroline heard a voice in the hallway and winced. Misty strolled regally into Caroline's office, dressed for the summer heat in a flowing white skirt, loose pink blouse over a black bra, white three-inch high-heeled strappy sandals, her wild red hair tied hastily back with a scarf, the wrong shade of red lipstick and smeared mascara on her cheek. *Money can buy expensive clothes but not class,* Caroline thought.

Misty held a large box filled to overflowing with off-white oversized envelopes. Watching her walk into the office, juggling the box and wobbling on her heels almost made Caroline laugh, so she turned away and pretended to be busy at her desk.

"Caroline, I have our wedding invitations ready to go into the mail today. There's only three weeks till the wedding."

Caroline quickly lost her sense of humor. "Why are you telling *me*?"

"Caroline, don't be obtuse. You have to mail them."

Caroline bit her lip to keep from opening her mouth and letting all kinds of arguments spill out. She swallowed and instead chose her words carefully. "I wasn't aware that *I* was going to mail *your* invitations. Richard hasn't mentioned it to me."

"That's your job. You're his secretary, aren't you?"

"Executive Assistant," Caroline said. She shuddered as Misty dumped the tangible proof that the wedding was still on, right on top of her desk. She moved as far away from them as she could get and still be seated at her desk. "I'll see to it that they get to the post office with the rest of the office mail."

"No, no, no, that's not going to work, Caroline," Misty said with a smirk. "I don't have time to go buy stamps, so you'll have to go to the post office and buy two-hundred and fifty first-class stamps and then stick them on."

Caroline looked at Misty, incredulous. "Misty, I have actual work to do here. I don't have time to bother with your wedding invitations!"

"Whatever you're doing will just have to wait. This is more important."

"More important to whom?" asked Caroline.

Misty stamped her foot and almost lost her balance in the process. "To Richard and me, of course!"

"And just what will *you* be doing while I'm putting stamps on your invitations?" Caroline felt like giving Misty a piece of her mind, but then she realized she couldn't, because once Richard was married to this woman, she'd have to be polite to her. *Maybe Mom was right about this job,* she thought. Misty was proving to be a huge thorn in her side.

"I've got a bridal shower to attend. Tell Richard to call me." Misty turned around and flounced out.

"Tell him yourself," Caroline muttered. She recognized the familiar stress-related nausea coming over her. She reached into her desk drawer and downed two antacid tablets, slamming the drawer shut afterward. Misty was using the wedding invitations to torture her.

Maybe I could 'forget' to mail the invitations? But Richard would expect her to honor his fiancée's request, and she couldn't let him down. She blew out a puff of air and got back to work proofing the Hamilton Hardware ad, hoping it would take her mind off the box of wedding invitations slash torture devices sitting on the edge of her desk.

Richard walked down the hall headed for his office, whistling a peppy tune. Caroline thought he looked more handsome than ever, well-rested, light-hearted. He stopped by her desk and fingered the box of wedding invitations sitting there.

"I see Misty's been here," he said, blushing.

"She wants these invitations to go out this afternoon, each with its own first-class stamp." Caroline could barely spit out the words. "Somehow she got the idea that, as your assistant, it's my job."

Richard started thumbing through them. He pulled out an invitation with her name on it, then found three more addressed to Susan, Allie, and Megan. He handed them to her with a weak smile. "I guess we can save some postage if I hand-deliver these. As for the rest, I hope you don't mind."

Caroline stared at her invitation, addressed to Ms. Caroline Benedict and Guest. "No, I don't mind." She couldn't look at him, because if she did he might see the tears she was fighting back. She stood and walked to the window, feigning a need for more light, opened the envelope and pretended to read it. When she'd composed herself, she put it down and looked him in the eye.

"What?"

Caroline swallowed hard. *Do I tell him about Chicago?* If she did, how would he react? Would he be angry at Misty? Angry at her for keeping it from him so long? She took a deep breath and said, "Richard, I saw…" She couldn't force the words out.

"You saw…?"

Caroline tried again. "I saw Misty, well, with, I mean, at…"

Richard shrugged. "You're trying to say you don't think Misty's the right woman for me."

Caroline looked at him in surprise. "Are you having second thoughts?" *I hope…*

Richard shrugged. "You're in good company. My

grandmother says the same thing."

"Your grandmother's a wise woman," Caroline said, "but that's not what I…"

Richard laughed softly. "Grandmother just likes meddling in people's love lives. She's a seventy-five-year-old woman with too much time and money on her hands."

"You should listen to her because…" Why couldn't she finish the sentence? Tell him about Misty and Mark? Even Adele Meadows saw the mistake Richard was about to make. Caroline silently berated herself for her lack of courage.

"Grandmother's an incurable romantic. She says it's a mistake but, well, Misty and I know each other really well. It's like our marriage was always meant to be, and it was what my mother always dreamed of." Richard looked pained at the mention of his mother.

Caroline's heart sank. "Are you sure? I mean, I know you're committed, but what about Misty?" Richard looked puzzled, so Caroline hurried on. "It's just that Misty seems so, I don't know, aloof, and Sharlene's planning the society wedding of the year, and if you aren't sure, maybe you should postpone."

Richard rubbed his forehead. "Believe me, I know. Every bridal shower, every luncheon, all of the elaborate preparations, the guest list that reads like the Indianapolis Who's Who—all dutifully reported to *The Indianapolis Star*, courtesy of Sharlene Meadows-Benedict." He let out a deep sigh. "It's just one day, I guess."

Caroline tilted her head as she thought for a moment. "But there's more to it than just a wedding day, Richard. What about the marriage?"

"Now you sound like my grandmother. Well, I guess I'll find out soon enough." Richard walked into his office, ending the discussion.

Caroline watched him go, shaking her head at the thought of this upcoming travesty of a wedding, and angry at herself for not telling him what she knew. She was afraid Richard was going to get hurt. In fact, after what she saw in Chicago, she was pretty sure of it. Would telling him be selfish on her part? She just didn't know.

"Caroline!" Lucy called as she strolled down the hall. "Look what's here!"

Caroline turned around and was surprised to see Lucy in her doorway with another bouquet of flowers. "Again?"

"Yup. They just came." Lucy smiled and set them on Caroline's desk. She put her fingers to her lips to signal silence and gave Caroline a conspiratorial wink. Then she cleared her throat and said loudly, "Lovely red carnations just delivered for you, Caroline!"

Richard came to his office door when he overheard Lucy and watched as she made a big show of smelling the freshly cut flowers.

"Oh, hi, Richard, gosh I didn't see you there," Lucy said. "Caroline has a secret admirer. We think it's Jared at Kinley Realty."

"Oh?" Richard's face was getting redder and redder as he stared at the carnations.

Caroline tried to read the look on Richard's face. *Is he jealous?* She couldn't tell because he turned around and went back into his office.

An email popped up in Caroline's inbox and she checked to see who it was from. Sharlene. *Great. Just*

what I need right now.
Caroline,

I desperately need your help planning the rehearsal dinner. I know how efficient you are, so I'm confident things will get done in a timely fashion. I need you to contact all members of the wedding party and confirm that they'll be in attendance. I've attached their email addresses or cell phone numbers, so you can easily reach them. Just so you'll know, the rehearsal dinner is scheduled for Sept. 1 at the Belford Country Club, immediately following the 6:00 p.m. outdoor wedding rehearsal on the Peterson estate. Call, text, or email if you have questions.

Caroline read and reread Sharlene's email. "Why me?" she moaned. She felt like crying. And yet she couldn't bring herself to let Richard down, even for something as odious as his wedding to Ms. Wrong. She replied to Sharlene's email.

I'll only agree to help if Richard asks me to. What about the wedding planner? What's wrong with her doing the work she's being paid for?

Caroline hit send and then sat staring at the computer. Not only was she supposed to individually stamp each invitation and mail it—tonight—but now Sharlene expected her to help plan the rehearsal dinner. This was all too cruel. Caroline had almost made up her mind to fill in her response card with a zero—none attending. She shook her head in frustration, gathered her handbag and the box of invitations, and headed out the door.

****

"Allie? Is that you?" Susan called. She stepped to the front door just as Allie came waltzing into the living room, music satchel weighing heavily on her shoulder.

"Yeah, it's me." Allie had a wicked smile on her face, but all she did was wink at her mother and head down the hall to her bedroom.

Susan followed her. "Well?"

Allie pretended innocence. "Well, what?"

Susan was exasperated. This meeting at Bradley University today may have been the most important in Allie's academic career. More important even than her audition for Bryce. "Don't play games, Allison. Tell me what happened."

Allie smiled and sat down on the edge of her bed, patting the corner for Susan to join her. "Okay, so I went to meet Brandon in his office, Thomas Hall, third floor. All the way up two flights of stairs, and boy was I sucking wind. Appendicitis is not for the faint of heart," she said.

Susan tapped her foot impatiently. "Go on."

"Brandon's office is pretty impressive really. Old, distinguished. Not how I would have pictured him, in a century-old building at a school at least that old."

"Allie…"

"Yeah, okay." Allie grinned. "I was nervous. I had to go through both a musical audition and an interview with the Dean of the Music school. My audition for Bryce was nerve-racking, but this was worse. I guess I didn't have as much at stake as I do now."

"So how did it go?" Susan asked, trying in vain to calm her nerves and hope for the best.

Allie smiled. "Okay, I think. Well, better than okay. I outdid myself, and considering I've hardly had any time to practice in the last few weeks, that's an accomplishment."

It certainly is. Susan and Allie hugged each other, laughing and crying all at once.

Chapter Twenty

Susan was in a deep sleep when the alarm went off. She blinked and stared at the clock, almost forgetting why she'd set it. Then suddenly she was wide awake. *My first day on the job!* She jumped out of bed as she shut off the radio, tossed on some khaki pants with a solid navy blue t-shirt she'd laid out the night before, and hoped she looked appropriate for this first day of new teacher orientation.

Mrs. Renfrow had emailed an agenda for the day and attached a list of items Susan would most likely need in order to set up her classroom. Susan had groaned at the unexpected expense, but printed out the list and went to a discount store to purchase the items.

"It's too bad I have to use my limited funds to buy school supplies," she confided to Megan as they stood in the long checkout line, "but I guess I'd better get used to it. I've heard teachers sometimes have to spend their own money to stock their classrooms." She texted her bank for her balance, and then frowned when the reply came back.

Megan thumbed through a fashion magazine and tossed it in the shopping cart. "You mean you haven't even gotten a paycheck yet, and you're already in the hole?"

Susan calmly put the magazine back on the rack. "Unfortunately, my first paycheck won't come for about three weeks, so we're going to be on a tight budget until then."

"Tight*er* you mean."

Susan had bought the bare minimum and had to put it on her credit card instead of the bank debit card, but now as she glanced at the numerous plastic bags sitting on her bedroom floor, she wondered if she'd bought enough supplies. But until Megan's child-support check came next week, this would have to do.

Susan adjusted the straps on her sandals and glanced at the clock again: six-thirty a.m. She was trying to estimate how much time she needed for driving since the school was only two miles away. She was nervous, could hardly sit or stand still, and food was the last thing on her mind, but she went to the kitchen anyway to try to drink some orange juice. Honey came bounding in from Megan's room, so Susan reached down and patted her on the head.

"Hey, girl, you need out?" Honey wagged her tail, and Susan opened the backdoor to let the dog out into the yard.

"Hi, Mom. Want some coffee?" Caroline stretched and stumbled into the kitchen as she headed straight for the cabinet to retrieve a mug. "I made extra last night when I set the timer."

"It smells heavenly, Car, but I think I'm nervous enough as it is. Besides, Mrs. Renfrow said there was a continental breakfast this morning."

"Nervous, huh?" Caroline stifled a grin as she absent-mindedly fingered the *Meadows Advertising* logo on the coffee mug.

Susan got up and opened the fridge, forgot what she wanted, closed it, and then opened it again when she remembered the juice. "Yes, a little. I'll be even more nervous next week when the kids come back to school."

"You'll do fine." Caroline poured herself a steaming mug of coffee and stirred in some sweetener.

Susan poked her pencil at the newspaper crossword, but couldn't concentrate on it. Finally she tossed the pencil aside and said, "You're up early, Caroline."

Caroline blew on her coffee and took a sip. "I'm going to work early this morning so I can take a long lunch. I've got a couple of appointments to look at apartments today. Hopefully I'll be out of your hair in the next two weeks."

Susan closed up her paper in surprise. "You're not in my hair, Car. Not at all. And I don't know what I would have done without you while Allie was in the hospital."

"That's what families do, Mom. No matter where I live, I'll always be around if you need me." Caroline gave her mom a quick hug, and then topped off her coffee mug so it was brimming full. "You have a nice first day at work, and I'll talk to you this evening." Caroline headed toward the bathroom, balancing the hot coffee gingerly.

Susan put her empty juice glass in the sink, opened the backdoor to let Honey in, and went to her room to gather her supplies. It seemed like such a normal day for everyone else. *So why is my stomach doing gymnastics?*

****

Okay, it only takes seven minutes to get here. Susan couldn't decide whether to sit in the parking lot and listen to the radio for fifteen more minutes, or just go ahead into the building early. Just as she was turning off the ignition, her cell phone rang. She answered without glancing at the caller ID.

"Good morning, Teach!" a cheerful voice said.

Susan laughed. "Good morning, Patrick."

"I'm just calling to wish you luck on your first day, even though I know you don't need it. Are you nervous?"

"A little. Well, all right, a lot! This school is so big, and I don't know my way around, and I don't know any of the other teachers."

"Everyone feels that way the first day on a new job. How about I meet you for coffee this afternoon and you can tell me how well it went?"

"I'd like that." Susan smiled at his encouragement. She got out of the car, gathered her belongings and her courage, and headed for the school building.

****

Caroline heard her phone ping with a text, but she was driving and couldn't look at it. She pulled up in front of the apartment complex where she was scheduled to tour an available unit and surveyed the building. It was a small complex, probably less than one hundred apartments, but the grounds were well-maintained with flower beds attractively arranged around the perimeter, and trees neatly trimmed. The building itself was all brick with a wood roof, probably built in the 1980s. She glanced at the dashboard clock and knew she'd be late for her appointment if she didn't get out of the car right then, but she wanted to check her text first. It was from Megan.

—*Car, Sharlene wants me to meet her at the mall*

for a dress fitting for that stupid bridesmaid dress. Can you come get me?—

Caroline rolled her eyes. She replied—*Ask Allie.—*

Megan typed back—*She's going to Brandon's and she's being a b...about Honey.—*

Caroline narrowed her eyes. She'd have to speak to her sister about her cyber language. *Honey? What's up?*

Megan sent a frowny face and said—*Honey chewed up one of Allie's sandals.—*

Caroline made a mental note to explain to Megan, again, that Honey was her responsibility and that she'd have to keep the dog out of Allie's belongings.—*I'm looking at apartments and then back to work. Call Sharlene?—*

A minute or so elapsed, and then Megan replied—*I'll get Allie to take me. NOT Sharlene.—*

Caroline smiled, stashed her phone in her pocket, and went inside the apartment's leasing office.

****

Susan and Patrick met at Peterson's Coffee Emporium. Since it was an easy one-block walk from Rosslyn High School, she didn't even bother moving her car from the school's faculty parking lot. Patrick gave Susan a quick kiss on the forehead as they walked in the door together.

"What'll you have, ma'am?" Patrick asked in his best Texas drawl.

Susan loved that they were from roughly the same part of the country, giving them all the more in common. "The usual, sir," Susan drawled back with a wink. But then more seriously she added, "But I'd prefer my latte frozen today. It's really hot outside."

"One frozen mocha latte coming up." Patrick

winked back as he went to place their orders.

Susan watched him walk up to the counter and marveled at how she'd gotten so lucky. She now had the exciting teaching job she had waited her whole adult life for, three wonderful and talented daughters, and three years after an ugly divorce, a nice man who wanted to be with her.

"So tell me how your first day went." Patrick set their frosted cups on the table and held Susan's chair for her. "Better or worse than expected?"

"Much better." Susan was charmed with his chivalry. "After I got over being nervous, my only problem was getting lost in the halls, which I did several times. I very nearly missed a meeting because I couldn't find the room."

He squeezed her hand and smiled. "One thing at a time. You're going to be a great teacher."

Susan felt completely safe and happy for the first time in years. They chatted, sipped their lattes, and enjoyed each other's company, but eventually they had to part.

"I don't want to let you go," Patrick said as he walked her out into the late afternoon heat.

Susan felt the same, but she had so many demands on her time. "Thanks again for meeting me, Patrick, for bolstering my spirits…"

He gave her a sweet kiss. "Go home and take care of your girls. I'll call you tomorrow."

Susan arrived home both tired and exhilarated, and went straight to the kitchen. She opened the fridge and stared into it. "What's for dinner?" she asked herself as she perused its contents.

"Mom!" Allie called as she came in the front door.

"You home?"

"In here," Susan called back. She decided the heat called for a cold dinner. Caesar salad would be perfect. She pulled some leftover grilled chicken out of the fridge, grabbed some lettuce and grated cheese,

Allie bounced into the kitchen, grinning.

"I thought you were at Brandon's," Susan said, "practicing." She pulled some croutons out of the pantry, got a large salad bowl out of the cabinet, and set all her ingredients next to it.

"She was."

Susan flipped around to see Brandon standing behind Allie, also grinning and exchanging glances with Allie. "What's up, you two?"

Brandon smiled adoringly at Allie and took her hand. "I spoke to my friend in the Admissions Office at Bradley this morning."

Susan held her breath, eager to hear the results of Allie's audition. But the two of them just stood there grinning at one another. She tapped her foot impatiently. "And?"

Allie threw her arms around her mother. "And... I'm in!"

"You're *in*?" Susan wasn't sure she heard right. "You mean...?"

"It means," Brandon told her, "that Allie really impressed both the Dean and the music committee."

"I've been accepted for the fall semester, and they awarded me the full ride scholarship!" Allie said. "Can you believe it, Mom? I'm in the Music School at Bradley University!"

"As soon as you go over to Admissions and sign the paperwork," Brandon reminded her, squeezing her hand.

Susan felt light as a feather. Her daughter had been accepted to a prestigious private university, with a music school that rivaled Bryce, and all with no added expense that Daniel could balk at. Susan pulled Allie in for another hug. "I'm so proud of you."

Allie stepped back from her mom and turned to Brandon, giving him a big hug, too. They stood in a silent embrace for a moment, Susan watching with a critical eye. "I can't thank you enough," Allie said.

"I'll consider myself thanked when I hear you play a solo in Central Hall."

"Can I talk you into staying for dinner?" Susan asked him. "It's the least I can do.

Allie shook her head. "No, thanks, Mom, we're on our way out. I lost track of time practicing at Brandon's and skipped lunch, so we're headed out for a sandwich now." Hand in hand, Allie and Brandon walked to the front door.

Susan almost called out for Brandon to take care of Allie, but she stopped. Of course he would. Allie was safe with Brandon.

****

Caroline fairly danced into the house, a folder full of papers under her arm. "Mom!" she shouted gleefully. No answer. She went through the house, eventually locating Susan and Megan in the backyard playing with Honey on what had turned out to be an unusually warm late-summer evening.

"Mom! Guess what!" Caroline announced. "I signed the lease on an apartment!"

Susan dropped the stick she was about to throw for Honey to fetch. "I knew you had some showings lined up, but I thought you were just looking." Honey danced in circles until Susan threw the stick, and the dog took off after it.

Caroline walked to the picnic table and poured herself a tumbler of iced tea. "It's a small two bedroom/one bath, about three miles south of here, affordable, really clean. And it's right on the Monon Trail! There were some other people interested, so I hurried up and put down the security deposit. I plan to move Labor Day weekend. Of course, I need to think about furniture and…"

"Labor Day weekend?" Susan interrupted her. "That's the weekend Richard's getting married, isn't it?"

Caroline took a big gulp of tea and looked down at Honey, dancing playfully around Megan's ankles. She would miss being with family, but it was time she got out on her own. And moving September first worked for several reasons. "I've been thinking about maybe skipping the whole wedding thing."

"Caroline, you have to go," Megan insisted. "I'll never be able to show my face in public wearing that hideous bridesmaid dress Sharlene picked out if you're not there."

"I know Richard wants you there," Susan said. "But I understand if you feel you can't go."

"Hey, tell me about your first day at work," Caroline said to her mother.

Megan threw the stick for Honey to chase. "Back off, Mom. That's Caroline-code for she doesn't want to talk about Richard's wedding."

Caroline opened her mouth to contradict Megan, but she couldn't get a sound out, and anyway Megan was right. Tears came to her eyes. "Oh, I just remembered a call I needed to return for work." It wasn't true of course, but she didn't want her mother and sister to see her crying. She hurried to her bedroom, shut the door, and let the tears flow.

"Car, I've got great news!" Allie stopped in her tracks. "You look miserable," she said, coming the rest of the way into their bedroom.

Caroline looked up. She hadn't even heard Allie enter. "How long have you been standing there?"

Allie took the box of tissues off the dresser and handed it to her. "Long enough. Is this about Richard?"

Caroline took a tissue and dabbed at her eyes. "No. I just told Mom I'm moving out and…"

"You're moving?"

Caroline nodded and sniffled. "Labor Day weekend. It's perfect timing, really. I get my own place…"

"And you get to duck out on Richard's wedding." Allie shook her head. "So it *is* about Richard. Why don't you just tell him how you feel?"

Caroline lifted an eyebrow. "If you mean tell him I hope he's going to be happy, he already knows."

"You want him to be happy?" Allie looked puzzled. "With Misty?"

"Well, of course." Caroline swallowed the lie and went to the mirror to wipe mascara from under her eyes.

"Caroline! Are you listening to yourself? You can't even look me in the face and spout that nonsense." Allie came up behind Caroline and looked at their reflections in the mirror. "Be honest, Caroline, you're in love with him!"

Caroline closed her eyes to blot out that thought. "Love? Impossible. He's my boss, and he's about to be married." The last part got stuck in her throat, causing her a coughing fit.

"Yeah, and if you don't speak up, he's going to marry the wrong woman." Allie patted Caroline's back till she quit coughing. "Richard doesn't know he has options."

Caroline sighed and shrugged her shoulders. "It hurts too much, but it wouldn't matter anyway. He's determined to marry the woman his dead mother handpicked for him." She stifled a sob. "I want Richard to be happy, I really do. I guess I could even watch him get married if I thought he was marrying the right woman. But Misty is *not* the right woman for him! Even his grandmother told him so."

"I agree with Adele." Allie gave her sister's shoulder a squeeze. "Did you ever tell Richard about seeing Misty in Chicago?"

Caroline began reapplying her smeared makeup. "I tried, but I just couldn't get the words out."

Allie sat down on the side of her own bed, her feet propped on the edge, elbows on her knees. "Try again. Before it's too late."

Caroline gave up on her makeup when the tears started falling down her cheeks again. She grabbed a fresh tissue and blew her nose. "It's already too late, Allie." She didn't want to hear *I told you so* from her sister or anyone else, but she was beginning to second-guess herself about taking the job at Meadows. "Alienating the boss's new wife would make my life miserable."

"If you can't tell Richard about your feelings, you

at least need to tell him the truth about Misty and Mark. Let him decide what to do with the information."

That was good advice, but Caroline doubted she had the courage to go through with it. She dabbed at her eyes and let out a huge sigh. "I guess I'm stuck. I'll have to go to the wedding, and once he gets back from his"—she nearly gagged—"honeymoon, I'll have to deal with the new Mrs. Meadows."

Allie brightened up. "Hey, you know the wedding invitation said we could bring a plus one, right? Why don't you invite some hot guy to be your date?"

Caroline sat with that a minute. "Well, I guess I could ask Jared at the realty office. Lucy thinks he likes me."

"See? There you go."

Caroline finally smiled through her tears, feeling like there might be hope after all. "I guess if I have to go, I could do worse than go with a hunky guy who's got a crush on me."

"And you could double with us," Allie said.

"Us?"

Allie grinned. "Mom and I have dates—Patrick and Brandon!"

This time Caroline raised her eyebrow. "Brandon?"

"Yeah, Brandon. He's been such a good friend to me. That's *my* good news. He helped speed up the paperwork and got me admitted to Bradley for the fall semester, full ride and all."

Caroline was happy for her sister, but wary of this new friendship, especially on the heels of her disastrous relationship with Mark. "Well, that's great, but did you ask Brandon out of gratitude, or is there something else going on?"

"Yes and no," Allie said. "Yes, I'm grateful, and no, we're just friends right now, but…" she stopped and looked at her sister.

"But…?"

Allie sighed. "I thought I'd found the love of my life when I met Mark. He was everything I thought I wanted in a boyfriend, but he turned out to be so shallow. At first I thought Brandon was just an old guy with a piano, but as I've gotten to know him, I've seen what a decent man he really is. He was there for me the whole time I was sick. So I'm taking my time getting to know him, which I didn't with Mark."

"Wow, near-death has given you all kinds of insight," Caroline said with a wry grin.

"So how 'bout it, Car? Ask Jared to be your date?"

Caroline thought about it, but she couldn't go through with it. An idea came to her. "Hey! I know the perfect 'date': Emily and Sara!"

Allie laughed out loud. "Well, I guess you can't invite one without the other!"

The more she thought about it, the more she knew that asking two close family friends to the wedding would give her the moral support she needed. "Richard won't mind, and it'll drive Sharlene nuts to have to add one more to the seating arrangement!" Caroline and Allie high-fived.

Chapter Twenty-One

Susan woke up before her alarm went off. Thoughts of all the classroom preparations she'd made for today's start of school, coupled with a bad case of nerves, had kept her up half the night. So she was up and dressed with time to spare.

"Megan!" She called down the hall. "Are you ready for breakfast yet? We have to leave here on time!"

Megan called back in a whiny voice, "I don't know what to wear!"

Susan walked into her youngest daughter's bedroom and surveyed the scene. Clothing was strewn all over her bed, yet there stood Megan, still in her pajamas. "What do you mean you don't know what to wear? You have a closet full of clothes and lots of new outfits Sharlene just bought you."

"I'm so used to just putting on my school uniform and not thinking about it," Megan said, pouting.

Susan put her hands on her hips. "Well, as much as you complained about those uniforms I'd think you'd be happy to wear something else."

"But what do kids in public school wear? Jeans, skirts, shorts, pants, what? I wanna fit in, but I don't know how!"

Susan understood Megan's frustration, because she was just as nervous as her daughter. "Well, Megan, you saw lots of students there when you went to get your schedule and books, and they mostly dress like you do when you're going to the mall." Susan pawed through the pile of clothes on Megan's bed. "Here, wear these new jeans and this solid white t-shirt, and some comfortable flats because it's a big school and you'll be doing lots of walking." Susan glanced over at her daughter, but Megan didn't look convinced.

Megan threw herself down on the bed, landing on top of the clothes. "What if all the other girls are wearing skirts?"

Susan sighed. "Then you'll wear a skirt tomorrow. But I really don't think these kids are going to be as judgmental as Willowby kids." She reached down and patted Megan's knee. "I know you're anxious about the first day in a new school, but we've got to get going. I can't be late."

Megan looked dubious but picked up the jeans her mother had suggested and held them up in front of her while checking the mirror. Susan quietly closed the bedroom door and said a silent prayer to the wardrobe gods. She went back to the kitchen to try to quiet her nerves but accomplished just the opposite by gulping down a cup of black coffee. Megan appeared a few moments later, dressed in a jeans skirt, a pink camisole underneath a white button-down shirt, and high-heeled sandals.

Susan, in her best noncommittal parent voice said, "You look nice."

Megan shrugged, poured herself a bowl of cereal, and sat down to eat.

"Do you have your book bag all ready to go?" Susan asked. "School supplies, schedule, lunch money?"

"Yes, Mom," Megan said as she rolled her eyes. "I know how to do that much at least."

Oddly enough, that classic Megan eye-roll was reassuring. "Okay, then I guess we're ready for our first day." At least she hoped so.

****

The first bell rang, signaling the start of the day, and a small number of students shuffled into Susan's classroom, shy and giggling. Her name, Ms. Benedict, was written on the whiteboard, along with the day's date and, in bold block letters, "Welcome to Freshman English." She looked around the room at the diversity of her students and smiled, both at them and to herself. There were African Americans, Asians, Hispanics, whites, and one Native American child, all with eager eyes trained on her.

It's showtime. "Good morning, ladies and gentlemen."

The first class of the day went smoothly, the next class was Susan's planning period, and then the third class arrived, a talkative group of very bright students. Some of them seemed to know each other already, probably from middle school Susan assumed, but as she listened to their conversations, she learned several students had come straight from a private K-8 Catholic school. They seemed as intimidated as Megan about entering a big public high school for the first time.

Susan walked to the front of the classroom to begin her lesson. Just as she had them quieted down, a voice on the PA said, "Good morning, Rosslyn Wranglers, and welcome to a new school year!" Susan sighed and hoped the announcements wouldn't go on too long, so she could get her lesson started. Unfortunately, they did and she didn't.

Before Susan knew it, the morning was gone, lunch was over and the class right after lunch was a test of her patience. She had thirty-five chairs in her room, and so far forty-two students had shown up. And they were still coming! Clearly there was some sort of clerical error here, but she didn't have time to stop and call the main office because the students were very loud, rowdy, and jockeying for seats like a game of musical chairs.

She tried speaking over the din. "Students, can we please quiet down and be patient till the office straightens out the scheduling problems?"

"Miss, uh, Teacher, can you sign my schedule change?" A very tall and thin young man thrust a form under her nose. "I'm supposed to be in athletic conditioning this period. Basketball."

Five more children came into the room, laughing and waving their schedules. The noise level rose as they all greeted one another after the long summer break, shouting and jockeying for an empty space.

"Mrs. Benedict!" shouted one kid in the back of the room. "There ain't no more chairs!"

She took a calming breath before speaking. "Yes, I'm aware that we have a problem, but it can't be taken care of until tomorrow. In the meantime, please try to find a seat somewhere and get quiet."

"Miss Benedict," said a very large young man with a booming voice, "can we sit in the windowsill?"

Susan was ready to tear her hair out, because three more students just arrived, bringing the total to fifty. "Yes, I suppose. If you don't have a seat, find someplace to sit. *Not* on top of the desks!" Susan noticed several girls sitting two to a desk and said, at the top of her voice, "Only one person to a seat, please!" Fixing this fiasco was at the top of her to-do list the minute the final bell rang today.

"Ms. Benedict?" A timid girl with thick glasses near the front of the room raised her hand. "Do we have any homework?"

Susan smiled at her and announced, again very loudly, "Your homework assignment is on the board." Somehow she doubted the work would get done.

"It's got to get better," she muttered to herself as the final dismissal bell rang. She slumped into her desk chair in exhaustion, kicked off her shoes, and rested her head on the wall behind her chair.

Susan realized she hadn't seen Megan all day except for a quick glimpse in the hallway before lunch. She wondered how her daughter had gotten along in this huge school. Susan forced herself up from the chair and began straightening desks, picking up trash, and stacking books.

"Hi, Mom!" Megan said as she bounced into the room.

Susan saw that Megan was smiling and hoped that was a good sign. "How did it go today?"

"*Great*! I like most of my classes except for math, because I hate math anyway, and my teachers seem nice and I really *really* like my art teacher! I have two whole hours in art class because you put me in the advanced art program—thanks by the way—and we're going to do all kinds of stuff in there this year. And the teacher says there are competitions we can enter and everything. And next year I can take drafting because I want to be an architect, and in history we're going to study Roman architecture and I already made some new friends. Emma and Ashleigh want me to go with them right now to Peterson's, and we're meeting some more kids I don't know, but Emma says they're cool. So can I go?"

Susan felt a huge sense of relief. Despite Megan's misgivings, and her own, things had apparently gone well. Susan tried her best to sound like this was exactly what she'd expected. "Sure, that's fine. I have work left here to do, so I'll pick you up there in an hour."

"Thanks, Mom! Oh, yeah, can I have five dollars?"

Susan unlocked her closet and took out her handbag. Megan grabbed the money and fairly danced out the door.

There was only one thing left to do. She pulled out her cell phone and pushed a speed-dial button. "Hey Patrick, it's Susan. I survived Day One—barely. Call me when you get this message." She smiled as she hung up the phone.

****

"Caroline!" Lucy giggled, standing in the office doorway, "guess what?"

Caroline looked up from her laptop and saw Lucy displaying a single yellow rose in a tiny bud vase like it was a trophy.

"Oh, my God, this is getting ridiculous!" Caroline got up and walked around the desk, digging for a card. "When I called the florist last time they said the customer paid cash and it couldn't be traced." She unpinned the card from the blue ribbon around the vase and opened it.

"Well?"

Caroline's eyes got wide and she sucked in her breath. "It says, 'Meet your secret admirer tonight at eight p.m. sharp at La Bella Italy. And bring this rose with you.'" She looked up from the card. "Isn't that a pretty expensive restaurant?"

"Yes, yes, yes!" Lucy exclaimed. "It just happens to be the most romantic place in all of Indianapolis! They have a high volume of marriage proposals."

Caroline blanched. "But if I go, this would be a first date. A blind date, and I'm certainly not planning on getting married. So why there?"

"*If* you go?" Lucy lifted an eyebrow. "Girlfriend, you're going. Wear your prettiest dress and let your hair down out of that infernal ponytail, because it's time to meet Mr. Right!"

****

Caroline smoothed her lime-green sundress, ran her fingers through her strawberry blonde hair hanging loose about her shoulders, gathered her courage and walked into La Bella Italy near Monument Circle in downtown Indianapolis. As instructed, she carried the yellow rose her secret admirer had sent, grasping it by the plastic holder. She looked nervously around the room, expecting to see Jared sitting somewhere nearby.

"May I help you, Miss?" the host asked.

"I'm meeting someone, but I don't see him yet. I'll just wait here till he arrives." She sat down in a chair near the front entrance host stand, alongside other guests waiting to be seated, while the butterflies in her stomach did somersaults. The door opened a few agonizing moments later.

"Richard!" Caroline said. "What are you doing here?" Instinctively she craned her neck to see if Misty was coming.

Richard looked just as surprised to see Caroline. "I got a message from my grandmother to meet her here at eight sharp."

Caroline breathed a sigh of relief. "Oh, you're meeting Adele."

"What are you doing here?" Richard asked. "You look really nice. Not that you don't always..." He stopped and blushed.

"I have a date," she said, blushing as well.

Richard frowned. "With the guy who's been sending you flowers?" He was silent a moment as he stared out the window that looked out on the historic Civil War monument. "Funny, yellow roses were my mother's favorite."

Caroline felt awkward about that coincidence. "Oh, well..."

Richard sat down in the chair next to hers and they didn't talk, just waited and watched as other couples were seated and busy waiters carried plates of steaming food to their tables. Caroline felt her stomach start to grumble. Finally Richard pulled out his cell phone to check the time. "I guess Grandmother's running late."

To break the awkward silence, Caroline asked, "Where's Misty tonight?" Not that she cared, but for the sake of their future working relationship, she thought she should be polite.

"Truthfully, I don't know, but Grandmother said come alone. You know how she is, always speaking her mind about..." Richard's voice trailed off.

"So you think this is about your wedding?" Caroline asked.

Richard didn't answer that question. "So where did

you say you got the rose?"

Caroline felt her face turn crimson with embarrassment. "A 'secret admirer,' and we were supposed to meet at eight o'clock sharp." She anxiously searched the restaurant one more time. "I think I've been stood up."

"Mr. Meadows," the host said, standing before the two of them, menus in hand, "your table is ready."

Caroline turned to the door, expecting to see Adele Meadows coming through it, but Adele wasn't here and neither was Jared. Her shoulders slumped.

Richard frowned, but then he suddenly slapped his forehead and burst out laughing. "Uh, Caroline, I think we've been had. Grandmother set us up."

Caroline's jaw dropped. "What? No!"

"Well, think about it. Both of us told to be here at eight o'clock, and you holding a rose that meant so much to my mom. It has to be Grandmother."

It was either an odd coincidence, or Richard was right. "Why would she do that?"

Richard stopped laughing. "She's an incurable romantic."

At that, Caroline stood up, clutched her handbag to her chest while she shifted the rose to her other hand, and said, "Well, then, I'd better be going."

Richard stood as well, but instead of holding the door for her he said, "Say, as long as we're here, and both hungry, and you look so pretty, and Grandmother's arranged a table, why not have that dinner?"

Was that a good idea? Caroline wasn't sure, but she *was* hungry, and Adele had gone to a lot of trouble. "Um, well, I suppose…"

Richard allowed Caroline to precede him as they followed the host. They were shown to a secluded candlelit table in the back of the room, a bottle of merlot already opened and ready to pour. "Compliments of Mrs. Adele Meadows," the host said. "I'm to tell you to order whatever you wish and that the tab will be covered."

Caroline realized that Adele had thought of everything, overlooking the fact that Richard was engaged to another woman. She was filled with conflicting emotions—disappointed to find out she had no secret admirer, but thrilled that she got to spend some alone time with Richard.

Richard held Caroline's chair for her and said, "Grandmother certainly knows how to set the mood. Wine?"

He nodded for the waiter to pour them each a glass, and Caroline was soon laughing and talking, almost like it was a real date. Except it wasn't a real date because it was with her very-soon-to-be-married boss, and she couldn't let herself forget that.

After the meal, she and Richard walked outside into the balmy air. Richard took her hand and squeezed it. "Do you have to go straight home, or could we walk around a little?"

Caroline quietly withdrew her hand. "I'd like that. I need to walk off some of that dinner."

The two of them strolled leisurely through downtown Indianapolis for the next hour. They walked around the Circle, stopping to read the inscription on the memorial and study the statue at the top. A horse-drawn carriage ambled by, transporting a young couple obviously in love. She and Richard went over to the

Canal Walk and joined the many people walking, jogging, or roller-skating along the river, all enjoying the summer evening. They made a loop back and ended up near the Capitol Building and headed to the mall parking garage.

"I can find my car from here, Richard."

Richard shook his head. "No, a gentleman always sees a lady safely home, or in this case to her parked car." He reached for her hand before Caroline realized what was happening, held it for a moment, and then just as quickly dropped it. "Sorry. I just got caught up in the moment." He blushed and Caroline looked away. "Isn't that your car over there?"

"That's it." Caroline turned to face Richard. "Thanks for a lovely evening, even if your grandmother did play a prank on us."

"It was great." Richard opened the door on the driver's side for her, and then leaned in as if to kiss her goodnight.

Caroline pulled back in surprise. "Richard!"

He jerked himself backward. "Oh, my God, I'm such an idiot." They both stood by her car door staring at each other in embarrassment, and finally Richard broke the silence. "Good night, Caroline. I'll see you at the office tomorrow."

Caroline backed her car out of the parking space, waved at Richard, and drove off down the ramp as tears threatened to spill down her cheeks. She looked in her rearview mirror and saw Richard still staring after her. She put a CD into the player and turned up the volume, hoping to drown out her thoughts.

"I've got you under my skin," crooned the vocalist.

****

"Well? How'd it go last night?" Lucy demanded as Caroline walked through the front door of Meadows Advertising. Caroline was juggling her travel coffee mug from home in one hand and her over-stuffed handbag in the other, hoping to get to her office without spilling the coffee or having to discuss the date.

"I'm running late, Lucy," Caroline fibbed as she hurried past her, head ducked as she all but ran to her office. She carefully set her coffee and bag down on her desk, opened the window blinds to let in some much-needed sunlight, and started to close the door.

"Oh, no, you don't." Lucy pushed the door aside and strode into the office, her hands on what would have been her hips if she weren't so pregnant. "Now spill!"

Caroline slumped down in her desk chair. "It was…" She looked around to see if anyone else—like Richard—was listening, and then put her fingers to her lips, shaking her head.

Lucy grabbed Caroline by the arm and dragged her through the reception area and down the hall to the women's restroom shared by all the first floor offices. Once inside Lucy finally let loose of her arm. "Okay, now spill!"

Caroline rubbed her arm. "Why did you do that?"

"Come on, Caroline. I'm dying to know what happened."

Caroline sighed and said, "It was a setup."

Lucy's head bobbed up and down. "Uh-huh. So tell me about *the guy*!"

Caroline folded her arms and tapped her foot. "There is no guy. It was Richard, and his grandmother thought she was playing matchmaker."

"Oh." Lucy looked deflated. "That sucks."

"Lucy, this is ridiculous! We're not in high school. Why are we whispering in a public restroom?"

"If you didn't care who overheard, we could have talked in your office."

Caroline stamped her foot, not so much in petulance but to keep her emotions in check. "I don't know what to do. It was a wonderful evening, but it didn't change anything."

Lucy cocked her head to one side. "Are you sure?"

Caroline threw her hands up in the air and walked out the door.

Chapter Twenty-Two

"Knock knock." Caroline tapped on Richard's open office door, waited, and finally went in when Richard didn't reply. "I'm leaving now, unless you have anything else you need me to do." Richard didn't answer. "I need to get home and start packing. You know I'm moving this weekend, right?"

Richard sat staring out the window, tapping his fingers together. "You know I'm getting married this weekend, right?" he countered.

Caroline bit her lip and looked down at her feet, trying to compose herself. "Of course," she said, somehow managing a smile, "and you leave for your honeymoon on Monday, so I'll see you back in the office on September fifteenth."

Richard turned around from the window. "Moving day or not, you'll be there, won't you? At the wedding, I mean?"

Caroline sighed. She'd already come to terms with this, and was steeling herself for the moment just a few days from now when Richard and Misty would say 'I do' in front of friends and family. And the society page reporters. "Emily and Sara will be in from Chicago sometime this evening, and since they're my plus ones, sort of…"

"Caroline, I *need* to know you'll be there," Richard insisted.

Caroline studied him closely but couldn't get a bead on what he was thinking or feeling. "Why is it so important I be at your wedding?"

Richard didn't answer but went back to gazing out the window and drumming his fingers on the armrests.

"Are you having second thoughts about the marriage," she asked, metaphorically crossing her fingers, "or is it just last-minute bridegroom jitters?"

Richard sighed. "I just want some friendly faces there in that sea of society gawkers, that's all."

Caroline wilted inside but plastered a brave smile on her face and said, "Since my dad is your brother-in-law, and *my* sister Megan is a bridesmaid because *your* sister Sharlene insisted, and I work for you, there's no way I could decently miss your wedding."

Instead of laughing, Richard went back to his silent brooding.

"Good night, then." Caroline left quietly, closing the door behind her.

****

It was a sticky, cloudless evening, with the sun still broiling and little shade available on the Peterson estate, with the exception of the gazebo which was a short distance away from the rehearsal site. Sharlene was becoming frazzled, what with the excessive humidity, the petulant bride, and the groom running late.

"Why are we out in this summer heat?" Misty complained. "Where are those tents anyway?"

Sharlene was determined to humor Misty, who was proving to be a bit of a Bridezilla. "Misty, dear, there was a bit of a mix-up, but the wedding planner will arrive first thing tomorrow morning with her crew.

Unfortunately, this evening the rehearsal has to be out in the open. Sorry, dear, but it'll be over before you know it and we'll be inside the country club."

"Not if Richard doesn't get here. We're all roasting out here while we wait for him!" Misty scooped her hair off the back of her neck with one hand and fanned herself with the other.

Sharlene said nothing but reached over to adjust Megan's ponytail. Megan pulled away and went to sit next to her father on a bench near the garden as Daniel took a swig from his bottle of beer. The whole wedding party was milling around, sweating, and waiting for Richard to arrive.

Sharlene watched as Misty paced back and forth, grumbling, and then found a likely victim to vent her frustration. "Mother, for heaven's sake, lay off those wine spritzers! And wake Daddy out of that lawn chair!"

Tildie Peterson ignored her daughter and kept sipping.

The matron of honor, Krystal McAlister, was leaning against a tree, tugging at her sandals. "Misty, I swear I'm walking through this rehearsal barefoot. These new Jimmy Choos you talked me into buying are rubbing blisters on my feet!"

"But they're so adorable, Krystal," Sharlene cooed. "Doesn't Misty have good taste?"

Misty scowled at Sharlene and bellowed into her phone. "Richard! This is Misty *again,* and you're late. Where are you? I'm mortified. Call me back *ASAP*!"

Sharlene went to the minister and quietly whispered in his ear.

Reverend Roberts nodded and tentatively

approached Misty as she disconnected her phone. "Miss Peterson, would you like to start the rehearsal without Mr. Meadows, allowing one of the groomsmen to stand in for him?"

"No," she growled, but then stopped, smiled, and said, "We'll wait for my fiancé."

The reverend's face looked pinched. "I'm afraid I can't stay past seven, because I have another wedding to perform this evening that begins at eight."

"He'll be here." Misty looked out toward the street just as Richard's car pulled up. "Finally," she muttered, and hurried off to greet him.

"Thank goodness," Sharlene said. She clapped her hands loudly. "Places, everyone."

Misty hissed something in Richard's ear, but Sharlene was grateful they were out of earshot, because neither of them looked happy. Noticing that Sharlene and the whole wedding party were watching them, Misty suddenly grabbed Richard and kissed him passionately.

Richard's eyes opened wide in surprise, but before he could react, Misty pulled away, beamed at him, and waved to the members of the wedding party. Richard sputtered as Misty took his arm and walked him back to the waiting group. He nodded to the minister, gave a thumbs-up to his best man Jack, and winked at a grinning Megan standing behind all the other bridesmaids. She winked back and giggled.

"Richard, dear," Sharlene said, "being late to your own wedding rehearsal—it's such poor manners. Couldn't you have called? Hopefully you'll arrive at the country club on time for dinner."

"Is that a question or an order?" Richard asked her.

"Richard, dear, always such a kidder." Sharlene clucked sweetly while Misty narrowed her eyes at her fiancé.

"Shall we begin?" Reverend Roberts asked.

****

This was Sharlene's moment. She was the hostess for this carefully-planned, elegant evening at the country club, all in honor of her brother's wedding to the Peterson heiress. She almost wished she were the guest of honor, since her own wedding had been such a hurry-up affair. But no matter; tonight would definitely land her in the society pages of the *Indianapolis Star,* lauded as Daniel Benedict's wife and capable hostess. Dinner was originally scheduled to be served at eight, but Sharlene had already informed the wait staff that it would be delayed at least a half hour, due to Richard's late arrival for the wedding rehearsal.

Sharlene surveyed the room. The bar was up and running in a reception area adjoining the private dining room at Belford Country Club, with waiters dressed in black tuxedo pants, white shirts and black bow ties. Since Daniel had driven himself and Megan from the Peterson estate while Sharlene rode with her cousins, he had a head start at the bar, working on a scotch while Megan stood next to him sipping a ginger ale. Adele Meadows, drinking her martini and barely concealing a scowl, sat in an overstuffed chair in one of the many cozy lounge areas scattered around the large room near the picture window that overlooked the eighteenth hole of the golf course. Mr. and Mrs. Peterson stood passively near Adele's chair, barely acknowledging her or each other while guzzling drinks. Sharlene hadn't yet had a chance to speak to the bride's parents, so she stepped over to join them and her grandmother.

"Hello, all," Sharlene said. Adele scowled, Tildie took a swallow of wine, and Merrill Peterson rocked back on his heels while sipping his cocktail and gazing out the window.

"Tildie, dear," Adele said, "would you pass me some peanuts? And perhaps you should have a few yourself, to soak up some of that alcohol."

Tildie shoved the bowl toward her but ignored Adele's suggestion and drained her glass of chardonnay. She calmly took her husband by the arm and led him back to the bar, turning to give Adele a dirty look as she went.

Sharlene cringed, embarrassed that her grandmother was already insulting the bride's family, but she'd learned long ago she couldn't tell Adele Meadows what to do. So she took a head count. The four bridesmaids were all clustered together on a sofa by the picture window. But the men were missing, as were the bride and groom. Sharlene sidled up to the bridesmaids. "This is going to be an absolutely spectacular party," she told them, then took a step back when all four of them gave her dirty looks.

"What kind of wedding rehearsal was that?" Sierra, an old school friend of Misty's, asked her. "I've never seen two people look more miserable."

Sharlene's hand flew to her chest. "Why, whatever do you mean?"

"Don't worry, Sierra, Misty has..." Krystal, the matron of honor, stopped herself and gave her friends a half smile. "Never mind."

"What were you going to say, Krystal?" Sierra asked. "Come on, you know more than you're letting on."

"Let's just say Misty has a plan."

Sharlene frowned, but quickly recovered. "I hope her plan is to enjoy this evening and tomorrow's gala wedding."

"Hey, look, the guys are here!" Krystal stood up and waved at her husband Scott, who waved back.

Richard and Sharlene's twin cousins Gary and Greg, brothers of the remaining bridesmaids, went straight to the bar, followed by Eric, Richard's basketball-playing buddy from the gym. Jack Anderson entered, hands in his pockets, and called out, "Hey, folks, nice night for a wake." No one laughed. Jack shrugged and went to join Scott and the bridesmaids.

Scott brushed Krystal's lips with a quick kiss and sat down on the sofa next to her. "I hope dinner goes better than the rehearsal."

"What is it they say? Bad dress rehearsal, great opening night?" Krystal took a swallow of her daiquiri.

"Except this isn't a play, it's real life," Scott said. "Why did Richard look so pained through the whole thing?"

Sharlene felt her face turning bright red. She left the young people to their gossip and went to her grandmother, took the martini out of her hand and barked, "Where is Richard?" before remembering herself. She stood up straight and smiled graciously to her guests. "He must be with Misty. Those two lovebirds!"

"I'll thank you to not treat me like a spoiled child, Sharlene," Adele said. Sharlene handed the drink back to her grandmother, who held it up in a mock toast.

"They were in separate cars," Jack volunteered,

"and they were right behind us guys. Traffic maybe?"

Daniel downed his drink at the bar and started to order another one. Sharlene shot him a dirty look and made a beeline across the room. Daniel put his arm around his wife as he turned to Megan. "Would you like another ginger ale, Megs?"

"No thanks, Dad. This is the most boring party I've ever been to. Can't I just go home? I'm sure Caroline would come get me."

Daniel gave Megan's shoulders a hug. "Sorry, Megan, but if I have to stay, so do you." Despite his wife's disapproval, he ordered a third drink.

Richard and Misty finally arrived after fifteen agonizing minutes—agonizing for Sharlene anyway—Misty's arm tightly linked in the crook of Richard's elbow. His stoic expression complemented the plastered-on smile on her face.

"The happy couple has arrived!" Sharlene announced. The rest of the wedding party applauded and whooped it up. She just hoped the 'happy couple' hadn't had an argument on the way over.

Misty smiled as she addressed everyone. "Just a few more hours till we're husband and wife." Richard blanched as she steered him toward the bar. The bartender handed her a white wine and Richard a beer. As soon as they had their drinks they parted company, Richard to talk to his best man, Misty to chat with her bridesmaids by the picture window.

Sharlene followed Richard, smiling graciously at her guests as she crossed the room, but when she reached his side she grabbed his arm and pulled him aside. "Richard, what in heaven's name is wrong with you tonight?"

He sighed and scratched his head. "I'm tired, Sharlene, and all this"—he indicated the country club, dinner party, and open bar—"is just so pretentious."

"Pretentious? Richard, surely you know how hard I've worked to plan this evening. I don't care how tired you are. Couldn't you at least act like you're having fun—*with* your fiancée?"

"I'm with her, Sharlene, but can't you see she wants to talk to the girls?"

"Richard Meadows," Adele said sternly as she joined her grandchildren, "I must speak to you in private."

"What is it, Grandmother?" Richard took her arm and patted it lovingly.

"I said *privately.*" Adele shot Sharlene a warning look as she led Richard out of earshot.

Sharlene gave them a few moments, although she was pretty sure Grandmother was trying yet again to convince Richard to postpone the wedding. Sharlene decided she'd had enough of this nonsense and stomped over to the two of them. "Richard, dear, you're behaving as if you aren't a man about to marry the girl of your dreams. Please feel free to mingle with the guests." She gave her grandmother a withering look.

Richard sighed and patted Adele's arm. "Sharlene's right, Grandmother. I'm being rude." He slowly rose and looked around the room. Jack waved him over.

The headwaiter whispered in Sharlene's ear. She nodded and announced, "Ladies and gentlemen, dinner is served. Please go in and find your seats."

The waiter opened the large white folding doors to reveal an elegant table with seventeen place settings, a seating arrangement Sharlene had agonized over for days. Unfortunately, none of the guests moved toward the private dining room.

She tried again. "Folks, dinner's ready!"

Daniel turned to the bartender yet again, holding up his empty glass. Megan pulled out her cell phone and started texting. Krystal and Misty had their heads together, and the Petersons both looked too drunk to acknowledge much of anything.

Sharlene panicked. "Everyone, the dinner will be ruined if we don't…"

Jack gallantly went over to Richard's grandmother and offered his arm. "Shall we?" Adele allowed him to help her to her feet, but instead of heading to the dining room, she adjusted her purse on her shoulder and went straight for the exit.

"Grandmother, wait!" Sharlene called. "Oh, this is not going well," she muttered.

Jack poked Richard's back and pointed toward Sharlene. "Your sister's waiting." When Richard nodded and started for the dining room, Jack put his hand on Richard's shoulder to stop him. "Dude, your bride."

Richard sighed, doubled back and offered Misty his arm.

There was an interminable silence. Sharlene stepped over to wave the bride and groom toward the dining room, hoping the others would follow suit. But then Krystal stepped between Richard and Misty, who were in a heated discussion.

Sharlened edged closer. "Could we…?"

"…bachelorette party at the Jazz Corner in Rosslyn Village," Krystal was saying to Richard. "You know, scene of your romantic proposal to your bride-to-be."

Richard shifted uncomfortably from one foot to the other. "Right."

"Richard," Misty said, "you didn't tell me where you and the guys are going tonight."

"Someplace where the happy couple won't see each other on the night before the wedding," Jack volunteered. He looked from Misty to Richard and back to Misty. "You two don't need the bad luck."

"Well, I certainly hope you all make an early evening of it," Sharlene said cheerfully as she attempted to shoo them into the dining room. "Everyone has a busy day tomorrow, but tonight of course, we haven't even had the rehearsal dinner. Would everyone like to…"

Richard didn't look at her. "I guess I'm not hungry after all, Sis."

"Nervous bridegroom, I suppose," Sharlene tittered, but it didn't relieve the tension building in the room. She cleared her throat. "Why just today in *The Indianapolis Star,* they raved about what a gala affair this wedding will be. *"*

"You'll have to excuse me, Sharlene," Misty said. "As you said, tomorrow's a big day and I have a million things to do." Misty turned her back and walked toward the exit.

"What about the bachelorette party?" Krystal called after her.

Misty called over her shoulder, "I'll meet you there."

Sharlene looked helplessly at Richard. "But the dinner…"

Jack stepped up once again. "Come on, guys,

Sharlene's gone to a lot of trouble, and I for one am starved."

This was a disaster, but Sharlene was determined to put a happy face on it as she led her remaining guests into the dining room. The seating chart would be all wrong now, of course, what with her grandmother and the bride gone, the bride's father MIA and the bride's mother passed out on a sofa. The salad course had been placed on the table ages ago, and now it was looking wilted. "Please, everyone, enjoy your meal," Sharlene said in frustration. The dinner and wine were expensive, but she'd thought it was worth the expense to be the hostess of the perfect dinner party. Now the evening was in shambles.

Richard was the last to head to the dining room. Sharlene watched as her brother stood transfixed, his back to the guests in the room. She got up from her seat at the head of the table and went to the doorway. "Richard, really, I...oh, Caroline!"

Sure enough, Caroline was there, dressed casually in shorts and sandals. She and Richard were staring at each other.

Sharlene let out a huge sigh. "Caroline, dear, your father didn't mention..."

"I didn't mean to interrupt, but..."

Richard actually broke into a smile. "Caroline, finally a friendly face!"

Caroline nervously shifted her handbag onto her other shoulder just as Megan walked between them.

"Hi, Car, thanks for coming to get me," Megan said. "This is the worst party ever."

Chapter Twenty-Three

Caroline fought back the nausea as long as she could but finally got out of bed and made a run for the bathroom. She didn't think she was actually sick, unless being sick with misery counted, but she decided to sit and wait out the queasiness. A couple of minutes later, she heard a quiet tap on the closed door.

"Caroline," Allie whispered, "are you okay? I heard you get up…"

Allie opened the door a crack and peeked in. Caroline was sitting on the floor near the toilet, a wet wash cloth draped over her forehead.

"Are you sick?" Allie went to Caroline, felt her forehead, and helped her stand.

Caroline shook her head, hung the wet cloth on the towel rack and ambled back to her bedroom, Allie trailing behind. Caroline sank onto her bed and leaned against the pillows. "It's just nerves."

Allie scrutinized her. "Nerves? I don't know, Car, you don't look good."

Caroline closed her eyes. "It feels like a bad case of dread."

Allie thought for a moment while she eased herself down on the bed next to Caroline. "Then maybe you should skip Richard's wedding today. I'm sure Emily and Sara would understand. Especially if you're not feeling well."

Caroline slowly shook her head. "No, I'll be okay. I just need to rest."

"But that's a lot of pressure you don't need."

Caroline lifted herself onto one elbow and faced Allie. "I've thought about it, and I think if I actually see Richard marry Misty, then I can quit fantasizing about a life with him and move on."

"Well," Allie said, "if you're sure, but I say you should stay home if you don't think you can stomach that whole circus Sharlene has cooked up."

****

Sharlene arrived late in the morning to check on the final preparations for the wedding at the Peterson estate. After last night's dinner fiasco, she was determined that nothing would go wrong today. She was barking orders at everyone, including the wedding planner who was nearly in tears. The caterer, florist, and hired wait staff had been there since nine a.m., setting up for the six o'clock wedding, and staying out of Sharlene's way as much as possible. The wedding planner may have thought she was directing the activities, but Sharlene set her straight on that, including where to position the arbor in order to deflect the late afternoon sun from the guests.

Sharlene didn't like how the chairs in the tent where the ceremony was to be held were arranged, so the wedding planner had to rearrange to make a wider aisle between the bride's and groom's sides. A wet bar was originally set up under a shade tree and stocked with only the most expensive brands of alcohol, but Sharlene ordered it moved to the patio under the awning. There was a separate tent for the reception, with an area designated for the musicians to play, adjacent to the dance floor. But the floor was a laminate material and Sharlene insisted on polished hardwoods, so it had to be swapped out. And Sharlene didn't think the area inside the tent where the guests would enjoy their meal looked festive enough, either, so the staff bustled around rearranging chairs, ribbons, flowers, china and crystal, silverware, linen napkins and serving dishes to Sharlene's satisfaction, all to accommodate approximately two hundred and fifty guests.

After hours of hard work, Sharlene looked around the grounds and decided it looked like the wedding wonderland she'd envisioned. She called out to the wedding planner, "The gazebo still needs to be decorated! And where are the Petersons? They should be here, too!"

The wedding planner timidly approached Sharlene. "Mrs. Meadows-Benedict, Mrs. Peterson's maid said she's taking a bubble bath and gave instructions not to be disturbed, and Mr. Peterson is holed up in his study. Miss Peterson hasn't come out of her bedroom all day."

Sharlene shook her head. "Find them! They need to come out and at the least, sign off on all this." The woman stood there motionless as Sharlene clapped her hands. "Go!"

****

Caroline parked her car in the Peterson's circular drive. She and Megan got out, walked to the front door, and rang the bell. Megan had her bridesmaid's dress in a plastic bag on a hanger, and another tote bag with accessories in the other hand. A maid answered the door.

"Hi, this is Megan Benedict," Caroline said, indicating her sister, "and she's one of the bridesmaids."

"Yes, ma'am, please come in. I'll show you the room where the bridesmaids will be dressing." The maid led them into the house and up the winding staircase to a large bedroom suite with its own bathroom. "Please make yourselves comfortable. Would you like anything to drink, Miss?" she asked Megan, ignoring Caroline.

"Diet Coke?" The maid nodded and left the room. "Wow! This room's as big as our whole house!" Megan exclaimed, doing a full circle to take it all in.

Caroline looked around. "You're right, it's a nice room, but I don't think it's quite that big." It had two full-size beds piled high with tastefully chosen green decorative pillows and coordinating pink duvets. The off-white dresser and nightstands each held a large onyx vase of freshly-cut pink roses, to coordinate with Misty's chosen wedding colors of pink and black. What Caroline assumed was a genuine Monet hanging over a desk in one corner, and in the other corner stood a full-length swivel mirror framed in white. The bathroom next to the closet had a shower as well as a large soaking bathtub, floor-to-ceiling mirrors and a chandelier! The walk-in closet door was open, all racks empty, inviting the bridesmaids to hang their belongings.

"Am I early?" Megan asked. "Sharlene said to be here at two for the hair and makeup people."

Caroline checked the time on her phone. "Right on time. I guess all the other girls are late. Probably too much celebrating last night." Caroline got a pang in her stomach, remembering her glimpse of the wedding party at the rehearsal dinner and how excited Misty's friends seemed to be.

Megan rolled her eyes. "Maybe, but Richard and Misty…"

"Stop, Megan. I don't want to know." Caroline went to the closet to hang Megan's dress, opening the bag with her sister's shoes and undergarments, and removing the earrings and matching necklace she was to wear, taking more time than necessary so she wouldn't have to listen to Megan's rendition of the previous evening one more time.

"Hi, Megan." Krystal walked into the room and threw her things on one of the beds.

Caroline stuck her head out of the closet to see who had arrived. From what little Caroline knew of Krystal, aka Misty's co-conspirator in the proposal entrapment, she didn't like. Krystal was married but didn't seem to have any more direction in life than Misty.

The housemaid returned with Megan's soda, opened it for her, and poured it into a crystal goblet.

"Oh, good," Krystal said to the maid, "as long as you're here, I'll have a Perrier, and I'm sure the other girls will want the same when they get here."

"Certainly, Mrs. McAlister." The maid hurried out again.

Krystal turned her attention to Caroline. "We met last summer. You're Richard's secretary, huh?"

Caroline bit her lip. "Executive Assistant."

Krystal shrugged her indifference. "So I guess you know him pretty well?"

Caroline thought about that. She almost blurted out that she knew Richard better than Krystal and any of these second cousins in the bridal party. She even thought she knew Richard better than Misty. But what she said was, "Yes, I've worked with him a couple of years now."

"Hmmm." Krystal rummaged through her satchel. "Well, maybe you can explain why Richard seemed so, I don't know, out of sorts last night."

"Um, maybe he had some business thing on his mind," was all Caroline could come up with.

Megan took a gulp of her soda. "It was really weird last night."

Krystal looked askance at Megan. "Weird how?"

Megan shrugged. "I don't know, just weird, because Richard and Misty don't seem all that much in love and it wasn't much of a party." Caroline picked up her purse off the bed and looked for her car keys. "Can't you stay awhile, Car?" Megan pleaded.

Caroline didn't know how much more of this wedding chit-chat she could take, but for Megan's sake she hesitated. "Well, I…"

"You can't go, Caroline," Megan whined. "There's no way I can get into that dress and stuff by myself."

The look Megan gave Caroline said *Please don't leave me alone with her.* Caroline glanced over at Krystal, who was ignoring both of them and texting. "Well, I guess for a little while, Megs, but then I need to go home and get dressed myself."

Caroline was definitely uncomfortable. Krystal certainly hadn't made her feel welcome, and she couldn't help Megan get into her bridesmaid dress until her hair and makeup were done. So she sat down quietly on the edge of the bed where Megan was sipping her diet soda. Megan offered her sister a sip and Caroline gladly took one.

"Finally!" Krystal said, waving her phone in the

air. "Only a half hour late."

Jessica, Natalie, and Sierra stormed into the room carrying their bridesmaids' dresses and bags of accessories. They nodded to Megan, ignored Caroline, and wordlessly began claiming spots for their belongings in the closet and on the beds.

Megan watched all this quiet busyness and whispered to Caroline, "Shouldn't everyone be excited or something?" Caroline put her fingers to her lips and shook her head, so Megan asked them, "How was the bachelorette party last night?"

"It never happened," Krystal said, not looking at her.

Jessica threw her handbag on a chair. "Boy, that made me mad! Hanging around Jazz Corner for over two hours waiting for Misty to show up, and she never did."

"We called her cell about a million times and sent dozens of texts," Sierra added.

Caroline was stunned. Misty never showed up for her own bachelorette party? And didn't even bother letting the others know? Something was definitely up, and the tension in the room was palpable.

"Do you think she and Richard had some kind of fight? Misty didn't even stay for dinner," Natalie said in a poorly-concealed whisper.

"Richard's got cold feet, that's my guess," Krystal said. "Because I *know* Misty's determined to get married today, since her father..." she broke off, glancing over at Megan and Caroline.

"...since her father what?" Caroline asked.

"My lips are sealed." Krystal did the fake zipping motion and pretended to throw away the invisible key.

Yup, something's really fishy about this wedding, Caroline thought.

"Well, has anybody talked to Misty today?" Jessica asked.

There was a chorus of *not me* from everyone, followed by another awkward silence. The door opened, and the maid came in again with the bottles of Perrier in an ice bucket, along with more crystal goblets. She began pouring the water.

"Um, do you know if Miss Peterson is around?" Krystal asked the maid.

"No, ma'am, she hasn't been out of her room, but she did order a breakfast tray midmorning."

"Well, at least she's still alive," Sierra muttered.

"When are the hair and makeup people supposed to be here?" Natalie stared at her reflection in the full-length mirror. "My hair's a disaster, and it's going to take hours on me alone."

"I believe they've just arrived, ma'am. I'll show them up."

Caroline couldn't have been more relieved. As soon as Megan was dressed, she was outta here. This whole thing was really odd. The bridesmaids mad at the bride? The groom with cold feet? The bride herself refusing to come out of her room? Yet the grounds were all set for an elaborate wedding. Caroline had no explanation for any of it.

An hour later Krystal tossed her cell phone down on an end table. "Okay, I've had it. She won't answer my texts." In her bathrobe, with curlers in her hair, she strolled down the hall and banged loudly on Misty's bedroom door. Caroline, Megan, and the other three bridesmaids listened and watched with eyes wide.

"Misty, it's me! Open up—we need to talk!"

"I'm busy, Krystal!" Misty shouted through the door. "I'll see you later." The volume on the music in Misty's room suddenly got louder, so Krystal tossed her hands up in disgust and went back down the hall to finish dressing.

"Megs, I think I'll be going," Caroline said. She picked up her handbag and hurried out the door and out of the house.

****

"Two hours until the wedding!" Sharlene surveyed the grounds with approval. Everything was beautifully decorated and the weather was clear and warm. The bar was stocked, and a bartender stood nearby, ready for early arrivals. Valets were stationed out front of the house in the circle drive, ready to park cars in the nearby church parking lot that had been rented for the occasion.

Sharlene smiled at her accomplishments and started walking toward the house. She'd been wearing capris and a designer t-shirt all morning, and now she was drenched in sweat, certainly not an attractive look. It was time to take a bubble bath and get into the pale pink couture silk suit she'd spent days shopping for. She was on her way in through the back patio when she saw Daniel from a distance.

She waved her arms in the air, signaling his attention. "Daniel, darling, I'm just about to go inside and get changed."

Daniel waved to her and headed toward the bar. "Daniel," she called out again, but he either didn't hear or was ignoring her. She shook her head, hoping her husband wouldn't embarrass her on this of all days.

She opened the slider and stepped into the refreshingly cool living area. There sat Adele in an overstuffed chair, two hours early. Sharlene braced herself.

"Good afternoon, Grandmother." Sharlene walked over and kissed her on the cheek, shuddering when she saw the deep lavender summer pantsuit and large red garden hat Adele was wearing. Sharlene tried to overlook her grandmother's obvious eccentricities and smiled sweetly. "Are you feeling better today? You must have been dreadfully ill last night to leave so abruptly." As Adele eyed her warily, Sharlene added in a less pleasant tone, "And please tell me you haven't invited The Red Hat Society."

Adele sat up straight and faced her granddaughter. "I feel fine, thank you, dear. And, yes, two of my fellow Red Hatters will be here. This day's going to be painful enough as it is, so I need my friends to bolster my spirits."

"Grandmother, surely you didn't arbitrarily add people to the guest list!"

Adele patted Sharlene's hand. "I assured them you could squeeze them in."

Sharlene bit her tongue. She decided to just let it go and inform the caterer about the extra guests. She took a deep breath and tried again to be civil. "Why are you here so early, Grandmother?"

"I need to speak to Richard. It's too hot outside right now, so I'm waiting in the air conditioning until I see him."

Sharlene inhaled a calming breath. "Grandmother, please don't put any undue stress on Richard. I know you don't approve of this wedding, but he's made his wishes clear." She paused and nearly added more, but decided this day was too important to be spoiled with an argument.

Adele gave her granddaughter a stern look. "No one ever kept me from speaking my mind before, so don't you try now."

Sharlene shook her head. All the hard work and planning that had gone into this wedding and she had no intention of letting Grandmother's opinions of the bride ruin everything, so Sharlene decided it would be prudent to head off Richard before Grandmother got her hooks in. She pulled out her phone to send him a text, but got distracted when she saw an incoming one from the reporter covering what he referred to as "this important society event."

She regained her composure and pointed to her phone. "Grandmother, it's from *The Indianapolis Star,* and they'll be here today to cover this wedding. So everything has to be perfect."

"Hrmph," muttered Adele.

Sharlene walked off, envisioning her picture in the Society section, her name captioned underneath, along with quotes about how hard she'd worked to make this a memorable day for her brother. *Sharlene Meadows-Benedict, wife of Truitt Wellness Corporation's CEO, sister of the groom.* It had a nice ring to it.

Richard walked in from the main entry at that moment. Sharlene stepped over, kissed Richard's cheek, and planted herself between him and Adele. He was already dressed in his wedding tux, complete with a white boutonnière in his lapel.

"Richard, dear, where have you been?" Adele asked, craning her neck around Sharlene.

"What do you mean? I'm not late." He pulled out his cell phone and checked the time display. "Actually I'm early."

"No, you're late—almost too late. This is important, dear. Sit down here and listen to me. Sharlene, move." Adele patted the oversized ottoman facing her. "You can still call off this wedding, you know."

"Grandmother!" Sharlene exclaimed, a lump rising to her throat as she nonetheless stepped aside.

Richard sighed as he sat down. "Grandmother, I gave my word. I agreed to marry Misty, maybe in a weak moment, but it's done, and one thing my mother taught me was to honor my commitments."

"See?" Sharlene said to Adele. "He's going to do the honorable thing."

"Your mother was a fine woman," Adele said, ignoring Sharlene, "but she died way too young. She had no way of knowing…" She sighed as she broke off.

Richard took her hand between both of his. "Grandmother, I know you're concerned, and I've been giving it some serious thought, I really have."

Sharlene tapped her foot. "Given what serious thought?"

Richard waved his arms around. "All these preparations, gifts sent, food prepared, and the guests will be arriving soon. It's too late to call it off."

Sharlene smiled to herself. Okay, so maybe Richard and Misty weren't passionately in love like her and Daniel, but they were friends and could fall in love later. They had a whole lifetime ahead of them. As soon as this wedding was accomplished, that is.

Adele shook her head. "It's easier to call off a

wedding than a marriage, Richard. You're marrying the wrong woman."

Richard sighed. "We've already had this conversation, Grandmother."

"End of discussion," Sharlene added.

Adele withdrew her hand from Richard's. "I've seen how you look at Caroline Benedict, Richard. That's why I planned that little surprise dinner. Didn't you see which woman you really want?"

Sharlene's jaw dropped. "What? You sent Richard on a date with another woman? Grandmother, really!"

Richard rubbed his forehead, looking from Sharlene to Adele and back again. "Good cop, bad cop, huh?" He smiled, but it soon drained away. "I guess I need to speak to Misty. Do you know where she is?"

"She hasn't been out of her room today," Sharlene said, chagrinned. "Bridezilla" didn't begin to describe Misty's behavior.

"Well, if you put off the discussion any longer, you'll be bound in wedded bliss to the wrong woman." Adele stood and adjusted her hat. "Now please do the right thing and go speak with your fiancée."

Richard nodded thoughtfully as he stood. "If you'll excuse me, Grandmother."

He walked out of the room, up the stairs to Misty's closed bedroom door, and knocked. "Misty? Misty, it's Richard. Can you open the door?"

Sharlene stepped to the bottom of the stairwell and stared up at her brother. "Well? Any luck?" she called.

Richard shook his head and knocked again, shouting louder this time. "Misty, turn down that music and at least talk to me through the door."

Sharlene went all the way up the stairs. "Misty,

dear, your fiancé is concerned about you."

"Fine," Misty called from her side of the door. "Okay, I'm here but I'm not opening the door. What do you want?" she snapped.

Sharlene was a bit surprised at Misty's tone, but hoped it was just wedding jitters. "Misty, I know it's bad luck to see the groom before the wedding, but may *I* come in?"

"No!" Misty shouted.

She and Richard heard muffled whispers, and they exchanged puzzled glances. Then the volume on the music increased to a deafening level. "I can't hear you. Go downstairs and let me finish getting ready."

Richard stared at the door and hesitated a minute, letting go of the knob. He turned to Sharlene, opened his mouth to say something, closed it, and ran down the stairs and out to the lawn.

****

The doorbell rang, and Susan went to answer it. It was Patrick, carrying his coat and smiling as he tugged at his collar to loosen the tie. Susan invited him in.

"Whew! It's a scorcher out there." He looked at her with approval. "You look gorgeous!"

Susan blushed. She had on a blue flowered sundress with a matching solid-colored shrug and low-heeled white sandals. "Everyone's about ready."

"How's Caroline doing?" Patrick asked.

"Not too well," Susan said. "This is hard on her. Anyway, Emily and Sara are here from Chicago, so hopefully we have enough troops rallied around her." Patrick gave a low whistle, and Susan turned to look as Allie walked into the room.

Allie had chosen a crisp pale yellow linen pantsuit

with black strappy sandals, the spike heels adding to her already statuesque height. Her dark hair was pulled back with an elegant clip, tiny diamond stud earrings shone brightly, and she was carrying a small black clutch bag.

"*Wow!*" Patrick exclaimed.

"Do you think Brandon will like it?" Allie asked, turning around to display the entire effect.

"What man in his right mind wouldn't?" Patrick grinned broadly. "The bride had better watch out." There was a knock on the door, and Brandon let himself in. Patrick elbowed him. "Are your ears burning, old man?"

"What?" Brandon asked, and then he saw Allie.

"Kind of takes your breath away, huh, Phillips?"

Emily and Sara walked into the family room from the kitchen. Sara was dressed in her usual dark blue, conservative business suit, and Emily had chosen a sleeveless little black dress, understated in its simplicity. They looked at Allie and gasped.

"Who's the star of the show today—you or Misty?" Emily joked.

"Is it too much? I can change."

"Don't you dare," Susan said.

"And Emily," Allie said, looking chagrinned, "I owe you an apology. For last month. You, too, Sara."

Emily folded Allie into a bear hug. "You owe us no such thing. You didn't get sick on purpose."

"But I used visiting Brittany as an excuse to go see Mark, and then I moped for days, all while getting sicker and sicker. I should have spoken up sooner."

Emily released Allie from the hug. "We're both just glad you're okay now. Did you talk to Brittany?"

Allie nodded. "We video-chatted We're getting together at Christmas. But I just feel so bad…"

"Nonsense, Allie," Emily said as she winked at Sara. "Love makes women do nutty things. Besides, look who you're with now!" Emily slapped a blushing Brandon on the back. "Say, where's Caroline? Is she ready?"

Susan frowned. "Ready to watch the man she loves marry another woman?"

"I'm giving it a good try." They all turned to see Caroline standing in the doorway, nervously tucking a stray hair behind her ear. Her sleeveless lime-green garden dress accentuated her slender waist and strawberry-blonde hair.

"What are we waiting for?" she said with a forced smile. "Let's do this."

They sorted themselves into two cars and the seven of them arrived in tandem at the Peterson estate. They had to wait in a short line of cars ahead of them. "This is going to be a big wedding," Susan commented as she looked at all the cars waiting to be parked.

The valet opened the front passenger door and handed Susan out. Brandon helped Allie out of the back seat, while Patrick turned over his car keys in exchange for a claim ticket. The valet hopped into Patrick's sedan and drove it to the church parking lot across the street.

"Shall we?" Brandon asked Allie, offering his arm.

"Yes, we shall," she giggled in response.

Susan put her hand up to shade her face, since the sun was beating down and causing a glare. She pointed to the far side of the parking area. "Emily's van had to go way over there."

"They'll catch up," Patrick said as he offered Susan

his arm. Likewise, Brandon escorted Allie toward the wedding festivities.

"It's breathtaking," Allie said as she took in the decorations. "There must be two hundred people here already."

Susan followed Allie's gaze around the grounds. Some guests sat in the white plastic chairs awaiting the ceremony, some loitered at the bar, and some just milled around the grounds. "Too bad the wrong people are getting married."

Patrick nodded and squeezed her arm reassuringly. "Do you want something to drink?"

"Not just yet," Susan said. "Let's wait for Emily, Sara, and Caroline."

"Look at the gazebo," Allie said, pointing off in the distance. "It's gorgeous over there." She again linked her arm through Brandon's as the four of them chatted happily, admiring the decorations and keeping an eye out for the rest of their party. Suddenly Allie gasped. "Ohmigod!"

"Allie, what's wrong?" Susan looked to see where Allie was pointing, grasped Patrick's arm tighter and whispered, "What's Mark Townsend doing here?" Of all the times for her daughter to run into the man who'd broken her heart...

Mark walked over to join them, never taking his eyes off Allie. He seemed to fumble for words, but finally said, "You look good, Allie."

"Mark, what are you doing here?" Allie demanded. Brandon glared at Mark who shifted from one foot to the other.

"I'm... uh... I'm a guest of the bride."

"You're a guest?" Susan asked. Mark was

underdressed for a wedding, to say the least, wearing khaki shorts, a golf shirt, and loafers. His whole appearance made her suspicious.

"Uh, Allie, can I talk to you a minute?" Mark asked. "In private?"

"Whatever you have to say, you can say in front of my family and friends," Allie told him.

Mark scratched his head and shoved his hands into his pockets. "I guess I just wanted to say I'm sorry for the way I treated you in Chicago."

"Apology accepted." Allie coolly turned on her heel, tightened her grip on Brandon's arm, and the two of them started to walk away. But then she stopped, let go of Brandon, and turned back around. "That's it? Just 'sorry'? You really hurt me, Mark."

Mark looked down at the ground. "I know. And when I heard you were sick..." He was silent for a moment. "If it makes any difference now, I did have feelings for you. But there were things going on in my family..."

"There were things going on in my family, too."

A look of anguish spread over Mark's face. "What are you doing with Brandon?"

"I'm right here, man," Brandon said, scowling.

Susan saw Emily, Sara, and Caroline approaching and was about to suggest they all go find their seats. The wedding couldn't be any more uncomfortable than this.

Allie tilted her head in Brandon's direction. "He's been a good friend, both to me and my family. And by the way, I'm starting at Bradley University next week, thanks to him."

"Bradley?" Mark lifted an eyebrow. "But I thought

you were going to Ball State."

"Things changed. Lots of things. I'm not that naïve little girl anymore that you rescued at the symphony."

"Allie, I'm, uh…" He shrugged. "Just be happy, okay?" Mark shoved his hands in his shorts pockets and slowly walked away.

Susan asked, "You okay?" at the same time Brandon asked Allie the same thing.

Allie stood up straight, pushed a stray hair out of her face, and nodded. "Mark caused me a lot of pain and disappointment, but I don't have any feelings for him anymore." She shrugged. "Maybe I never did."

"I'd still like to know what he's doing here," Susan said as the four of them watched Mark disappear into the crowd.

Caroline walked over with Emily and Sara, and put her hand on Allie's shoulder. "Was that Mark Townsend? Surely you're not…"

Allie firmly shook her head. "No way, Car. Besides," Allie smiled at Brandon, "I have new friends."

Brandon blushed.

"Hi, Dad." Caroline greeted her father and Sharlene as they sauntered over arm-in-arm.

Now it was Susan's turn to squirm. She'd like to just pay her respects to the hosts as quickly as possible and go to their seats. But Daniel was hugging both Allie and Caroline, so she stood aside with Patrick.

That's when it struck her: Sharlene was the perfect wife for Daniel. Susan had never felt she fit in with his social crowd, and Daniel frequently seemed embarrassed by her down-to-earth approach to life. Sharlene was dressed in an expensive polished linen suit with pearls at her neck and a diamond tennis bracelet on her wrist, which accentuated the large five-carat diamond in her wedding ring. Her young, curvy figure, all the bling, the whole package, were exactly what Daniel needed to make himself stand out among his peers.

"Caroline, Allie, you both look very pretty," Daniel said.

Sharlene looked down her nose at the group. "Hello, Benedicts and friends. Who do we have here?"

Susan made introductions. "This is Patrick Williams, a professor at Bradley University, Allie's friend Brandon Phillips, also a music professor there, and I believe you know Emily Martin and Sara Whetstone from Chicago."

"Oh, yes, I remember seeing your names on the guest list." Sharlene dismissed them all with a wave of her hand. "It's lovely to see you all."

"Lovely day for a wedding," Emily said.

"It certainly is," Sharlene muttered as she scanned through the crowd.

Susan assumed Sharlene was looking for someone better to talk to. She sighed and said politely, "The decorations look beautiful, Sharlene. Patrick, shall we…?"

"Well, of course they do, Susan, after all my hard work. Don't you agree, darling?" Sharlene dug her nails into Daniel's arm and he winced.

Sara casually reached into her handbag, pulled out one of her business cards, and offered it to Sharlene. "I handle divorce cases, Mrs. Meadows-Benedict, if you should know of anyone needing my services."

Sharlene gasped in indignation, stomped her foot,

and dragged Daniel away.

****

The chamber orchestra started playing and those guests not already seated moved toward the tent where the ceremony would be held. Richard's groomsmen, Eric, Scott, Greg and Gary, also doubling as ushers, offered their arms to escort women to their seats on either the bride's side or the groom's. Susan, Allie, Caroline, Emily and Sara were each deposited on the groom's side, with Patrick and Brandon following behind.

Once seated, Allie whispered to Caroline, "Do you see Mark anywhere? Why isn't he seated on the bride's side?"

"Shh. It's starting." Caroline felt that familiar wave of nausea as the musicians began playing Pachebel's *Canon in D Major*. All the guests were now seated and awaiting the arrival of the families of the bride and groom. Eric escorted Adele Meadows to her front-row seat. Caroline almost laughed aloud when she saw Adele festively adorned for a meeting of the Red Hat Society, and knew Sharlene must have been beside herself over that. But then Caroline noticed Mrs. Meadows' grim expression and remembered how hard Adele had tried to get her and Richard together. She let out a slow, defeated breath. She couldn't see Merrill Peterson from where she sat, but that was probably because he was preparing to walk his daughter down the aisle. Sharlene was escorted by Greg to her place next to Adele, followed by Daniel who sat down next to his wife. Lastly, Tildie Peterson was ushered down the aisle by Gary, clinging tightly to his arm as if she might stumble. As soon as the mother of the bride was seated,

Eric, Greg, and Gary rejoined the wedding party at the top of the aisle.

The groomsmen and bridesmaids came down the aisle two by two. First came Megan on Gary's arm, each peeling off to opposite ends of the makeshift altar inside the wedding tent. Megan caught sight of her mother and sisters and winked at them on the way to her place. Megan was followed in even-paced succession by three more pairs of attendants, and lastly by the matron of honor Krystal and best man Jack. Once the bridal party was in position on either side of the altar, the minister, dressed in a black suit with clerical collar, entered discreetly from the left, followed by a nervous-looking Richard. Caroline thought he looked as nauseous as she felt, and her heart went out to him. *Please let him be happy* she prayed.

The orchestra paused once the wedding party was in place, and transitioned to the traditional wedding march. Reverend Roberts said in a booming voice, "Ladies and gentlemen, please rise and greet the bride."

Here comes—my lunch. Caroline turned with all the other guests to watch for Misty. The wedding march played through, started over, played again...

"Has anyone seen my daughter?" Mr. Peterson poked his head in and did a visual search of the tent. A murmur went through the crowd when the guests realized something was wrong. "Where's Misty?" Caroline whispered to her mom. Susan lifted her shoulders imperceptibly.

Reverend Roberts leaned over and quietly said something to Richard, who nodded. "Ladies and gentlemen, I believe the bride has been delayed. If you'll take your seats for a moment, I'll go check on her." Richard ran off toward the house.

What had been quiet whispering among the guests turned into loud conversations and speculations, and a few people even stood up to leave. Richard had been gone for several minutes when Sharlene stormed over to the musicians. "Play something, you fools! Anything!" They quickly took up their instruments and began playing a lively aria.

Allie hugged Caroline. "Could we be so lucky?"

Because her throat was choked and tears of hope were coming to her eyes, Caroline just nodded and breathed deeply.

Chapter Twenty-Four

Caroline had been holding her breath, but now she exhaled as a combination of panic and relief overtook her. Panic that Misty might still appear and relief when she didn't, because Richard rushed back outside alone to rejoin his confused guests. He had a piece of paper clutched tightly in his hand.

"Hey, folks," Jack called out as he waved his arms to get attention, "let Richard speak."

Richard walked to the front of the tent. His brow furrowed and moist with sweat, his expression pained, he opened his mouth to speak, but nothing came out. Richard took a deep breath, cleared his throat and tried again. "Ladies and gentlemen, I regret to inform you that the wedding's off. Misty has left town, but she asked me to invite all of you to stay for the party that's been planned. I apologize for the inconvenience and urge you to take your gifts with you when you leave. I hope you'll feel free to enjoy the buffet and dancing first, though."

The crowd buzzed with the news. Tildie Peterson stood up and seemed close to fainting, but her husband caught her and helped her to the house. She cried out, "My baby!" as Merrill had to practically carry her away.

Caroline turned to Allie in shock, and Susan came over to hug both her daughters. Megan danced out of the bridesmaid formation and joined her mother and sisters in a group hug. All of them jumped up and down, laughing and crying at the same time.

"Yes!" said an exuberant voice in the front row. Adele adjusted her red hat and walked out, heading straight for the champagne table set up for the reception.

Murmuring guests slowly stood. A few of them followed Richard's suggestion that they move to the waiting reception tent, while others headed for their cars.

Richard pulled his sister aside. "Sharlene, could you help the guests…"

"Richard, how *could* you?" She was shouting at him, oblivious to the fact that people were staring. "What did you do to Misty? I'm so embarrassed! I'll never be able to show my face in public again!"

A well-dressed young man stepped out of the crowd and stuck a recorder in Sharlene's face. "Mrs. Meadows-Benedict, may I ask you…"

"No!" she shouted at him.

"Sharlene…" Richard watched in confusion as his sister ran off toward the house.

Without Sharlene to take charge, no one seemed to know what to do. Finally Krystal stepped forward. Taking her husband's arm, she said loudly, "Folks, there's a buffet supper waiting for us, champagne and cake, music, a party! Let's go!"

"Mom, should we…?" Caroline glanced around at all the commotion, wondering if she should go to Richard, take her family and quietly leave, or what?

The other bridesmaids and groomsmen followed Krystal's lead and headed to the reception. The chamber orchestra gathered their instruments and moved into the reception tent to join the larger band, reset and started playing again, this time contemporary dance music. Gradually the remaining guests dispersed. Richard grabbed Caroline's arm, dragged her away from her mother and sisters, and hurried her off in the opposite direction to the deserted gazebo.

"Richard, what happened?" Caroline tried to catch her breath as they stepped onto the gazebo. "What happened when you went to the house? Misty left town?"

Richard ran a hand through his hair, nervously mussing it up. "I got to her room and found the door ajar. Misty's wedding dress, with the ten thousand dollar price tag attached, was still in its bag on her bed, untouched. Her dresser drawers were empty and hanging open, and there was nothing in the closet either. Everything was gone, even in the bathroom."

Caroline was bewildered. "But how do you know she left town? Maybe she just got cold feet, and she's waiting for you to come find her someplace." Caroline hoped that wasn't true, but this was Misty, so who knew what she'd do?

Richard shook his head. "There was an envelope with my name sitting on the nightstand, propped up against the lamp. Inside were these." Richard pulled Misty's engagement ring out of his pocket and waved the letter at Caroline. "Dumped by a *Dear John* letter," he said with a huff.

"Dumped?" Caroline had never trusted Misty, but this was out of character even for her. "Why would she dump you?"

Richard shrugged. "Here, read it for yourself." He

thrust Misty's letter into Caroline's shaking hands.

Dear Richard,

Sorry about the short notice, but I had to be sure all my plans would work out first. I don't love you, and I'm pretty sure you feel the same about me, so neither of us will cry if we don't get married. I've fallen in love with another man. In order to get my hands on Grandmother Peterson's trust fund, I have to be married to a man who is my social equal for at least a year. You did just fine until he came along, so we're eloping. I'm sure you'll be happy with that insipid Caroline, because you two bores deserve each other. Give my engagement ring back to Daddy, since he paid for it, and ask our guests to stay for the party that my parents paid for. As for me, I'm off to Chicago to start my new life with Mark Townsend.

XOXOX Misty

Caroline gasped as she read and reread the letter. "Mark Townsend?" She looked up at Richard, who seemed just as stunned. "Misty ran away with Mark?"

Richard shoved the hair out of his face. "Wasn't he the guy dating your sister earlier this summer?"

"Yeah, and Mark dumped Allie because she was broke, saying he needed an infusion of cash from somewhere." Caroline looked up from the letter. "I guess he found it."

Richard looked bewildered. "When did all this happen?"

Caroline hesitated. Should she tell him? It didn't seem like it would make a difference, now that he and Misty had broken up. The words came tumbling out of her mouth, explaining how she'd seen Misty and Mark together last June, and then saw them dancing in a

Chicago bar right before he dumped Allie. "And Mark was here this very afternoon, claiming he was a guest of the bride," she finished.

Richard looked stunned. "You saw Misty and Mark together this summer? Why didn't tell you me?"

Caroline sat down on a bench. "I tried, but I just couldn't get the words out. I thought maybe you really loved her. The first time I saw them, they were in a group of people just talking, but in Chicago it was obvious something was going on between them, judging by the way he was holding Misty in his arms."

Richard sat down on the bench next to her. "So Misty and Mark have been carrying on all summer." He was quiet a moment, staring down at his feet. "I guess that makes me a clueless idiot."

"You trusted her." Caroline felt devastated for Richard, who had been taken in by Misty's con, but shook her head, still dismayed at the quirky turn of events. "Your grandmother was right, you know. Misty never loved you at all."

Richard took her hand and brought it to his lips. "I'm sure Grandmother is dying to say 'I told you so.'"

Caroline smiled when she felt his light kiss on her trembling hand.

"But what I don't understand is why Misty didn't put a stop to all this," Richard waved his arms around, indicating all the wedding preparations, "if she was so in love with Townsend the whole time. It would've saved everyone a lot of trouble."

Caroline's heart broke for Richard. She reached for his hand and held it tight. "I'm sorry she hurt you."

Richard shook his head. "I'm not hurt, I'm angry, mostly at myself. I should've listened to you, *and* to my grandmother, *and* Jack. I knew I didn't love her, but I thought I had to follow through with the promises I'd made." He took a deep breath and exhaled slowly. His shoulders rose, making him appear inches taller, and then the tension left his face. "I feel like a weight's been lifted off me."

Caroline smiled. "I think it has."

Richard looked into Caroline's eyes as he held both her hands. "That quirky dinner date we had made me realize I'd fallen in love with you, but I found myself in an impossible situation, trapped between Sharlene and Misty. Can you ever forgive me?"

Caroline blinked in surprise. "Wait. You love me?"

He gave her a wry smile. "I know it's poor form to profess love to a woman on the day I was to marry another one, but do you think you could ever love me back?"

"You love me? Can it be true?"

"Yes, Caroline Benedict, I love you!"

Tears came to Caroline's eyes as Richard pulled her close. He lifted her chin, pulled her lips to his, and kissed her, slowly at first, and then with more urgency, until they seemed to melt into one another. She sighed with happiness.

They pulled apart when they heard music playing in the background. "Come on," Richard said, helping her to her feet, "we're missing the party!"

The 'reception' was in full swing. The guests were eating, dancing, and thoroughly enjoying themselves despite the lack of newlyweds. The wedding cake sat untouched atop the buffet table, a silent monument to the failed nuptials.

Allie and Brandon were salsa dancing with total

abandon. Daniel was dancing with Megan since Sharlene was nowhere to be seen. Emily and Sara were joyously swing dancing, and Jack danced over with Natalie just as Richard and Caroline rejoined the party guests. Caroline was beaming, and Jack gave Richard a thumbs-up.

Allie grabbed Caroline's arm and pulled her aside. "Well? What happened?"

Caroline hesitated for a moment. "Do you mean to the wedding or to Misty?"

"Either. Both." Allie stamped her foot. "Caroline, spill!"

Caroline felt like smiling and laughing, but for Allie's sake, she didn't. "Brace yourself, Allie. Misty ran off to Chicago—with Mark!"

Allie gasped. "What? Wow!"

Caroline studied her sister closely. "Are you okay?"

Allie had to take a minute to let that sink in, then burst into a wide grin. "I'm better than okay! Mark did me a favor. His breaking up with me was the reason I took a second look at Brandon, and it's because of Brandon that I now have a full-ride scholarship to Bradley."

"There sure was a lot of pretending going on this summer," Caroline mused. "Mark pretending to be in love with you, Misty pretending to be in love with Richard, and Richard pretending he wanted to get married."

Allie frowned. "I guess it was all about the money, like Mark said."

"If it makes you feel any better, I think you were spared a lifetime of heartache," Caroline said, squeezing Allie's shoulder. "Mark doesn't strike me as the kind of guy who likes to make sacrifices."

Allie nodded in agreement. "Sometimes things work out for the best. Misty and Mark deserve each other." She suppressed a giggle.

"Hey, there's a party going on here!" Richard interrupted the sisters as he happily led Caroline out onto the dance floor.

Allie walked over to the orchestra and said something to the leader, who nodded. Allie sat down at the piano and began playing "Feeling Good." As Richard held Caroline while they danced closely, they both smiled at the lyrics while he sang off key in her ear. From her vantage point on the dance floor, Caroline could see Adele and her Red Hat friends guzzling champagne, and Patrick with his arm around her mother.

Daniel abruptly stopped dancing with Megan and walked her across the floor to her mother before making his way to the bar.

"Double scotch," Daniel yelled at the bartender, his voice reverberating through the tent.

Megan sat down at her mother's side for a moment, but popped up again with teenage exuberance and headed for the dance floor, grabbing a pre-teen boy to dance with her as the band switched to a more modern tune. Allie sat happily accompanying the other musicians on the piano, and soon Patrick offered Susan his arm and led her out onto the dance floor.

"Uh-oh," Caroline whispered to Richard. "Mom's kinda rusty at this. She hasn't gone dancing in years." Then, to her utter surprise and amusement, Patrick pulled Susan close and began to waltz her around the floor, despite the fast music. Caroline burst out laughing.

Brandon sat on the piano bench next to Allie. He whispered something in her ear. She smiled and nodded as Brandon joined her in a duet on the keyboard.

"Richard!" Megan shouted over the music. "What about the cake?"

Richard took Caroline by the hand and led her to the table with the artfully decorated wedding cake. "I say we eat it!" Richard shouted back. He took up the carving knife which was set aside for the bridal couple, and sliced a large piece of cake off the bottom tier. Without bothering with a plate, he stuffed a bite into his mouth while the guests looked on in amusement. "It's delicious!" he announced with his mouth full. "Come on, everyone, help yourselves!"

The orchestra struck up a rendition of a rowdy dance tune as guests swarmed around the cake. Jack picked up a glass of champagne and jumped up on a chair to make a toast. Richard looked at him askance.

Jack winked at Richard. "Hey, it's the best man's job to propose a toast." Addressing the guests, Jack raised his glass. "To Richard. May his future be less sensible!"

Caroline said a silent amen.

Chapter Twenty-Five

Sharlene was highly agitated as she sat at the breakfast table in her newly-decorated kitchen. Susan's idea of good taste, if you could call it that, had been pale blue walls, a round antique breakfast table with deliberately mismatched antique wooden chairs, and a lightweight curtain with no distinguishable pattern that Sharlene could see. She had been understandably horrified, and with Daniel's blessing had proceeded to redecorate with white paint, white curtains, brand new stainless steel appliances, and a white breakfast table with matching chairs in a complimentary oak/white combination. All from the most exclusive stores in town, naturally.

She was drinking a mimosa and poring over the society section of the newspaper. "No!" she shouted, and then "How dare they?" and "unbelievable!" followed by several loud groans.

Daniel stumbled into the kitchen, opened up a cabinet, and pulled out a large bottle of ibuprofen. He grabbed a bottle of designer water from the refrigerator and downed three of the tablets in one gulp.

"Is there any coffee?" he croaked.

"Make it yourself," Sharlene growled.

Daniel sat down at the table opposite his wife and rubbed his throbbing temples. "What are you reading?"

Sharlene continued flipping the newspaper pages in

disgust. "This is just awful, Daniel! Richard and Misty's non-wedding is on the front page of the Society section!"

"Be careful what you ask for," Daniel muttered.

Sharlene looked up in shock. "Is that all you have to say?"

Daniel carefully placed his elbows on the table and leaned his head in his hands. "What else is there to say? It was a fiasco."

"Listen to this!" Sharlene said as she indignantly read aloud from the paper. "'SOCIETY WEDDING PUT ASUNDER! The wedding billed as the social event of the season was called off last evening when the bride unexpectedly left for Chicago with a male friend. Richard Meadows, the jilted groom, had this to say: *I hope Misty is happy.* Misty Peterson, daughter of coffee baron Merrill Peterson, was unavailable for comment.'" Sharlene pounded her fists on the table. "Happy? What was Richard thinking?"

Daniel started to shake his head but then groaned in pain and rested his head in his hands once more.

"And here's the part that really makes me angry," Sharlene huffed. "'The groom's sister, Sharlene Meadows-Benedict, wife of Truitt Wellness Corporation's CEO, Daniel Benedict, refused to comment.'"

Daniel looked at his wife through bloodshot eyes. "You wanted to be in the Society section."

Sharlene threw the newspaper on the table and jumped out of her chair. "I'm going to the mall!"

Daniel looked up in surprise. "It's Sunday. The mall doesn't open for hours."

"I'll wait!" Sharlene stormed out of the room.

****

Susan heard a knock at the front door and came out from the kitchen. She couldn't believe her eyes. "Daniel?" Daniel was peering through the locked screen door. "What are you doing here?"

"Uh, hello, Susan, may I please speak to Megan?"

"She's in the backyard. I'll show you through." Susan flipped open the door latch and Daniel followed her into the kitchen, onto the screened-in back porch and out to the yard.

"Megan," Susan called. "You've got company!"

Megan was sitting in a wooden Adirondack-style lounge chair, sketching on her drawing pad as Honey dug holes in Susan's carefully-planted vegetable garden. She looked up from her work. "Hi Dad!"

Daniel walked over and awkwardly hugged his daughter. "Hi, Megs. What are you drawing?"

"Well, I'll just leave you two alone," Susan said, turning to go back in the house.

"No, Susan, stay. You should hear this, too."

Susan didn't know what Daniel wanted to talk to Megan about, but if she was honest, she was glad he'd asked her to stay because she was very curious.

Daniel stood quietly, looked around, shuffled his feet and stared at the trees. "It's nice out here."

"Thank you," Susan said, although she didn't think he'd come to compliment her on her gardening skills.

"What are you doing here, Dad? You didn't even call first."

"Well, I, uh, wondered..." At that moment Honey came bounding up to him and jumped on his legs, her paws soiling his clean khaki pants. "Ugh! Get down, dog!"

"Sorry, Dad." Megan picked up Honey, opened the back door, and gently set her down on the porch floor. "So what were you saying?"

Susan picked up her pruning shears and pretended to be engrossed in culling her bushes.

Daniel dusted his pants and tried again. "I've been kind of unfair to you, Megan. I haven't spent enough time with you since the divorce and I was hoping to make that up to you."

Susan looked up just in time to see Megan's face light up. "Are you asking me to dinner? When?"

"Well, certainly, if that's what you'd like, but I have another offer."

Uh-oh, Susan thought.

"Uh-huh…" Megan said.

"I know you were unhappy about having to move out of the Belford house and go to a public high school after spending all your life at Willowby, so I thought… How would you like to move back into the house with Sharlene and me and enroll at Belford High School?"

Susan gasped, then coughed to cover her shock. Daniel looked over at her and frowned.

Megan's jaw dropped. "Now you ask me? After I finally got used to living here and even made some friends at Rosslyn High? Dad!" She looked her father square in the eye, hands on her hips. "And what about Sharlene? She's cool with this?"

Daniel shifted his weight uncomfortably. "Well, I haven't actually spoken to her, but I'm sure she'd agree."

Megan rolled her eyes. "Dad, you know Sharlene isn't gonna like this! And what about Honey?"

Daniel cleared his throat. "Well, the dog will

definitely have to stay here, but you can visit her, and your mother, on weekends."

Susan could feel her blood pressure rise and her pulse increase with his sudden turnaround, and the fact that he just assumed Megan would pack up and move made her want to scream. She was about to step in to set Daniel straight on his thinking. She opened her mouth, but Megan beat her to it.

"No! I won't do it!"

"Daniel, don't you think this is something you and I should've discussed first?" Susan asked, her jaw clenched.

He held up his hand. "It's fine, Susan."

Megan took several deep breaths, took the ponytail holder out of her hair, wrapped it on her wrist, took it off, and put it back in her hair again, and at last confronted her father. "Dad, it's too late. If you'd asked me in June then yeah, maybe, but now I'm happy here with Mom and Allie, I like Rosslyn High School, and I won't give up Honey!"

Daniel looked off into space, searching for words. "You're growing up so fast, Megs, and I haven't really been around to see it, so I just thought…." He started to hug her but she backed away. "Well, then, maybe we can set up regular visits on the weekends if you want to."

"Yeah, like Sharlene's gonna let that happen."

"Come on, Megan, can't we try?"

Megan kicked the garden dirt under her feet and mumbled, "Maybe."

Daniel slowly walked out of the yard while a stunned Susan watched him go.

When he was gone and Susan had had a chance to

calm down, she asked, "Megan, are you sure?"

"I'm sure, Mom." Megan picked up Honey's stick and tossed it for the dog to fetch.

****

Another moving day, twice in one summer Caroline thought. She couldn't believe it had only been three months since the last, traumatic move from Belford to Indianapolis. How different things seemed now.

She surveyed the disarray in her new apartment—boxes stacked everywhere, furniture from the discount store, recently delivered and none of it in the right place yet. She now had a sofa, a matching upholstered chair, coffee table, and one floor lamp in her living room, plus a small dinette table with two chairs in the kitchen. In her bedroom she had splurged on a queen-sized bed, but then bought a used dresser and nightstand at a garage sale. She plopped down on the sofa in exhaustion, gazing out the window at the walkers, bikers and joggers on The Monon Trail. She hugged herself, feeling snug in her new surroundings. *Mine, all mine.*

Caroline looked at the clock. Only a few more hours till Richard would be here to pick her up for their flight to Hawaii. She needed to rest a few more minutes before rummaging through the boxes to find enough items to pack for a ten day trip. After months of misery, Caroline could barely believe her good fortune.

"You want me to go on your honeymoon with you?" Caroline had asked Richard in astonishment after the reception last night.

"Yes! Just say you'll go. It's all nonrefundable anyway—plane tickets and hotel reservations. No one wants to go to Hawaii all alone." He'd stroked her cheek. "If you say yes, I'll just make one small adjustment and get you your own suite in the hotel. It's a five-star hotel right on the beach," he coaxed.

"But what about work? I had all those projects while you and..." Caroline had caught herself before saying Misty's name, "while you were going to be away."

"Who works while they're on a honeymoon?" Richard joked.

Caroline lifted an eyebrow at his attempt at humor. "I don't know..."

"I want to take this trip with you, Caroline. Come on, quit thinking honeymoon and start thinking vacation!"

Caroline's hands felt clammy as she contemplated Richard's offer. "I haven't been on a vacation since, well, since before my parents got divorced. But who'll run things at the office?"

Richard gently pulled her into an embrace. "For once, Caroline, let's be spontaneous instead of practical. I want some time off, and I want it with you."

"But..."

"No buts. It'll all be here when we get back. If anyone needs to reach us, that's why we have cell phones and email." Richard had stepped back, taken both her hands and looked into her eyes. "Please say you'll come with me."

Caroline couldn't refuse Richard anything. She glanced at the clock again. She needed to quit daydreaming and start packing her suitcase. They had to be at the airport by six this evening to check in for their eight p.m. flight. Despite being physically tired from lifting and moving boxes all day, she bounced off the new sofa and into her cluttered bedroom with an exuberance she had rarely ever felt.

****

The flight board said the plane to Los Angeles was on time, so Caroline sank into a chair in the airport waiting area near Gate Five, Intercontinental Airways, and placed her carry-on bag beside her on the floor. They had a few minutes to wait before the official boarding call, and Caroline wanted to savor all that had happened to her in just one, amazing weekend. *I'd pinch myself, but I know I'm not dreaming. It's real!*

Richard sat down beside her and took her hand in his. A tingle went up her spine as she squeezed his hand in return. "I can't believe we're really here."

"I can't believe how much time we wasted getting here." Richard smiled. "I mean, finding our way to each other." He gazed into her eyes for a long time. "What's the first thing you want to do when we get to Maui?"

She laughed softly. "Walk barefoot on the beach!"

"Then that's what we'll do. In a perfect world, it'll be sunset and the most romantic walk we'll ever take."

"I'd be happy just walking along the Canal in Indianapolis with you again," she said, leaning her head on his shoulder.

"We've got lots of time," Richard replied, "and we'll do that, too. We've got the rest of our lives to take romantic walks together."

Caroline closed her eyes, their hands still clasped. This was better than anything she ever imagined. She noticed an elderly couple sitting across from them, smiling at the two of them as if remembering young love.

Caroline's stomach leaped, and this time the butterflies were excitement for what the future held for the two of them.

****

Susan closed the front door, collapsed onto the sofa, and allowed herself to relax in front of the TV. Just as she was dozing off, her phone rang. She picked it up, smiling when she recognized the caller ID.

"You just left, Patrick."

"Quite a weekend, wasn't it?" He chuckled.

Susan grabbed the remote and clicked off the TV. "It's been quite a summer. But now that the girls are settled, I feel like I can finally relax."

"I know it's late on a school night, and I won't keep you, but I was wondering about next weekend," Patrick said.

"Wondering what?"

"Well, we've been seeing each other for a while now, but we haven't had much time alone. How about driving down to Madison, Indiana, and doing some sightseeing? I hear it's a quaint, historic town, and I know of a great bed and breakfast." He chuckled. "Okay, I Googled it."

Susan smiled, realizing she was ready for this next step in their relationship. "I'd love it. Next to literature, history's my passion."

"Great. I'll pick you up after school on Friday."

Susan smiled as she hung up. Looking back over the summer, she thought about all the changes she'd gone through, finally coming of age as an independent woman. She had gotten a job on her own and was good at it, bought a home of her own, be it ever so humble, and was managing her life with confidence. Her three daughters were happy, each reaching a new level of maturity as they carved out exciting lives for themselves. And best of all, she had a deepening relationship with Patrick. The future was looking pretty bright for the Benedict women.

Honey nuzzled Susan's legs, so she reached down and scratched the dog behind her ears. Susan turned off the lights in the living room as Honey pranced happily at her side. She looked into Megan's room and found her asleep with her ear-buds in, clutching her iPod. Susan quietly turned off her daughter's bedside lamp, and then went to her own bedroom and shut the door. Sleep would come easily tonight.

****

Caroline's phone buzzed with an email.

"If that's business," Richard said, "don't open it."

"But you said…"

Richard pulled Caroline in close and kissed her forehead. "I know what I said, but we're on the most beautiful beach in paradise at sunset, so work can wait."

Caroline stole a peek at her cell. She shook her head. "It's Allie." She looked up at Richard as they walked along, their toes sinking into the soft sand. "Do you mind?"

Richard squeezed her hand and shook his head, so Caroline opened Allie's message.

Caroline—

Hope you're having fun on your, uh, vacation! I'm sure by now that Sharlene has told Richard how furious she is with him. She's so mad that she's done nothing but shop. I'll bet she's maxed out all Dad's credit cards by now! And Dad called me to say I can now use the piano any time I want. Finally! He's standing up to Sharlene!

Next weekend Megan's staying here with Honey

and me while Mom and Patrick go out of town. Dad said something about taking Megan out to dinner, so I told Megs to make reservations at the Skybridge Club so he couldn't cancel at the last minute without paying a penalty. Megan's going to a Rosslyn High School pep rally with some new friends later this week.:)

Tomorrow I start classes at Bradley University. Commute time: 5 minutes, instead of 3 hours. (Nathan's seriously mad at me because I didn't give him a heads up, but he's found a ride up to Chicago with someone else. A female someone!) Car, I've come to appreciate Brandon Phillips a lot, and I never would've gotten to know him if Mark hadn't dumped me. (You're welcome, Misty!) I'm looking forward to both my music and academic classes and to spending more time with Brandon. He's meeting me for lunch tomorrow at the student union! And yes, you do detect a hint of romance. :)

I look forward to hearing all about your Hawaiian vacation. I saw the pics you posted on Facebook. You two are so cute, and Richard's a lucky guy.

I'm more excited about the next few months than I've been about anything in the last three years. Happy endings just make sense!

Allie

Caroline hit reply.

I agree. From your reformed sensible sister,

Caroline

A word from the author...

I am a former high school English teacher and author of *Confessions of a Teenage Psychic* (TWRP 2010) which was a 2011 Epic Ebook Contest finalist. My just-released YA novel *Genius Summer* was a finalist in the 2013 San Francisco Writers Contest and received high marks in the 2013 Pacific Northwest Writers Contest.

I live in Carmel, Indiana, just north of Indianapolis.

Thank you for purchasing
this publication of The Wild Rose Press, Inc.

If you enjoyed the story, we would appreciate your
letting others know by leaving a review.

For other wonderful stories,
please visit our on-line bookstore at
www.thewildrosepress.com.

For questions or more information
contact us at
info@thewildrosepress.com.

The Wild Rose Press, Inc.
www.thewildrosepress.com

Stay current with The Wild Rose Press, Inc.

Like us on Facebook

https://www.facebook.com/TheWildRosePress

And Follow us on Twitter
https://twitter.com/WildRosePress

www.ingramcontent.com/pod-product-compliance
Lightning Source LLC
Chambersburg PA
CBHW051519260626
47170CB00003B/685